LOVING COUPLES
Stories of Love and Marriage

Also edited by Alfred Bradley and Kay Jamieson
DANDELION CLOCKS Stories of Childhood

LOVING COUPLES
Stories of Love and Marriage

Edited by

Alfred Bradley and Kay Jamieson

Michael Joseph
London

First published in this edition
in Great Britain by Michael Joseph Ltd,
44 Bedford Square, London WC1
1981

© in this collection 1981 by Alfred Bradley and Kay Jamieson

The Red Dress © 1981 by Frances McNeil; *Buzz Buzz* © 1981 by Dave Sheasby;
Proper Uncertainty © 1981 by Brian Thompson; *Christmas is Over*
© 1981 by Alan Bleasdale; *Folie à Deux* © 1981 by David Mercer; *A Job for the Silversmith*
© 1981 by John Wain; *At the Brasserie* © 1981 by Peter Tinniswood;
Three, Three No Rivals © 1981 by Anne Spillard; *You Get What You Ask For*
© 1981 by Jo Gill; *People for Lunch* © 1981 by Beryl Bainbridge;
The Pity of it all © 1981 by Stan Barstow; *Anybody's* © 1981 by Keith Waterhouse;
The Sea Rose © 1981 by Sid Chaplin; *The Companions* © 1981 by Robert Furnival;
The Monument © 1981 by Alun Richards; *A Walk Before Breakfast*
© 1981 by Joan Bakewell; *Coming Home on the Bus* © 1981 by Margaret Seymour;
Alice Out Loud © 1981 by Paul Allen; *Juice* © 1981 by Elizabeth North;
Pastoral © 1981 by Rachel Billington; *The Train* © 1981 by Liane Aukin;
Proceedings © 1981 by Chris Barlas; *A Patched Jacket*
© 1981 by Jean Binnie

ISBN 0 7181 2037 X

Typeset in Hong Kong
Printed and bound by Billings, Guildford and Worcester

Contents

FRANCES McNEIL

The Red Dress

It was one of the sights of the city. Like eating in the high restaurant — not for spectacle as tourists did but to increase your notion of the geography of the place. Like taking the boat at night down the inky river, ceilinged by stars and sodium lighting. Like visiting the private museum with the fountain, the artificial plant and the Goya. Until on a Sunday evening, seven-thirty till eight-fifteen, you witnessed 'The Performance', you were uninitiated — a mere tourist, not part of the city at all. Gwyneth waited for Michael who was to take her to The Performance. She stood by the window and watched for him.

She had first telephoned him a month ago, on her arrival in the city; as directed by her aunt but reluctantly. Reluctantly they had arranged to meet. Cautiously they did the things two people do in such a situation — ate in the high restaurant, he pointing out the landmarks. Rode on the tops of buses. Visited the zoo. Liking her appearance, he had taken an interest in her. For her part, well, after work she had nothing else to do and he was pleasant and talkative — took her out of herself. All in all she was glad her aunt had made the suggestion: 'Ring Michael Tierney, I have the number from his mother.'

Gwyneth wondered whether she would fall in love with Michael. But the thought was speculative, unengaged — as she wondered when she came up in the lift at work whether there was something between the lift-man and the tea-lady. Idle speculation. Not much curiosity. Anyway, she was not ready for such an eventuality, still recovering from a passion for the lad who unloaded boxes at the supermarket back home. More precisely, she was still recovering from the passion's aftermath. It had proved difficult and messy to extricate herself. There had been quarrels, violence, recriminations from him. She saw herself at some villain from a Victorian melodrama and dreamed disjointed, ugly dreams featuring mud, toads and chemical lavatories until in the end she got a book from the library on dreams and kept it by her bed until it was long overdue and a card came saying she had a fine to pay. By then the worst was over. But even after that, from time to time she woke in the middle of the night, looked from behind her curtains and saw him standing across the street. Her aunt said he would lose his job, but fortunately he did not. And then she left to come to the city. But something told her it would not be like that if she fell in love with Michael Tierney. How it would be she did not know.

When Michael arrived he smiled and said, 'You are always ready.' There was mock amazement in his voice. Or perhaps it was simply mockery. A month ago Gwyneth would not have known the difference; she had learned things in the city. They set off for The Performance.

It was because of what she had learned that she did not wear the red dress. She and her aunt had looked through the catalogue to find her some clothes to go to the city. Turning the pages, they spotted the red dress at the same time. It was described as a 'pretty floral dress'. It had a ruched bodice, puffed sleeves, a full skirt trimmed with broderie anglaise and a flounced hem. Red floral. A red background the colour of the poppies just out in the fields was spread with bursts of golden flowers, the colour of marigolds. Looking back, Gwyneth thought that she and her aunt were attracted less by the dress itself than by the optimism they experienced when they looked at it. It was the only thing she bought from the catalogue — she waited and bought other clothes in a boutique when she arrived. She had put on the red dress the first evening Michael Tierney was to call for her, just a month ago, and had stood by the window to watch for him. When he approached, older than she remembered and dressed with impeccable casualness and sophistication, she knew the dress was the brash sign of a more simple world and that he would recoil from her in it. She quickly changed her clothes and shut the wardrobe door as he knocked. The dress hung there in the dark of the wardrobe. Absurd. Incongruous. Soon the weather would change.

The dress reminded her of Mrs Moody's registry-office wedding.

Mrs Moody had wanted a church wedding but the priest regretted he could not marry them. Mrs Moody was divorced and so was Mr Carter. Her three children, his two and their own one were to come to the ceremony. She wanted a white wedding — a veil and all the trimmings — in spite of gentle persuasions to the contrary by her friends. In truth, neighbours and friends were a little put out by the inappropriateness of it all and there was a big turn-out on account of that. But when they saw her there, a great hulk of a woman in flowing tulle and satin and an embossed veil, people said 'Well more power to her if she can get away with it. Good luck to her.' Gwyneth's own dress was as inappropriate as that. But she was not a Mrs Moody.

On the way to The Performance, Michael was talkative as usual. He talked about his friends, none of whom she had met but all of whom led interesting lives. One was a writer of travel articles and had contributed to the *National Geographic* magazine. Another was a photographer who had taken the pictures to accompany the article for the *National Geographic* magazine and had also won a prize for a still-life study. The third had a serious drink problem, and a fourth — an air hostess — ensured the others a good supply of duty-free cigarettes and drinks — except for the friend with the serious drink problem. Over the weeks Gwyneth gathered that the air hostess, Jane, was Michael's girlfriend and that probably their own meetings coincided with Jane's departures. When he had promised Gwyneth a bottle of duty-free *Je Reviens* she thought he did so more from a sense of intrigue when generosity, but said nothing.

Tonight he talked more quickly than usual. He was jumpy. When the conductor gave him the change from the fares he dropped it and the three of them scratted about for it on the bus floor. Suddenly he said, 'I'm sorry about the *Je Reviens*. I can't get you any duty-free.'

'It doesn't matter.'

'But it does. I'll get you some myself.'

'It really doesn't matter.'

'I hate to say this about Jane but she's got incredibly jealous and possessive. She's totally unreasonable. It was never meant to be that kind of relationship.'

'Meant to be?'

He took her hand. 'You're very perceptive.'

She looked out of the window, suppressing an urge to laugh. The scenery changed. Banks. An insurance company. Warehouses.

'What are we going to see?'

'Wait and see.'

'The Performance, I know. But of what?'

'Dancing.'

'Who dancing?'

'Charles LaPage, if that makes you any wiser.'

Usually Charles LaPage prepared his room in the morning — arranged chairs in horseshoe rows with space for standing at the back, erected a screen, gathered props. He covered his divan with a white counterpane which he had come to believe was crocheted by his maternal grandmother — so often had he said it was. On top of that he placed a carved wooden box and on either side two candlesticks. There was no particular significance in placing the box there. But it was his most cherished possession. Fine workmanship — carved grapes and leaves. A good smell. Someone once told him it was pine. It contained prized mementoes: lucky coins, a shell ring, a tiny box of snuff, a tortoiseshell comb and a broken fob watch. He had not prepared the room this morning because he felt unwell. Usual trouble. Bowels. Waterworks. He felt a little better now but a clammy sweat clothed him beneath the white robe. His audience would not be late. People knew he started on time. He had a reputation.

Gwyneth and Michael got off the bus and walked towards a warehouse. As they entered the building he said, 'You'll notice people don't look at each other. They don't want to laugh. Whatever you do don't laugh. No one ever has.'

He pressed for the lift and she read a small, hand-written poster which said:

Charles LaPage in
The Performance
of
The Dance
Sunday evenings
7.30-8.15
Fifth floor

The lift came from a great way off. It clanked about up in the roof, then bumped its way down. It was a goods lift with two gates and had a sour smell like dustbins at the back of a restaurant.

'Why does he live here?'

'He's always lived here.'

The lift filled with people, eyes downcast, voices low. The atmosphere was conspiratorial. There was a shared knowingness, and between them the distance of guilt, or sophistication.

'Tell me what to expect.'

'I've told you. He will dance.'

'Dance?'

As the lift stopped, Michael said, 'He likes polite applause. Enthusiasm tires him.'

The square room was lit by candles. At one end was a kind of altar, with what resembled a small coffin in the centre, a candlestick on either side. In front of the altar was a broad area of floor space and to the right a large, shabby screen behind which a white-clad figure disappeared as they entered. Sitting on the front row, Gwyneth heard the white-clad figure take deep, regular breaths. The room filled. At seven-thirty someone closed the door and Charles LaPage appeared from behind the screen, holding a large egg basket. He passed it to the person at the end of the front row and stood, arms folded, until it was brought back full of notes. A silent collection. He took the basket behind the screen. When he re-emerged, it was with one arm raised above his head and the other extended. He sidled out, turned this way and that, bent his knees and swung his left arm like a man striking blows. His right arm made reaping motions. He took fairy steps across the room and giant steps back. This was repeated several times. Gwyneth thought it was the dance of death. He was an old man. About seventy. Huge veins tried to burst from the skin of his arms. His face was discoloured, yellowish, worn. Suddenly he stopped, faced his audience and said 'The Dance of Spring. And now the Dance of Summer.'

He began again. It seemed to her to be the same dance, but after the giant steps across the room he disappeared behind the screen for some moments and Gwyneth did not know whether the sound they heard was meant to be a summer rainstorm or whether he was peeing in a tin. Beside her, Michael allowed himself to shake silently until Charles LaPage reappeared. The Performance ended prompt at eight-fifteen; after the dances of Autumn and Winter.

Outside people talked rapidly and laughed nervously.

'What do you think?' Michael asked. 'Isn't he a gas?'

'I hope he has no income-tax men in his audience.'

He laughed as if she had made a highly witty remark. She laughed herself. Relieved to be out of the place.

They went back to his flat for something to eat, and the Irish boy came in from the flat next door and listened to an account of The Performance. Gwyneth realised that he had been invited in advance to meet her, and could tell from the way Michael acted and talked in front of him that she was now meant to be Michael's girlfriend in place of Jane. She thought of her old boyfriend — the quarrels, the violence, the recriminations. She remembered the disjointed, ugly dreams. Then she thought of what she knew about Michael's friends — their gossipy intimacy warding off the loneliness of the city. She thought of the old man, face discoloured, yellowish, worn, and of Michael shaking silently beside her. She thought of these things and felt a deep despondency. When the Irish boy left, Michael played some records and talked about the love affair of a woman he worked with, conducted on Wednesdays and Fridays twelve-thirty to one-thirty. She told him about Mrs Moody, Mr Carter, the six children and the white wedding.

She thought perhaps she had imagined that she was meant to be his girlfriend until a little later, going back on the bus, when he took her hand and kissed her and she saw that the shape in his top pocket was his toothbrush, put in on the off-chance no doubt. It was not difficult to send him home, but when some days later he asked her to a party at which she would meet all his friends, and mustn't mind Jane who probably wouldn't come anyway, she could think of no good reason to refuse. For if she did not meet them at the party there would be another occasion.

'What kind of party?' she asked.

'Oh nothing special. Just a few drinks. Wear what you normally wear. Casual.'

That night the dreams returned. She walked in mud. Mud to her ankles. Charles LaPage nearby. Michael calling to her, giving her directions but wrongly.

The evening of the party arrived. She had tried to say, 'I do not want to be your girlfriend,' but could not, for nothing had happened in words. Just gradually — in moments, in experiences. Nor could she cut him off without words, because she did not know how. It was time to get ready. She went to the wardrobe.

There she saw it — the red floral dress. Red the colour of poppies, sunburst flowers the colour of marigolds, ruched bodice, puffed sleeves, full skirt delicately trimmed with broderie anglaise, flounced hem. She put it on. Somewhere she had a pair of flame sandals. She rooted them out. A great clash. Then she went to the girl in the room next door to borrow a coral-coloured necklace. The girl looked at her doubtfully. They did not know each other well but she took a chance and said lightly, 'A touch of red might help, Gwyneth. Know what I mean?'

'It's all right,' said Gwyneth. 'I know what I'm doing.'

Michael was late as usual. He came in carrying a small package which he almost gave her until his eyes took her in, then he forgot the package and said 'What . . .?'

'Is anything the matter?'

'No. No.'

He had the dazed look of a man struck.

'Shall we go?'

'Yes.'

'I thought I'd put on something a bit decent for a change. Since it's a party.'

He said nothing. She picked up her coat and he seemed relieved to see her button it. Her coat was not red. Then he took a breath, and steadied himself to speak.

'Look I don't feel like going to this party. Do you mind if we don't? We could go for a meal instead. I know a nice quiet Italian restaurant . . .'

The restaurant had plush seats and large mirrors on the walls. She saw herself opposite. When he went to the men's room she picked up the small package he had left on the table and opened it with curiosity. Inside a brown paper bag was a box containing a *Je Reviens* perfume spray. Not duty free. She sprayed herself liberally, since it was meant for her and now she would not have it. Then she put it back, replaced it by his side plate and surveyed herself in the

mirror, remembering the optimism she had felt when she first saw
the red dress in the catalogue all those weeks ago. It was really not
the weather for it now.

Michael shuffled back wondering how they would get through the
evening. But Gwyneth smiled at her reflection in the mirror and
said to herself, 'More power to you if you can get away with it.
Good luck to you.'

DAVE SHEASBY

Buzz Buzz

In her handbag Linda carried two books. One was a slim volume of poems by Ted Hughes which Ed had given her last Tuesday on the bench by the swanpool. Next to it nudged a small pocket guide to the paintings of Marc Chagall. This was her present to Ed. It was like that at the moment. Total. She hurried down Tamworth Avenue. The Honeybee coffee bar was ten minutes' walk away, but she kept to the back streets to be on the safe side. Stoughton was like a village sometimes; you could never be sure you were not being seen and noted from passing cars or from behind shop windows. She felt in her handbag to make sure the book was still there and hurried on through the grey November streets. It was twenty past ten.

Ed Bain, at that moment two minutes nearer the Honeybee than Linda, told his secretary Myra he had a meeting in the main block and slipped his coat on. He didn't say exactly what meeting or which room. 'See you later, then Mr Bain.' Myra watched him go. Not a nice man; not at all sociable. She knew there was no meeting in any main block, but she didn't particularly care. She wondered why he bothered to tell lies. There was no need. She heard the woman on the phone with that dull, flat voice which always seemed so near to tears, asking to speak to Mr Bain please. Still it gave her some time on her own with Mr Lucas being away. She took out *Rutters Gold*, and propped it up against the typewriter.

Ed walked quickly across the large car park, noting the Volvos, his thoughts on Linda. They had met at a party. In a corner of a crowded room, with the Eagles slicing the atmosphere of wine and smoke, he had noticed most of all her perfume. It was at the end of the autumn term. A postgraduate Christmas party; the restrained frenzy of older students was unmistakeable. She had come with her husband, a journalist who was buried somewhere in the throng. 'No doubt trying to get back at his youth,' she said, smiling. 'If you see what I mean?' Again the smile. He found himself gaping at her and was glad of the dim lighting. Afterwards he cursed himself, his age and his predictability, but by then it was too late. Finding the time and opportunity to see her had been a constant problem. It was April now. Guilt was another problem. It came daily into the hollow of his chest and by night into his thumping dreams. The hag in his head. He was born with it, grew up with it on his tail. He counted four Volvos. How did they do it? He remembered the guilt at the age of seven when he had let his mother win at rummy. And the guilt when he had beaten her. It was quite hopeless. Not that Janice suspected anything. His gloom was part of their life together. 'A crow,' Linda called him once. 'An old, black crow.' Without a car he was always having to walk to their secret meeting places or wait for buses which never came or, when they did, stopped endlessly for aged crippled citizens with impossible loads of shopping.

Linda was alone in the Honeybee when he got there. She looked pale and unhappy. They quite often met here.

'It's what we are, isn't it?' she once said. 'Honeybees buzzing away at each other. Buzz, buzz.'

She was sitting with her back to him and he paused for a moment in the café doorway to take in the sheaf of fair hair which fell smoothly across her shoulders.

'Hello.'

'Hello.'

'OK?'

'Yes. You?'

'Yes. OK.'

'Did you have any trouble getting away?'

'No, not really. You know us academics. Our time is our own.'

'It's lovely to see you. I've got you a coffee.'

She reached out her hand, touched his and pulled away again. He looked at her. Bloody beautiful. The air jangled and the distance between them yawned open. It was always so difficult, each new meeting. He searched round desperately to fill the gaping silence. The world emptied and drained. They were unspeakably alone. He heard himself say: 'You liked the poems?'

'Super. The one about the calf was very powerful. Smashing stuff. I've brought you this.'

She gave him the Chagall book at least fifty times earlier than she had planned to. The moment was slim and no bells rang. The delicious rehearsals faded.

'Thanks,' Ed said. He rippled the pages. 'I like him beaucoup.'

She smiled. 'I know. All those dreamy blues and yellows. That's what you talked about at the party.'

'Too much wine,' he said. They laughed, just for a moment relaxed. Then silence again. He sipped his coffee.

'How's the kids?' she asked.

'Fine. You should meet them. You'd like them.'

'You always say that,' she said.

'You always ask.'

The coffee machine screeched and the woman at the counter gave it a bang with the flat of her hand and grinned across at them.

'What are you doing today?' Linda asked.

'I've got a lecture at two. Final-year lot. Spanish foreign policy since the war.'

'I didn't know they had one.' She tried to smile.

'I didn't either until last Monday,' he said. 'It's a filler for Lucas. He's away. Not my period at all, really.'

The woman at the counter dragged a dishcloth through the grease under the row of white cups.

'What will you be doing today, then?' Ed asked.

Suddenly Linda stood up. 'I don't feel so good. I'm going outside. Catch me up after you've paid Miss Sunshine 1980.'

She snatched up her handbag and hurried out. He caught her up outside Bellamy's fish and chip parlour. She was walking quickly, head down. There was a notice in white lettering on the window: 'Pies and Peas past all praise.' He put his arm round her shoulders.

'Shall we go for a walk?' he said.

'Sod walking,' she snapped back at him. 'And take your arm away. You know why. This town.'

'We could get a bus to Bowman Woods,' he suggested.

She turned to him, white-face and sad-eyed. 'Let's go back to the house. There's time. I haven't got to pick Jenny up until twelve.'

He looked at her, hesitating. He knew himself for a man who took risks grudgingly and she sensed his fear.

'Tom's at the Majestic fire. Have you heard? It's burning down. He went out early. It's a big one. An inferno as they call it. He loves fires. They're part of the fun of the job. Along with murders and missing kids. Girls preferably.'

They walked quickly, not speaking, desire hovering between them. They went straight upstairs, undressed quickly and dived shivering under the covers. Ed thought of the risks. He thought of Janice and Spanish foreign policy. It all cartooned across his mind as he groaned into her luscious warm hair. It was the eleventh time. For some reason he couldn't explain, he was keeping count. They lay together, palms touching, Linda near to tears. Outside an ice-cream van carolled wonkily. Suddenly she sat up, jerking the covers off him.

'Christ! There's someone downstairs.' She whispered this, her head on one side listening. Ed noticed her breasts, white and melony and slightly trembling. Then he was out of bed, dressing frantically.

'Who is it?' He mouthed the words and realised he was shaking. He registered cowardice. He had kicked off his shoes in his hurry to get into bed and now he found he couldn't get the laces undone to get them back on. He was going to be murdered in his stockinged feet. Tom Rolls was a big man. Ed had seen him at the party, dancing about to the music like a bear on fire.

'Hello? Linda are you there?'

A woman's voice from somewhere on the stairs.

'Who?' mouthed Ed.

'Louise. Next door. Stay here,' Linda whispered.

She was dressing in a windmill mass of arms, blouse, legs, stockings, elbows and zips.

'I'm coming down,' she shouted.

'Are you OK?' Louise called. She was coming up the stairs.

Ed dived under the bed and lay still. His corduroy jacket followed him a moment later. He held his breath, his face pressed down on the tufted green carpet.

Louise came into the bedroom. He saw her legs. Black, high-heeled shoes with straps and mid-brown stockings. He watched them, fascinated by their strangeness — belonging to nobody with a life of their own, like puppets.

'I was just having a lie down,' Linda said. 'Feeling a bit headachy. Let's have some coffee.'

They went downstairs. Ed felt his left side going numb and rolled over. His bladder signalled. He badly wanted the bathroom. A spider crawled on to his hand and he jerked up sharply banging his head on the bed springs. He hated spiders. He saw coloured lights for a moment and bit his lip against the pain. He rolled very slowly out from under the bed and stood up, then sat for about a minute on the bed, thinking out his next move.

It would have to be the bathroom first, no matter what. He could hear the two women talking downstairs and heard Linda shouting unnecessarily loudly. He was just stepping out on to the landing when he heard a car. He dodged back quickly into the bedroom and edged the curtain very slightly back to look out. In the driveway below, Tom Rolls was getting out of his car. Ed dropped back under the bed and lay still, trying to think clearly, listening. Two minutes must have passed before he heard someone coming upstairs. He took a deep breath and held it as Tom came into the room, sat on the bed and took his shoes off. Ed watched his hands fiddling with the laces. It occurred to him that he was two feet away from being shot in the stomach or strangulation. His bladder signalled stronger than ever and he started to sweat. Above him on the bed Tom started to hum the tune of London's burning. Linda came into the bedroom almost at a run. Ed saw her legs; she still hadn't put her shoes on.

'You're not going to sleep all day, are you?' Her voice was cracked and shrill.

'What's up with you?' Tom said. 'I'm bloody tired, kid, actually. I was up at five, remember?'

'I want to go to town,' Linda said.

'Go to town, then.'

Ed heard the sound of Tom stretching out on the bed above him.

'Are you coming?' Linda asked.

'What's up with you? Very edgy, aren't you? Why should I go to town? I've just been. The Majestic's a black shell. Don't you want to hear about it? Bloody incredible. An inferno. Everyone got out, though. No casualties.'

Ed thought he sounded disappointed. Then he felt the atmosphere in the bedroom shift and change. It was unmistakeable.

'Has that woman gone?' he heard Tom ask.

'Louise? Yes. I'll get you some coffee,' Linda said.

'Come here kid,' Tom said quietly.

Linda almost shouted the word coffee and went out of the room. Tom called after her.

'Coffee first then. In bed. Get one for yourself.'

He sounded revived from his night's work and Ed watched items of clothing dripping in a heap two feet from his face which he kept pressed down against the carpet. He must get to a bathroom soon. Any bathroom. The pain was intense.

In the kitchen Linda put a trembling heaped teaspoon of coffee in a cup and gripped the sink with both hands, white-knuckled . . . possibilities? Try to persuade him to come to town? No chance. Give him coffee and get out? Only provoke an argument and afterwards he would probably go to sleep leaving Ed trapped. Tom came into the kitchen, a towel knotted at the waist, and put his arms round her.

'Hey. We haven't done it for ages, you know that? I've been working it out. Ten days. What's up, eh? Am I slipping or something? Very remiss.' He hugged her to him. 'Come on, love. Leave the coffee.' A sudden possibility flashed across her mind and she clung to it. She turned round to him, nestling closer. He smelled of smoke.

'In the lounge then?' she said. 'Like we used to?' Tom grunted and hugged her closer but she pushed him away as firmly as she dared. 'I must go to the loo first. You go in and wait,' she said.

He went off down the hall, the flesh at his waist rippling above the purple line of the towel. 'I'll go and draw the curtains. That Jackson woman will no doubt be on the look-out. These open-plan estates weren't made for passion.' He went into the lounge calling back, 'And lock the door. I don't want a threesome with luscious Louise; not yet anyway.'

Linda shuddered, but it was the only way. She went upstairs. Ed heard her come into the bedroom and saw her legs. Without bending down she whispered into the empty air over the bed.

'Give me five minutes, then get out. Use the back door. For Christ's sake be absolutely quiet, though. The back door. OK?

We're in the lounge but ...'

Ed whispered back from under the bed, 'Right. I've made a bit of a mess on the carpet I'm afraid. Sorry, I had to. Linda?' He thought he could hear her crying.

'What?'

'I love you.'

He watched her legs move to the door.

'I love you too, so much!' She whispered this and then was gone. He heard her flush the toilet in the bathroom and a minute later some laughter and a door close firmly downstairs. He lay still. It was too late for the bathroom now. He lay there counting off five minutes, and then rolled swiftly out from under the bed and stood up. He put his jacket on and started downstairs. He paused for a few seconds by the lounge door and then crept past it along the hallway, opened the door and stepped out into the cold April day. He walked casually down the path at the side of the house and felt his trousers damp against his leg. He stood waiting at the bus-stop, aware still of Linda's perfume on him. It smelt of wallflowers and reminded him of the swanpool in the park. After ten minutes the bus came but it was full. He started to walk, dragging his mind to France.

Linda could feel the warmth of the radiator along her right side. She shivered slightly and stared up the ceiling, easing Tom's body round so she could breathe more easily. He murmured sleepily but didn't move. She lay still under his weight and felt tears stinging her eyes. Very carefully, so as not to wake him, she tried to brush them away, and it was then she noticed the time by her watch. Ten to. She had to pick Jenny up at twelve and she didn't want to be late.

BRIAN THOMPSON

A Proper Uncertainty

When Rose Brearley said a thing was unnatural, she meant rather that it was not socially acceptable; or perhaps, even, not usual.

'It's not natural for a child that age to want to read so much,' was an instance of how she used the phrase.

It was true that Melanie Brearley was an unusually avid reader. She enjoyed the privacy it afforded, for one thing. A book in the hand, at school or at home, was like a locked door. Upstairs in her bedroom, when other children were going into town for a Saturday roam around, she would prop herself against a huge cushion in the shape of a Heinz Soup label, her long thin legs stretched out before her, and cause the natural world of her mother to disappear — dwindle, from a complaint of hoover and washing machine, to nothing. In the language of Mrs Brearley, she could spend hours up there, daydreaming.

Her reading habits began to be noticed when she was fifteen, and in the fourth year of school. Mrs Brearley had heard that it was the year things could go wrong, words always spoken in that context in capital letters. At Melanie's school, quite a few had already Gone Wrong, if Melanie's account of them were to be believed. Kevin, who sat near the window, had been hoicked out of class by two uniformed policemen. Gary was a Rude Boy. Helen, of the broad flat face and nylon polo-necks, was pregnant. A boy called Gaz had been suspended by the Head for persistent breaking of wind.

'It isn't natural,' Mrs Brearley said.

'A form of dumb insolence,' Mr Brearley explained, recalling a phrase and a face from his time as a National Serviceman, RAF Lushington.

'I was talking about the girl who was in the Family Way.'

Melanie sat calmly at table, watching her parents and listening to

the tintinnabulation of their remarks. She had already grasped
something about the three of them that Mr and Mrs Brearley
seemed not to understand at all: they lived very sheltered lives, away
from the rush and the roar of the mainstream. They were like chips
of wood that were slowly circling the millrace — drawn to the force
of it and then flicked away in another lazy circle.

'I don't know what's becoming of the world,' Mrs Brearley said
with more than half a glance at her daughter, to see if the little
rhetorical gesture was understood. Melanie acknowledged only the
literal truth: her mother did not know what was becoming of the
world.

It was shortly after this conversation about Helen the pregnant
thickie that Melanie was surprised in her room by her father. He
came and sat down on the bed. Something about the way he did it
signalled what the chat was going to be about.

'Your mother thought we ought to talk, Melons.'

It was his pet name for her. She nodded.

'About Helen.'

'Yes and no. I mean, I don't much care what happens to her, you
see. About you.'

They both sat very still, aghast at the problem of talking to each
other.

'She's told you about your body, has she, your mum?'

'A bit.'

'And you have lessons at school?'

'To do with rabbits.'

'Yes, rabbits,' Jack said, sweating.

'I know what you're trying to say.'

'You do? Then I needn't say it, eh?'

'I know where babies come from. In her case — Helen's — from
a boy called Smurf.'

'Smurf?'

Her father did not know whether it was more shocking to hear all
this, or to hear it in Melanie's calm and faintly mocking tone. He
considered his shoes, reflecting on the unknowability of most things.
The fact that *he* was doing all this with Melanie, and not her
mother, had been the outcome of a lot of fierce whispering in bed at
night. He didn't like it, didn't like it one little bit.

'Can I ask you a question?' Melanie said suddenly.

'Eh? Yes, of course. If I can answer it I will, you know that.'

'Why do you call me Melons?'

'A term of endearment,' Jack said, angered. In fact, he was angered quite beyond reason, and flung out of the room, crashing the door behind him. His wife was at the foot of the stairs, peering up in apprehension.

'That bloody kid is made of ice,' he shouted, and then slammed into the spare bedroom and locked the door. He sat on the divan in there and trembled with irrational feelings. What the holy hammer his wife was doing sending him to talk to a girl about something as obvious to her as the freckles on her arms, he did not know. Rose had told him not to get bogged down in physical matters, but to put the moral issues. Jack did not know what the moral issues were, except that he did not want his daughter impregnated by someone called Smurf, or his pals, or anyone else. The thought of it was like a dirty picture. He took off his shoes and threw himself back on the divan, groaning. Sod them both, he thought.

In the room next door, Mrs Brearley and Melanie were speaking in whispers.

'What have you said to your father to upset him like that?'

'I don't know,' Melanie said truthfully, the tears running down her face. My godfathers, her mother thought distractedly, she even cries without effort, without a further visible emotion.

'Your father loves you,' she said, pointlessly.

'If she wants any help about the moral issues,' Jack bellowed through the wall, 'she can get a bloody book out the library.'

'Hush,' Mrs Brearley said to the curtains.

There was an apology, followed by a treat: the three of them went on a picnic. Melanie remembered not to bring a book, and thoughtfully put on some shorts her mother had bought her as a present. She was standing alone under the dripping boughs of an oak when her father came to her and put his arms round her, smelling of tobacco and soap powder. He kissed her on the hair.

'You're a wonderful kid,' he said. His hand rucked up her teeshirt, and he stroked the small of her back in what she thought to be an absentminded gesture. His thumb was like sandpaper. 'Just remember your old Dad loves you very much. With all his heart.'

When he disengaged her, there was the shadow of a resentment back on his face: Melanie was momentarily frightened by life. She took his hand and kissed it.

'You're a lovely dad,' she said. His pleasure was almost pitiful.

All this sharpness of observation came from books. Reading was not just oblivion. She had a funny phase when her habit took on more than a degree of self-regard. She used to sit against the Heinz Soup cushion quite naked, the book in her lap, her tiny bosom goosepimpled with cold, her knees far and away the most protuberant thing about her. It was her experiment with time. She was reading Henry Miller, and wanted to feel wicked. But imagining herself to be an urchin in a Paris brothel ended with her bottom and thighs being imprinted with the weave of the haircord carpet. She gave up the experiment.

She was a novel-reader who made deeper and deeper excursions into literary biographies and the letters of famous men. They were mostly American, these men. She had tried the British novel, but found it too petulant. Her admired writers were Hemingway, Scott Fitzgerald, and of course Miller. Much of all this was a kind of love affair with America itself — young though she was, she recognised the different Americas of her heroes as being filled with an innocence her own innocence might answer. These men, these sprawling and wryly upturned giants, fitted very well into her own imagined country, where things were huge and playful, and exuberant, where to die was not to die, and to love was painful yet not a clumsy act, but deft. America was not for Melanie a country to be reached on payment of money to a travel agent. America was a country of fictional geography — an island. She did not realise that her most favoured authors were all exiles, and some would say traitors. She was, after all, still very young.

'It just isn't natural,' Mrs Brearley said to friends. 'We've tried to wean her off this sort of thing. Jack made a special effort with her a few months ago' (which was how the bellowing hurt of talking to Melanie about Helen the thickie had been fictionalised) 'but she's just the same again. No change. None whatsoever.'

'She just reads,' Jack agreed, but with a secret swell of pride in him at having a daughter so elusive to the grasp. One of the crosses he was learning to bear was the occasional pang of lust for her, the

stir of something he felt ashamed to put in words. The two women
in his life: the one a nag, but as familiar as cloth; the other likewise
familiar, except that sometimes he caught himself looking at her
with a keenness he had instantly to erase. He asked around, cautious
and indirect, among pals who had daughters. It happened, apparently.

Melanie and her mother did not get on. They did not quarrel, but
they did not enjoy each other as perhaps was natural. The child
recognised a duty to both parents and was docile — irreproachable,
even. But she did not feel a scrap of warmth towards them. She had,
after all, never experienced it. Mrs Brearley had views about
cuddling and touching and all the things you heard other people
doing with their children. She loved Melanie. She loved her
sometimes to distraction, sobbing into the pillow long after Jack had
fallen asleep, sprawled on his back like a roofer who had crashed
through the ceiling. She wanted Melanie to succeed: she wanted her
daughter to conquer. But she would have liked (although she did not
know how to ask for it) Melanie's respect. For her, love and respect
were so closely intertwined as to be like the stake and the plant.

When she was eighteen, Melanie went to university. By now, she
had eleven 'O' levels and three 'A's — it was awesome, the calm
she showed when being examined, or placed under what for her
parents would have been extreme stress. She had grown into a tall
slim girl with no fashion sense and few contemporary manners:
there was a curt side to her that disconcerted those who wanted to
get to know her.

She still read. Her parents were older and in some ways more
satisfied with life — or more accommodated to it. She read downstairs nowadays, in the glass-green light of the front room. Her
father had built her a row of shelves in the alcove for her books, and
in her absence he would like to show friends from the bowls club
into that room and exhibit Melanie's books.

'Some of these are first editions. That makes them worth twenty
quid or more,' he would explain wonderingly. 'And some of 'em
have stuff in them you'd find hard to imagine. You know, the Paris
lot. The expatriates.'

His pals would stare at the spines of the books and try to understand what the hell old Jack was on about.

'And now she's up at Cambridge, eh, Jack?'

'Now she's up at Cambridge.'

She was reading English. The Brearleys went to see her in her rooms, and marvelled at the gleaming whiteness, the purity and silence. They exclaimed at the quality of the college lawns, and walked along the Backs, identifying in loud voices all the trees and shrubs in all the college gardens, too nervous to ask her how she was. Mrs Brearley commented fervently on the peace and calm of the surroundings. Melanie nodded. She did not know her mother was aghast to see that she had discarded her bra. Jack too was stunned. But there was something else with him. He felt the most uncomfortable sensations in watching Melanie covertly. The little commonplace lusts he had harboured for his daughter, which had made him so guilty, were now replaced by something very much like love. He could not take his eyes off his daughter. She seemed to float, and shimmer. She seemed a being utterly apart from him, not connected to him in any way, by bond or blood. He truly fell in love with her.

'We were half-hoping to see a young man in evidence,' his wife said to friends when they returned from one of these trips. It was like a knife in the guts to Jack. 'I mean, I'm sure it isn't natural the way she seems to exist without anybody else.'

'Don't go marrying her off,' he said, too gruffly. Mrs Brearley looked up, startled.

'Now who on earth is talking about marriage, these days?' she asked. 'Really, Jack, you can be so old-fashioned.'

But her laugh was a false one. Privately she was watching her daughter as a woman might sit under a distant tree, waiting for the castle to fall to the siege.

At the end of the first year there was a fortnight's hiatus after Prelims, and before going-down. Melanie was out walking in the fields beyond Grange Road when she met David, who had been born and raised as a member of the Plymouth Brethren, and had just thrown it all over. His mind, as she quickly saw, was in chaos. If anyone was like a sacked castle, it was David, that summer.

Like Melanie, he had a complete absence of conventional manners. He was reading Natural Sciences and talked a lot about lasers, and chip technology — indeed, anything that was new, and superior, and remonstrated with the common inefficiency and stupidity. He was the most terrific intellectual snob. Incoherent, but massively priggish. His youth's beard was springy and black and he wore, on the day she met him, football shorts and sandals, with an aertex shirt to protect his chest. There was something of the wild man about him. Melanie recognised, deep down in her bowels, that he could be a most dangerous man to know. She did not at first realise that he was very close to killing himself.

'I suppose you love your parents?' he accused.

She considered this in silence. David frowned. 'You may as well know I hate mine. I don't just mean temporarily. I hate them.'

'Have they made you afraid?' she asked, jolting him badly.

'What I want,' he said recklessly on the second time they met, 'is the experience of real love.'

'You want what?' Melanie asked with her customary sharpness.

They made a funny couple — she so tall, and with a cotton skirt and teeshirt flattened against her by the breeze; and he, massive and truculent looking, still wearing the dreadful shorts from which thrummed thighs like a weightlifter's. They were leaning over the bridge in Garret Hostel Lane, looking towards Clare. He studied the soupy green water for a long time, trying to clarify his remark.

'I want not to be afraid of my doubts,' he said.

She understood him perfectly, and instantly.

'You want a proper uncertainty,' she said.

People passing, just there for a day out, sniggered. Two bits of kids talking bullshit, mooning about with their lah-di-dah ideas.

She gave herself to him that night. It was very studied, her attitude (although she was frightened more than she liked to admit). He was the first, and she did not specially want there to be *that* much significance. The earlier remark about uncertainty was apt, too apt. Neither of them had any prior experience, and at the very last, when it was too late to retract, she was overwhelmed by terror. Life, after all, was not a book, and he was by no means Hemingway.

'I meant to wash my hair,' she said distractedly, lying on the bed and watching him fumble with his clothes. It was still light outside, and they could hear feet crunching on the gravel walks. Her naked body shuddered uncontrollably. The details of the thing were amazing her: David was folding his shirt and his shorts as though at boarding school. His underpants were the most terrible lime green, faded by washing. A semi-circular scar on his back gleamed like a bit of Arabic.

She woke at dawn, the delicate nacreous light of a fen sunrise. The birds chattered. Beside her, the fiasco of the night before. She slipped out of bed and washed herself with a cold sponge, crying. It was perfectly possible, though unlikely, that a cell of her body had been impregnated by a cell of his — *there*, under the pale flesh shimmering with pearls of water. She crawled back into bed, a gush of hot tears at the back of her nose, and fitted her body to his, her bony hips against his hugely square buttocks.

Mr Brearley discovered them at ten, when he came to fetch Melanie home in the Chevette. He steamed into the room in his new jumper from Marks and Spencer's, a wool and suede thing he had chivvied his wife into buying. He was silent, and apologetic, but pierced to the heart. David sat up in bed with a hasty fumbling for his glasses.

'I am so very sorry,' he kept saying. 'I can't tell you how sorry I am.'

'Shut up,' Melanie said.

She met her father for lunch at the Mill, discovering him with a sandwich and a half of bitter, squeezed out to the very edge of a crowd of students. He smiled wanly.

'It was going to be a surprise,' he said.

'Put all that down and walk me somewhere,' she commanded.

They walked out in the meadows beyond the Garden House Hotel, and sat with their backs to a honey-coloured wall.

'I can't talk about it,' Melanie warned.

'That's all right. It's none of my business.'

She turned to look at her father with a hopeless expression.

'Of course it's your business.'

'I don't see how,' he muttered, stubborn. The tears in his eyes must be, he thought, as big as rivers.

'I don't love him,' Melanie said.

Her father felt a momentary surge of relief that was more appropriate to a rival than to anything else; but then his natural prudence conquered it. He took her hand and kissed it.

'You can't say that,' he said, choking. 'It's a funny old thing, love.'

Something in the unfamiliar gesture of his having kissed her hand sparked a memory in her, without her being aware exactly what. She looked at her father in surprise and startled him.

'Dad, do you remember when we had a picnic once, down by the river, and there'd been some quarrel about something and you were so kind to me. Do you remember?'

He wrinkled his eyes as if trying to see that far back along the path they had come. For her the question was really rhetorical for, like Proust dipping a cake into his tea, the action of handkissing, which was not the Brearley's common way of going about things, had released the fragrance of a long-forgotten event. But Melanie's father was not and could not be her lover in the sense that David claimed he was. He drummed his fingers on her wrist, thinking of only what to do for the good. The practical problem was what to say to Rose when they got home, or whether to say anything at all. There was a moral issue here if only he could refine the chaos of his thought.

What he had felt for her that afternoon of her childhood and what he felt for her now were the beginning and end of a love affair — not the only one he harboured for his daughter, and not the last he would experience. But for the time being he was a man with his child, gassy with beer and watching the particular way his trouser leg flapped in the little breeze; and thinking. Melanie threw her arms round him suddenly.

'Oh Dad, I love you,' she sobbed, pierced by it all.

'There, he said, 'There, there.'

It was what people said to each other at times like these. Melanie sniffed suddenly at the cloth of his jacket.

'You've given up smoking,' she said.

'What the holy hammer has that got to do with it?' he asked, a bit exasperated. The warmth of her unencumbered breasts pressed unheeded against his anxious heart.

ALAN BLEASDALE

Christmas is over

Their reunions had become, over the years, very careful and calculated affairs. Or perhaps their affair had become a very careful and calculated reunion.

Sometimes in the late summer she would find a short residential drama course advertised in *The Teacher* and scheduled for the start of the Christmas holidays, terminating on Christmas Eve. She usually had a choice of courses and it always amused her to study each prospectus carefully before deciding on the most appropriate one.

Then, when the enrolment forms arrived, she would leave them displayed casually on the mantelpiece and at some point in the next few days her husband would, in her presence, pick up the forms, glance at her strong handwriting, search for the cost and silently agree. After all, there had never been any children to worry about. As she said herself, quite often, she was totally free.

Finally, silently too, in the season of great rejoicement for the birth of the Boy Child, she would leave her husband, taking the taxi to the station and the train to Harlech; the snow on the mountains far purer than her intentions.

This year, however, was different. Most decidedly different. But it wasn't a decision that she had made; there were no arguments to debate within herself. It was simply a fact of life. She had even, in her precise manner, checked the times of the trains for the return journey before setting off from Lime Street Station.

He, inevitably, would be waiting for her when the train shuffled into sight, past the rows of stone houses that seemed thrown in collision against the Harlech hillside. He had always thought it was his duty to be there first; to light the fire in the caravan and fill the shelves with Christmas groceries and then be there waving wildly on platform one.

Even now, at the age of thirty-seven, he needed the security of a ritual to wrap his life around, a spider's web to catch his fears. Absurdly and nakedly, his last actions before going to bed entailed touching the door handle and the light switch three times, while his final words to his wife as he climbed in beside her were, 'See you in the morning.' Almost certainly he would not have minded never actually seeing her again, but he always wanted to believe that he would still be alive in the morning.

This particular morning, this year, there was a drama course in Reading and a trades conference in Newcastle, but instead, as the morning mist turned to afternoon drizzle, they walked along a broken-fenced path through the sandhills towards the beach. At their backs, just below the skyline, on a mound that looked like an afterthought of nature, stood the empty Castle of Harlech.

As was their custom, they had just celebrated their Christmas dinner: turkey and the trimmings, Christmas pudding and Christmas crackers, the unwrapping of presents, and a bottle of brandy. Nothing unusual perhaps, except that outside their caravan, everywhere else in the world, Christmas Day was still at least seventy-two hours away.

They strode for some time along the empty beach while the tight-lipped waves drove against the shoreline. Occasionally she would stop and lift stones and prod the driftwood, while he walked towards the salt and the spray at the edge of the tide.

'It's like a cigarette advert,' she said, coming up behind him. 'All we need are two white horses, bleached jeans and three inches off my hips.'

They stayed silent till the tide began to trickle and then spurt across their overshoes. 'Come on,' he said, 'It's getting late and we need milk and eggs.'

'Good job it's not really Christmas Day,' she said as they turned and saw another, much younger, couple walking towards them. The boy wore a duffle coat and the girl a bright yellow mac and they clung heavily to each other, pretending it was for protection against the wind slicing across the beach.

He had once worn a duffle coat and she a bright yellow mac. And once, too, they had been ridiculously young. She lost her mac in the Cavern when it was still a jazz cellar, and his duffle coat he left behind on the Seacombe ferry one spring night in 1962 — the night she told him that she had found someone she liked 'an awful lot' at college in Bedford, and perhaps it would be better if they 'stopped seeing each other, you do understand, don't you?'

They did stop seeing each other, and he pretended to understand for as long as he could. He pretended so well that when mutual friends informed him of her eventual marriage, he sent a telegram, a dinner service and his best wishes. Her reply was formal but friendly, and the invitation to dinner if ever he was in London seemed genuine enough. However, he remembered the cold cheerfulness with which she had once dismissed him, hesitated for a few days, and then hurled her letter out of his attic flat window. A couple of hours later, when he searched the street outside, it was nowhere to be found.

'Let's go then,' she said, wakening him from his dreams and tugging him away from a tide that was now attacking their ankles. The other couple had started running across the foreshore, hair blown back by the wind, giggling like the schoolchildren they possibly still were. He wondered, as they passed in a flurry of laughter and splashes, whether she was aware of her own yellow mac and his lost duffle coat, their distant youth and the distance *still* between them.

Many times before, here on the beach, or there in the caravan, he had asked her to leave her husband and live with him. He was secure financially if nothing else, he would say, why suffer two barren and childless marriages when they could start again together? And she would smile and call him her little child, saying it in such a way that the desire to hit her was overcome by the most basic desire of all.

'What's the matter?' she said, seconds before he was about to ask her. Perhaps he had thought of the question first, but hadn't he, as always, hesitated? The bully of the boardroom became the blushing boy, bewildered by his first date whenever he was with her. Twenty years ago she had been his first date. When he had kissed her on the nose, in a bus shelter at the Pier Head, she had laughed and offered him a chocolate. And when they had met again, totally by chance, when he lived in London and she had returned to Liverpool with her husband, as they stood staring at each other in an Inter-City buffet car, he had said to her, 'It's so again to see you good.' Whereupon she had laughed and offered him a cigarette.

'Come on,' she said, 'what is the matter?'

'The fire's gone out,' he replied as they entered the caravan site.

'They usually do, eventually,' she said distantly, as if it was her turn now to be lost in her own imaginings. She took her hand away from his and stared across at the black clouds crouched against the shadowed mountains of Snowdonia, coming all this way merely to bring rain.

Briefly, as he walked with her through the dead winter grass, he struggled with an explanation for the reasons why he made this pre-Christmas pilgrimage every year. Part ritual, part memory and a small part passion, were the only answers he could ever give himself. And this year, the memory and the passion had seemed further away than ever.

'This could be the last time,' he whistled bravely to himself as they approached his BMW at the side of the caravan, but if she noticed at all, he thought, it was only to recognise the tune.

'We need some firelighters as well,' he said, taking hold of her hand again and walking towards the car.

'No,' she said, stopping and turning on him, almost pulling him off his feet with the abruptness of her action. 'No, we don't, I'm afraid.' She released her grip and walked slowly towards the doorway.

'What do you mean?' he asked, but she neither turned nor acknowledged his question, and he was forced to follow her into the cramped surroundings of the caravan. He found her, back turned, head down, her monogrammed suitcase already lying on the tiny divan couch, and they stayed silent for some seconds amid the miniature cupboards and utility furniture for midgets, until he stumbled into speech.

'You . . . you want to unpack first, is that it?'

'No,' she said flatly. 'I don't want to unpack at all.'

'Don't tell me you bought a day return?' he said, trying for laughter that lay stillborn. 'I know, you've left the oven on.'

She turned, glanced at her watch, and then looked at him until he averted his eyes, as they both knew he would.

'There's a train in twenty-five minutes,' she said.

'But *why?*' he demanded. 'Why now?'

'Look at me,' she said and unbuttoned her coat. 'Look very carefully. Do you not notice any difference?'

'Well, yeah,' he said, 'you're older than when we first met.' He
grabbed her but she pulled herself away. 'All right then, all right,
you've put on a bit of weight this year, no harm in that, suits you,
you said something yourself on the beach ... what was it? ''Three
inches off my hips ...'' So, we'll eat yoghurt and bran for the next
two days. You don't have to ...'

And then he stopped and stepped back, tripping over the half-
empty brandy bottle, while she stayed unmoved by his performance
and his sudden nervous giggle of realisation.

'You ... you're ...' he said. 'You are?'

'Three months. Perhaps four.' She picked her suitcase up and
walked past him through the curtained partition. He reached out
and put his arm around her shoulder, but, yet again, his affection
was misplaced, lost like a memory of events that never really took
place.

'It's another ending, isn't it?' he asked, still searching for
humour to cover the hurt as she stood stoically against him until he
released her. 'The end, in fact. It's all right, I'll send you another
dinner service. A Mothercare one.'

'Who knows,' she said, smiling for what seemed like the first time
since her arrival, 'perhaps when we're old and grey and bent double
with arthritis, we'll meet on a pensioners' outing to Llandudno, and
live happily ever after.'

'Great,' he said, 'shall we make that a date? Why leave it up to
chance this time? How about the er ... summer of 2007; let's say
August Bank Holiday, eleven o'clock at the corporation bus depot
on Edge Lane. Now, let me see, I'll be wearing a duffle coat, and if
you carry a yellow mac ...'

'And a walking stick,' she said.

'Yeah, and you can push me along the prom in my wheelchair.
Knock-out. I'll write it in my thirty-year diary when I get home,' he
said with a sudden unaccustomed harshness as he opened the
caravan door. And then waited to let her walk through first.

He didn't cry till they got to the station. While she went to the
ticket office, he stood behind a chocolate machine with his handker-

chief and pretended that the cold weather had got in his eyes. When
she returned he was blindly trying to put a fifty-pence piece in the
tenpenny slot of a machine that had been vandalised some years
before. And when he turned around, she said precisely the words
that would hurt him the most with the effortless flair that comes to
people with power and control over others. A careless, dismissive
authority he had used so often himself on everyone else, except her.

'I'm sorry,' she said. 'I am going to miss seeing you.'

It was a combination between a back-handed slap and a punch,
and although it was talked about for a long time in the staff rest-
room at Harlech station, where within the week it had turned into a
vicious uppercut that lifted her in the air and broke her nose, in
reality he barely caught the side of her face with his half-opened
knuckles.

There was no sense of elation or victory, for he knew that
violence was the last act of a defeated mind, and was no defence at
all. However, like the first time he grabbed his mother's wrists and
stopped her from hurting him again, the feeling of freedom as he
saw the surprise in her eyes was enough for him to be satisfied with
a plea of self-defence.

'No, you're not sorry,' he answered harshly, aware that this was
yet another of her carefully orchestrated plans, the conclusion of a
smooth operation. 'You won't miss me at all. You're going to have
a child, you won't need your memories of childhood any more, will
you?' In the dull half-dark of the late afternoon, he saw two porters
turn rapidly away and the train approaching, moving like an out-of-
season caterpillar across the ridge between stone and sea. 'I've been
your child for twenty-five years. Not so much a lover as a brother.
A baby brother.'

He leant forward, his turn to smile, kissed her carefully on the
nose, patted the cheek that he had hit, then brushed aside her hand
on his shoulder. As he walked away there was something about
himself that reminded him of Humphrey Bogart.

'No!' she shouted, her unhappy ending not achieved, and briefly
he heard her footfall behind him until the train came sighing into
the station. As he reached the end of the platform her voice echoed
with a desperate lightness out of the carriage towards him.

'Don't forget, the corporation bus depot, August Bank Holiday, a duffle coat and . . . '

The whistle went, a porter bellowed, he handed his platform ticket in, the train was released. And so was he.

DAVID MERCER

Folie à Deux

It's a bit of a sod when you're writing about somebody and you find they're writing about you. If it's intimate, I mean. Because the other day I was just going through Ossy's bureau and I finds this:

May 6: I really don't know what to make of it. An extraordinary thing! And now, I have to ask myself why I have not told my wife. I cannot avoid the self-accusation of dishonesty, but she looks so ill and fragile. This paralysis is a great trial to her — she was such an active woman. Besides, I think her sense of duty aggravates her conviction that I find it difficult to manage things without her assistance. Alas, it is true that Claire's devotion to Parish affairs has always compensated for my own somewhat dilatory approach to the problems which fall to the lot of an ageing vicar.

Yet in all my years I have never gone through quite such a harrowing experience as that which found me so ill-equipped to handle this evening.

I had spent a pleasant half-hour instructing the new server (a pleasant and intelligent boy), and was preparing to lock up, when it happened. Someone came into the church through the West Door (it should have been locked) and sat down in the sidesmen's pew. I had turned off most of the lights and was just opening the vestry door. I waited, in something of a quandary. People often do come into church like that to rest or pray, or merely to shelter; but it was nine p.m. and rather late, I thought, for the exercise of that amiable tolerance which is the most strenuous discipline of my calling. Tired and hungry, I felt in no mood to provoke an exchange which might turn out to be boring, or even starkly unwelcome. Then, whoever it was (I could hardly see) began to sob in the most heart-rending fashion. There was nothing for it but to investigate. An all too familiar situation, and one which I knew to my cost would put a humiliating strain on a charity already closer to despair than to God.

It was a woman, of course! A massive, pathetic creature huddled in the shadows — and, I suspected, in an advanced state of intoxication. Not a case for a few gentle, pious phrases. So much physical bulk and such obvious unhappiness made me timid, so I bowed my head and waited for her to notice me.

Now that, if you can make any sense of it, is how I entered Ossy's life. Him with his head bowed and me in the act of damning me immortal soul. Holy Mother of God, it was like being drunk — just the same feeling, so how should I expect *him* to know the difference? You know, when you've had one too many? Like falling down a hole. And there's this old priest, I suppose *they* call it vicar, come down the aisle and stood over me like a judgement. The old buzzard. Still, he couldn't have known I'd swallowed all them aspirins *and* had a bun in the oven *and* crawled into the wrong bloody church to die in a state of mortal sin. Jesus wept. I looks up and sees him standing there and thinks I shall die damned and lonely in a foreign country with this old streak to comfort me last hour. Had a wart on his chin with hairs sticking out. Couldn't make out if the place was dark or I was going already. I can laugh now, but Christ I had the wind up then and not enough sense to tell the old fool to fetch a doctor.

Katie, when you get this letter light a candle for Peg.

Well, after a lot of shenanigans he gets me into the vestry and sees this lovely bulge under me coat and the look in me eye. Gets a medical pal from down the street. Katie, that was an experience. I shan't forget it, no. They got it all up, the aspirins and me dinner and I prays they get *it* up as well, but no such luck.

You see his wife's got polio, that's how I think it all started. You'll kill yourself when you hear he's going on seventy. He must have seen a thing or two that night anyway, he's been after me like a goat ever since and never mind the bulge, oh no. He's a very learned man, I will say. All brain. But Claire, that's his wife, thinks it's immoral except for getting babies, by which I don't mean brain of course. She's barren or some such expression. Wish I was. But who's Peg to deny a man's natural appetites even if I am punished with this inside. I think it had a good old kick this afternoon, I wish it would kick itself to death — it's going to make a difference to *my* life. Still, he's good to me. I'm the organist here now and I live in and look after Claire as well. I don't think she knows what he's up to.

Don't ask me how it came about — you know how it is when you're up against it, and Ossy, I call him Ossy but his name's Ossian (Flint!), well, he's a scream really. These Anglicans. I've seen some funny things in Dublin and I shouldn't be surprised if that's where I got this inside, or Liverpool, but *he* beats the band. Comes up in his cassock after service, you wouldn't think she was upstairs all crippled and him looking like a sort of cross between a starved ram and a headmaster. It's hard to put into a letter but I get a few laughs what with him being so thin and peculiar and me, well, you know, *my* size. Like cracking nuts. Isn't it funny, though, the things you'd never expect from people who ought to know better. Then I told him how I've got no parents and came over here and the hell they make of your life. After all, servants aren't what they were, are they, to get kicked around. Not even in your opportunity state, I said. And then all that with knowing I was in the family way and getting depressed and taking the pills, because what is there to live for? I'm no Holy Mother.

Ossy's sweet, though, in his way. I really do think it's doing him good. And to look at Claire you can see she'd die sooner than let him, even when she had the use. His trouble is he seems to worry. I can't make it out and I don't know why he doesn't just enjoy it while he's got it. But there you are, he *is* a kind of priest isn't he? Wait till you see May 17.

May 17: I see that I was interrupted during my last entry, to minister to the unfortunate girl I described — who was ill and had to be put to bed in the vicarage. Even now I can hardly bring myself to speak of these things, and were it not for my proneness to an ironic masochism I would discontinue this journal. However, I have never been guilty of blindness to my unorthodoxies as a clergyman, even if I have been cynical of my responsibilities. As an agnostic of some forty years' standing I have not once baulked at self-examination, though it promised to exacerbate the pain of a guilty conscience which can turn nowhere for absolution. Doubtless I would have been happier had I been of the Roman persuasion.

And now Peggy (who might be described, perhaps, as a dubious colleen ... a Demeter of the Emerald Isle), Peggy is better, is so well indeed as to bring to my cloistered existence the delights of a somewhat prurient convalescence. We drink. We fornicate. I have become an ecclesiastical tosspot, and this a shameful document — the '*liber pornograficorum*' of a cleric so reduced and enfeebled by lust as to welcome the thought of his possible demise at the climax of the sexual act. In my young days, it was known among a certain clique of muttering youths as 'dying on the nest' — and it has taken me fifty odd years to detect the note of poetry in this laconic phrase, so characteristic of the *Lumpenproletariat*.

But such a nest. The flesh tints of Reubens, the spacial solidity of Titian, the ribald speciousness of Rowlandson — all combined for the terrible sacrament of my disintegration.

NB — Investigate: (1) Randy
                    (2) Get with it
                    (3) Dig (of idea, curious phenomenon etc.)

Back again. What a day. We spent most of the afternoon you-know-how, so I made him take me out afterwards. Ossy bought a camera that takes indoor photos (he'll come to a sticky end, this one), and some nylons for me. Said something about why don't we go off on his motorbike and spend a week rubbing brasses, which I suppose is his funny old way of saying rubbing Peg. Why should *I* mind? Rising twenty-two and my weight, you can't pick and choose. But I'll say this for old men — what they haven't got by way of you-know-what they make up for by cunning. Oh, he's full of ideas and talks all the time about something called pre-natal conditioning. Well, we went to the pictures in Leicester Square — a lovely film about a Thing. Came home on a bus. You've not lived till you've seen Ossy on a bus. What with the camera, his pipe and his umbrella and having to count out the fare. First thing I knew, he was yelling fit to wake the dead and skeltering down the gangway in a cloud of smoke. Burning ash from his pipe. It had dropped down inside his umbrella and the last *I* saw of Ossy, he was belting down Kensington High Street whirling a flaming gamp round his head. Well, it was a quiet ride home, but laugh! Turns up panting like a dog at half-past seven with a black face, and what was left of his brolly draped over his arm like a smoked haddock. No sooner washed and has his dinner than off we go again. *This* time she was beating on the bedroom floor with her stick. Thought it was burglars. So, instead of going up to tell her some story to set her mind at rest, he takes me into the vestry.

He has a sort of stuffed couch there and we gets down between the Mothers' Union banner on one side and the Church Lads' Brigade banner on the other. No sooner had we got nice and comfy than Ossy leaps up with his trousers round his knees and scuttles into the cupboard where they keep the surplices, shouting, 'Choir practice, choir practice!' And sure enough, there's voices outside and I've just time to nip in beside me man before they arrive. The next thing I know the little organ they have in the vestry's blowing away like a banshee with wind, and we're treated to a lovely rendering of 'Born is the lamb' or one of those.

I forgot to mention I had nothing on but me slip, and the rest of me clothes was under the couch there.

Well. We stands there shivering and they stands there singing and it goes on and on and on. Ossy said never a word. I just felt his bony old hand wandering over me bulge in the darkness with the surplices and cassocks waving round us, and thinks, Did you ever! Then he would have his pipe. Of all the times and places. He must have his pipe and be damned. Meantime I've pulled on one of the cassocks and I'm feeling a bit warmer. But I'd had a premonition ever since the bus. And sure enough the burning plug comes out of his pipe like a perm on the flaming head of the Devil himself. You'll not have smelled burning cassock, Katie, so I'll tell you now it's a moving experience. It's a revelation, as if they was setting fire to one of those old monks I should think that crossed the Holy Father.

I expect you've guessed the rest. Inside ten minutes we're standing there with the flames coming up round us, Ossy groaning and me wondering whether it's best to fry now or later. Then his shirt tail caught fire — he'd forgotten to tuck it in — and *that* set him off. He flings open the cupboard door and he's through that vestry like a jumping cracker with me not far behind him, only tripping over the cassock.

I wish you could have seen their faces. There'll be one or two in that bunch never sing another note for shock.

Now I'm in the bath, Ossy's locked in his study and the firemen are trying to put out the church, but it's expected to be a total loss. Will post this when I've seen Ossy's entry for tonight.

May 23: As I write, the sky over South Kensington is red with the apocalyptic glow of my burning church. Peg is taking a bath. My wife is shrieking for information, but I fear she will have to make do with Nembutal. The catastrophe is of such dimensions that no mortal grasp of the logical possibilities of life can do it justice. In such circumstances the mind is prone to clutch at detail. My collection of ikons (which I foolishly kept in the vestry) is lost. My Canterbury rubbings, which I transferred from the vestry to the house only this morning, are safe. The traumatic nature of the evening's events is mercifully obscured by a sense of their absurdity.

I console myself that my parishioners are at last aware of the salient inconsistencies of their spiritual shepherd! As I fled past the choirmaster in my halo of fire, I distinctly heard him say, 'Now the old goat's been and gone and done it!' Doubtless his reference was inspired more by the presence of Friar Peg in voluminous cassock than by the sight of my incandescent self. I defy any man alive to concoct an explanation of what happened that would satisfy the choirmaster. As for the Bishop — that dour and underfed man of labyrinthine dissimulations — the Bishop will certainly think it worth a gutted church to have such incontestable grounds for my liquidation. The Church of England has never known how to deal with its eccentrics, but has a nimble way with more purulent forms of dissent such as carnality and pyromania. The Bishop does not dig me, anyway.

Strange to sit here and watch those sturdy firemen going about their lawful business. Mournful to reflect that I had the joint ablaze within six weeks of the completion of the restorations. I can imagine the relief in high places that we failed to raise enough

money to purchase a Graham Sutherland altarpiece; thus is
philistinism ever at the service of thrift, and thrift at the mercy of
vulgarity. All the same, I would have liked to see something nice
and spiky in the place and I am sure we would have been able to
get it down before the flames reached the chancel.

The roof of the nave has just crashed in.

Perhaps I should cram wife and doxy on to the motorbike and
flee the country? Peg would like that, for her world has hitherto
been restricted to Dublin, Liverpool and London. But I cannot see
us arriving at a *modus vivendi* with Claire. I am inclined, in fact,
to abandon my wife to the mercy of that God in whom she has
still a certain weary faith. True, she is paralysed, and so entitled to
such consideration as would be insulting to a person in a state of
bodily health; and yet, apart from my respect for the integrity of
medical science, I wonder if such paralysis is not an expression of
the desire to yield volition and cower gratefully beneath the
umbrella of necessity?

For dearest Peg, on the other hand, necessity is the mode of
fulfilment. She is bewitchingly defined by her limitations. If their
postulated God had been a Jesuit, Eve would have been a sort of
Peg — would have renounced the apple and dreamed Original Sin
out of a sense of destiny. Or some such nonsense.

Now the head fireman (or whatever he is called) strides forth
from the holocaust bearing a chalice. I have never been partial to
symbolism, but the moment has its dignity. Perhaps vicars should
be burned with their churches, as captains used to go down with
their ships. Why, the good fellow is waving the chalice at the
crowd! Where does he think he is? Wembley? I presume he *is* the
head fireman, since he appears to have a larger crest on his helmet
than the others. Now the chalice has been snatched from him by
one of the sidesmen — a venerable banker, who is doubtless
grateful to be able to rescue our silver and the vessel of Christ's
Blood by a single stroke of the arm.

The doorbell has not stopped ringing since we found sanctuary
here after quitting the turbulent scene at the church. I must wash
and divest myself of these poor charred garments, and go down.
Tonight I must also inform Claire of the true nature of our little
ménage à trois. In a way, it is exhilerating to think that at sixty-

eight one can be so indisputably committed to the Way of Choice rather than the Refuge of Determinism.

Oh, Kate, what a time we've had! It's October now and I've got a little boy who doesn't look like any of his possible dads, and we've just come back from Europe where we went on Ossy's bike the morning after the fire. That morning! It turned out the old girl (Mrs Ossy) wasn't paralysed after all, would you believe it? She's up at half past six and takes all me things and throws them downstairs — you see Ossy had told her about Us the night before. Well, and the last to go is me little trunk that's been with me everywhere, and as she tips it over the bannisters she can't get her hand out of one of the handles and over she goes *with* it. A shackled and self-destructive soul, she's dead as a doornail when we picks her up and, as he says, these things are never accidental. There's those with the Will to Live and those without. 'So, let the dead bury the dead,' says Ossy and rings up Claire's sister and asks her to see to things. We put the poor old thing on the couch in Ossy's study, covers her with a blanket, locks the door and posts the key to his sister-in-law. There was no time to waste that day. Fancy, all those years in bed when she could have been up and about, just for spite.

We packed two suitcases and bunged them in the sidecar, then I got on the pillion and Ossy was just kicking the starter thing when he suddenly moans and claps his hands to his face. 'Now then,' says I, 'this is no time for second thoughts.' But he moans and moans, and finally croaks at me, 'Rigor Mortis!' It went to my heart the way he looked sitting there with wisps of grey hair floating round his ears and one foot on that pedal. So then it's back into the house and break down the study door, switch on the electric fire and get somebody to come and Lay her Out.

Well, we finally got to Europe which is a lovely place with many fine churches and paintings. But I got homesick and Ossy gave me a book to read which he said would remind me of Dublin. This book is very thick by a man called Joyce and its title is *Ulysses*, which I recommend you never to read if you are feeling likewise. If that is Dublin then I am a Dutchman, which as Ossy says is a logical impossibility since I am Irish, though not proud of it. According to him I have a Natural Intelligence which he says he will nourish, and

I will say the book has a moral which seems to be that if you do not know who your Father is you must not allow the fact to grind you down. Thus we come to my confinement, and talking of Fathers I wish the one responsible had been there, for it nearly ripped me in two when it came and now my bubbies look like mangled rubber balls, what with the way it eats. But lovely to be down to eleven stone again.

After Europe we came back to London and now go by the name of Travers. We have two furnished rooms in Highgate and Ossy is writing articles, at the moment one on a frog philosopher called Sart, I think, and one on a Cardinal called Newman. Also he is helping me to perfect my Literary Style as I have taken to showing him my letters to you and he says they are very Human documents. I cannot help wondering what would have become of me if I had not found Ossy that night in his church — and, indeed, what would have become of the old lecher himself. He is much the same, though, in some ways and will still have me morning, noon and night as the fancy takes him. But I am full of love and take his brittle old carcass and roll it between me flanks, though I stand in the full glare from the Devil's eye and dare not think of the prognosis for me immortal soul. At the same time Ossy is not an ordinary man and sometimes gives me a turn, as you will see from the following.

October 30: Today I says to myself it shall be Sartre! And Sartre is was, though I lost my favourite pen and pounded the rest of the day on a typewriting machine. Now, would it not be true to say that by a process of what you might call psychological exfoliation, Modern Man is reduced to the status of an Object? I have tried this out on Peg, who retorted that Modern Man is a figment of his own imagination! This delightful hunk of girl is revealing what the novelists of my youth used to call 'unexpected depths of character'. If it were not for her nauseating infant, what succulent morsels might we not disinter from the seething chaos of a mind steeped in the trivia of twentieth-century existence? For Prom (we have named him Prometheus in honour of our freedom, stolen like fire from the teeth of metaphysical opposition), for Prom I say, obscures the finer points of our relationship at the moment. Conceived in what slum, born in the Camargue, destined for the stultifying complications of mother love, this outrageous little parasite is a wily enemy. Rattle in hand, nipple clenched firmly between the gums, he insinuates his revolting person between us at every turn. Ah, Prometheus Travers, the struggle will be long and there shall be no quarter!

Holy Mother of God, I says to Peg, can we not give him away? Sell him? Barter him? Have him pressed and use him as a sentimental bookmark? She gives me one look, and I cower back over my article like any other demoralised hack. What a mercy it is that babies are so small and puny, for had they the physical stature of men they would quickly establish themselves as our masters and the world would be ruled by the rattle, civilisation held in bondage to the Pleasure Principle.

A Dynasty of Tots!

Yet when I see our politicians, men of power, promoters and neo-tycoons disporting themselves on the television screen, I am inclined to think that from their statements and various antics one can construe the beginnings of such an Infantile Revolution. Imagine beneath those well-cut suits — the Nappy! Behind those horn-rimmed glasses — the azure vacuity of the Tabula Rasa! Inside those damp mouths — the sour and milky regurgitation of a primitive organism! The final take-over bid of them all will surely set a rotund infant on the throne, to bubble the time-honoured platitudes at us and wiggle a biffy fist from the balcony of the palace.

Peg will not have it so, but what loving mother does not secretly wish to see her plump and dribbling youngster attain worldly honour whilst retaining precisely those characteristics he had when shot parboiled and yodelling from the womb?

But who is Ossy to deny a woman her natural aptitudes, even if I am punished with this little Prom on the rug? He gave me a good old kick this afternoon, I wish he would kick himself to death — he is going to make a difference to *my* life. Still, Peg is good to me and you know how it is when you are up against it. These Celts. This morning she decides to bake us a cake. Well, anyone who hasn't seen Peg in a kitchen hasn't lived! What with not understanding about gas cookers and trying to finish *Finnegan's Wake* and maundering over her cub — the last *I* saw of her before lunch she's hurtling downstairs with a flaming cake held aloft and screaming like a banshee. Most amusing. Turns up at half past twelve, tearfully clutching a few black and pathetic crumbs.

I wonder if Peg and I are pyro-prone, so to speak?

Oh, Katie, I don't know what to make of it. An extraordinary thing! Ossy looks so ill and fragile that I fear I have not the courage to pass on to him my observations regarding his Behaviour during the last few weeks. The fact is that on three occasions I have seen him deliberately place Prom (my baby) on a high stool in front of the fire and leave him unattended. It is a miracle that there has not been a Tragic Accident. Then yesterday, I had just finished some washing and I hears somebody sobbing in the most heart-rending fashion in the living-room. Ossy has lapses you know, and when he does, he often goes into the living-room to rest or to pray. Even though an agnostic of some forty years' standing I believe he still has a little weakness for the Ritual. Well, I rushes in — and there he was. Ossy, of course. Huddled on the carpet in front of the fireplace with Prom in his arms and what I can only describe as a sacrificial look on his (Ossy's) face. Not a case for a few gentle, pious phrases! But he lets me coax the child away from him. Even now I can hardly bring myself to describe it. That ancient man ... that spindly cleric ... is so reduced and enfeebled by jealousy as to be tortured, I'm sure, with plans for Infanticide. And my poor Prom the object of this madness! He is troubled with something wrong inside for sure is Ossy, and has the look just lately of a man destined for an overdose. Whether it be pills, insanity or murder I cannot say. Here is Jan. 13.

January 13: I look up and see her standing there. I look down and see the little babe in my arms, and the fire roaring in the chimney like a furnace. His nasty face, filled with naked hostility, is turned up at me. I give him over to Peg. I notice for the first time that she has a wart on her chin, with hairs sticking out.

How to wean Doxy from doxelino? Permanently?

Katie, I cannot write of the things that have happened this last week. I shall enclose a bit I cut from the newspaper about it all and leave my grief to your prayers. More when I have got over this terrible tragedy.

Interviewed outside the burnt-out ruin of her Highgate flat, 22-year-old Miss Peg Donovan denied the truth of reports that her child had wilfully set fire to the Reverend Travers. Her child, she said, was only a few months old and could not possibly have struck a match. She added that the Reverend was often careless with his pipe, and might well have set fire to the house himself.

Miss Donovan, a tragic figure in borrowed jeans and wellingtons, said that her baby Prometheus and the Reverend Travers will be buried side by side in the graveyard of St Matthew's, South Kensington. Recalling the curious coincidence that St Matthew's itself was destroyed by fire in May of last year, Miss Donovan went on:

'I can think of no finer resting place for my baby than beside the friend who had so devotedly loved him during the pitifully brief time of his stay on this earth.'

JOHN WAIN

A Job for the Silversmith

Young Mr Gregory Fairweather and his wife Elaine both worked for a living, and it was their habit to ride into Central London each morning on the same tube train. Leaving their flat after a quick, frugal and figure-preserving breakfast (and both he and she had the kind of willowy figure that is worth preserving), they walked through the grey, windy streets of Camden Town to get on the Northern Line. Then they went together as far as Euston, where Elaine changed to the Victoria Line to get to Green Park. She worked in the design department of a publisher who did very well out of children's books. Gregory went on to King's Cross because his studio was in a little side-street in the St Pancras area.

The citizens who assemble each morning on the platforms of the Northern Line are not, on the whole, a joyous throng. Starting out as they do from East Finchley or Tufnell Park or Kentish Town, and going in as most of them do to a day of working in an office to make profits for somebody else, they give the impression of people who are stolidly accepting their fate.

At any time from seven-thirty onwards they stand three-deep on these platforms, raincoated and briefcased, some reading news-papers, some staring straight ahead, some smoking — but all silent, immersed in thoughts that do not, evidently, please them much. Their taciturnity, and the patient stance of their sensibly dressed bodies, convey the attitude that life, in the form in which they know it, is neither unpleasant enough to rebel against nor pleasant enough to greet with a smile. They are good, dour, dutiful people, quite different at seven-thirty in the evening, when the same platforms often see them dressed up and on their way out for an evening's fun.

Among this dutiful crowd, morning by morning, in the fog of November, in the freezing slush of March, in the lyrical mornings of June when it was a worse pain than ever to have to go to work, Gregory and Elaine always stood out as exceptions. Her casual elegance, and his quiet but obvious joy in her presence, made them worth looking at and were a perpetual reminder to the most jaundiced onlooker of what lyrical happiness life could hold, if you were young, and good-looking, and healthy, and in love.

Gregory always bought a newspaper from the kiosk at the entrance to the station, but he never looked at it while Elaine was with him. She was more worth looking at than any newspaper. Even if he had achieved his ambition of staging a one-man show of his work in an important gallery in London or Paris or Amsterdam, and if the newspaper in his hand had contained a long and ecstatic notice of it, he would still not have looked at it as long as there was a possibility of looking at Elaine.

They had been married nearly two years and not one bit of the magic had worn off; in fact it had intensified.

So Gregory looked at Elaine and Elaine looked straight in front of her, turning now and then to meet his eyes with a little mysterious half-smile, as if she were remembering things that it would not be proper to mention out loud with people standing all round. When she did this, Gregory's heart beat faster and his eyes glowed with the intensity of his feeling for her. When the train came in, sometimes they managed to get seats and sometimes they had to stand. If they found seats side by side, Gregory would spend the journey looking at Elaine's earrings. She was not the kind of girl who hangs ornaments from herself at every available point — her elegance was of the stunningly spare, understated kind — but he had made two silver pendants for her ears and he loved seeing them below the rich brown of her hair. If she happened not to be wearing gloves, he would also look admiringly at the ring on her marriage finger; it was rather a large ring, with a heavy and chunky quality that stood out in contrast to the slim elegance of her hand, and it seemed to Gregory that this was an emblem of his love for her — strong, ardent, male, impulsive, against her feminine restraint and coolness.

Gregory was a silversmith whose work was already beginning to be noticed and talked about. Though he was only twenty-six, he had built up good professional contacts, notably with a Bond Street jeweller who sold his work and put commissions in his way, and he had hopes very soon of being permitted to set up his own hallmark. His studio in St Pancras was a dingy little room which had for years been the workshop of a dental technician, and the equipment still vaguely suggested false teeth, but to Gregory it was an enchanted place, shining with the rich light of opportunity. He sat for hours there, waiting for silver to heat to the right temperature, dreaming up new designs, and enjoying visions of himself as a modern-day Benvenuto Cellini. And it would all be for Elaine, in her praise and to win her approval.

He had courted her with silver. Soon after they met he had made her a brooch; that summer they had gone on holiday together and on their return he had made her a bracelet; when they married he had made her a ring; at the end of their first year he had given her the ear-pendants; for their second anniversary he had plans for an ankle-bracelet. She might need some talking into this. She was not the kind of girl who wore ankle-bracelets. But perhaps he could get her to wear it when they lay around for long afternoons, drinking cheap wine and making love. The thought filled Gregory with daemonic energy.

Every day, when Euston came near and the train slowed and then halted, Elaine stood up in her composed way, gathered her handbag and umbrella, and held herself ready to get out. Gregory stood up too, and kissed her: just on the cheek, because Elaine's lipstick, though of a natural shade that left the onlooker wondering whether she wore lipstick or not, was carefully applied and she did not want it smudged at the very beginning of the day. But modest though this kiss was, Gregory looked forward to it every morning, and savoured it as the last he would have until the evening blessedly restored her to him.

When she got off and the doors closed behind her, he would lean forward in his seat and stare through the window to get a last glimpse of her moving down the platform, and it always annoyed him if some bulky citizen innocently got in the way and deprived him of this final fleeting vision.

In short: Gregory was a young husband very much in love with his wife. Marriage, that usually reliable cure for infatuation, had not cured him.

On this particular October morning they took the train as usual, he gave her his parting kiss as usual, he went on to the studio as usual. He had switched on the heating, hung up his raincoat, and was just turning to consider the question of what work he could best do that day, when there was a knock on the door.

Surprised, Gregory opened it. No one ever came to see him at the studio. But there was a visitor, asking if he were Gregory Fairweather, and saying that the Bond Street gallery had supplied his address. Gregory let the visitor in and looked at him with interest.

He was a young man, this newcomer: large and smooth, as if he had been specially inflated and plumped out for some Christmas market. His bearing, accent and physique suggested a man who had been to a public school where, whatever they had done to his mind, they had made his body healthy and the health had not yet quite worn off.

'I want to discuss business with you,' he said, handing Gregory a card. 'I have a commission to offer you. The money's ready, the work's ready, and all it needs is for you to say that you're ready.'

He gave a routine winning smile. The card said *Glisters Ltd*, and gave a London address. Underneath, neatly handwritten, was added, *Rodney V. Barker*.

'This is you?' Gregory asked, indicating the name.

'I'm Rod Barker. I haven't been with the firm long enough to get my own cards printed yet. As a matter of fact it's a very fast-growing outfit and most of the people who work there are new. Business is building up so fast that we're taking on new staff all the time.'

Gregory Fairweather turned the card over and looked at the back. There was nothing there, so he looked at the front again.

'Glisters?' he said, trying to understand.

'I'll tell you what we do,' said Rod Barker. 'First, may I sit down?'

Gregory, embarrassed at his forgetfulness, urged the visitor to be seated. The studio held two kitchen chairs, but one was broken. He took the broken one himself; Rod Barker settled his broad frame in the unbroken chair, which creaked protestingly as he leaned back.

'Quite simply,' he said, evidently going into a well-rehearsed routine, 'we make and promote the kind of things that people give each other as presents. There's no better customer than the person who's rushed into the shop to buy a present, especially one they've forgotten till it's almost too late. You know, the husband who's in a panic because he's forgotten his wife's birthday and suddenly remembers it on the way home and leaps off the bus. He has exactly ten minutes before the shop closes and he daren't go home empty-handed. Or people panic-buying just before Christmas. Buyers like that'll snap up trash if they have to. Not that we offer them trash. All our ideas are good ones and the stuff is tasteful.'

'What kind of outlets do you have?'

'All sorts. London, the provinces, the Continent.'

'I often go into the gift department of shops and I don't recall—'

'It would take too long to detail all our outlets,' said Rod Barker, leaning forward till the chair creaked again. 'We're all over and we're growing every day. If you haven't seen our displays it could be you've been going into the wrong shops. Now, what we want you to do is design and execute some silver rings for us. Good-class stuff. Tasteful. We'll give prominence to your name because we think it's going to mean something very soon. It's a chance for you and a chance for us. We'll take as many as you can do and you'll get five per cent commission.'

'That doesn't sound much. What will they sell for?'

'Two hundred and fifty pounds. That way you'll get £12.50 for every ring you put in our hands.'

'And you'll pay for the silver?'

'We'll discuss that. We haven't a great deal of cash liquidity at the moment, compared to what we will have soon.'

Gregory Fairweather walked slowly across to the window, looked out of it at the blank wall opposite, and walked back. Then he said, 'What are these rings?'

'They're divorce rings,' Rod Barker said.

'They're what?'

'Divorce rings. A man gives a girl a ring when he marries her. What does he give her when they get divorced, as most people seem to do these days?'

Gregory Fairweather looked at his visitor with dislike. He wished now that he had not let him in.

'I don't get it,' he said slowly. 'Why should he give her any-thing? If their marriage hasn't worked and they're about to separate, surely he isn't in a mood to—'

'Have you ever been divorced?' Rod Barker interrupted.

'No, I haven't, and what's more I have no inten—'

'If you had been divorced,' said Rod Barker easily, 'or had talked to many people who had, you'd know that at the actual moment when the decision is taken, people often feel quite tender and generous towards one another.'

'It doesn't seem much like it from the sort of thing you read in the papers.'

'That comes afterwards. When the various agreements about money and property have been drawn up, and the wife's had a year or two to try to get along on what he's agreed to give her, and the husband has had a year or two of trying to run two households on one income, that's when the bitterness starts. That's why lawyers always advise people to smother their generous feelings and go hard for what they can get. At the time when the couple first go to a lawyer, they're usually feeling grateful to one another just because the in-fighting's over and they've decided to give each other a bit of peace. If she's been nagging him or he's been beating her, it's all over now and they're going to come to a nice amicable arrangement and be good friends.

'And that's the moment when we step in. He's looking round for something to give her. Pretty soon he'll be looking round to see if there's anything he can take away from her, but just now he's in a giving mood and he wants to spend money. So, a divorce ring.'

Gregory Fairweather was silent.

'What d'you think of the idea?' Rod Barker asked.

'I don't like it.'

'Why not, if I may ask?'

Gregory shrugged. 'I just don't.'

'Well, a lot of people will. It'll make a good gimmick and get talked about. We've got contacts in the press and the media and we can get it some really good publicity when the time comes. You'll wake up to find yourself famous.'

'I shan't. I don't want to do it.'

'Now, this is what we have in mind,' Rod Barker said. The chair groaned as he leaned forward. 'It won't be a ring in the strict sense, one that goes round in a complete unbroken circle. It'll be more like a clip. It'll go right round the finger but the two halves won't actually be joined. You've seen rings like that.'

'Of course.'

'And on the display side we want a really tasteful design. That's where you come in. And the words *Exire volo* engraved on it.'

'*Exire volo?*'

'Yes. That's Latin for "I want out".'

They would have taught him Latin, Gregory realised, at his public school, in between teaching him to play rugby and cricket and keep himself fit and wear the right kind of tie.

'I want out, too,' he said. 'I just don't want any part of it.'

'I'm surprised to hear that, I must say. It would be a good chance for you.'

'I don't have to take every chance that comes along.'

'Perhaps not,' said Rod Barker, getting up from his chair, 'but you may regret having missed this one.'

'No, I shan't.'

For a moment, as Rod Barker looked across at Gregory, a cold hostility showed in his face. Then it relaxed into a smile, and he laid his business card down on the scarred work-bench. 'I'll leave this, anyway. Our telephone number's on it, if you change your mind.'

'I shan't.'

'Well, if you do, you know where to get hold of us. We shan't give the commission to anyone else till you've had time to think about it.' He started towards the door, then stopped. 'There's just one thing I ought to warn you about, though.'

'Warn me?'

'When you turn the idea over in your mind and see what a winner it is, you might be tempted to design and market divorce rings yourself, without going through us. Well, don't be. The idea and the slogan are both registered for copyright.'

'You probably don't realise you're being insulting,' said Gregory. He held the door open and stood silently waiting for Rod Barker to take his leave.

That ought to have been that; the visitor was dealt with and his repulsive idea consigned to oblivion, and at barely ten o'clock the day still stretched invitingly ahead.

Why, then, did young Mr Fairweather find himself unable to make any use of the day? He pottered about the studio, he sketched a few design ideas that didn't look right even on paper and certainly would look hopeless in silver; he messed about for a time with modelling clay. But nothing happened. He walked back and forth, he stared through the window at the blank wall and watched it stare blankly back. Then he sat down in the broken chair, got up, sat down again in the unbroken one, and got up again. This was worse than useless. The day, for some reason, was shot.

Stale. Perhaps he was stale. He decided to do something he had never done before: to take a Green Line bus into the country and go for a long, mind-clearing walk. He could get a bus back and be home at the same time as Elaine. The day was rather cold for October, and the sun was shining only hazily, but the thought of the countryside tempted him. He closed the studio and went to the place in Victoria where buses ran into the country. Vaguely, he chose a destination that sounded countrified — Epsom or St Albans, or somewhere like that — and was actually sitting in the bus, waiting for it to start, when it became overwhelmingly clear to him that he did not, after all, want to go for a country walk. What he wanted was to set eyes on Elaine. He could not have said why with any precision — as he was the first to admit, he was not good at saying things with precision, at any rate in words — but he needed her. If only for five minutes, he must have the sight and the sound and the touch of her.

They had an agreed rule that neither must intrude on the other during working hours, but rules were made to be broken sometimes. If Elaine had been upset about something and had dropped in at his studio for a few minutes, he would have been glad to stop work and comfort her.

Gregory Fairweather tore up his bus ticket and dropped the two halves into a litter bin. Then he took the tube train to Green Park. It was now half past eleven. There was no danger that Elaine would be out to lunch yet. She would have had her morning coffee, gossiped for a while with the other girls in her department, and settled back to work. He went up in the lift and was directed to the design department. Elaine was not there. A girl he more or less knew by sight, a tall, lanky, rather pretty girl called Penny or Fanny or something, told him that Elaine had left at about eleven. She had said that because she had some designs she wanted to get on with, she was going to spend the rest of the day working at home, and since she wanted to concentrate hard she was not to be telephoned. If any messages came for her she would attend to them the next morning.

Gregory was mildly surprised at this, since Elaine never worked at home; she had none of her equipment there, and used to say that the flat would become too cramped if they tried to use it as a work-place as well as a place to live. But perhaps this was an emergency. Perhaps the girls in the office were talking too much, or the boss was interfering, and she needed the quiet of the empty flat. Well, he would not break in on her unannounced. He would telephone first, and then go home briefly, and afterwards go out for the rest of the day to give her peace.

Downstairs, he dialled their home number. No one answered. Elaine must be concentrating hard. Or perhaps some hold-up had occurred and she was not home yet. He took the tube to Camden Town and telephoned from the first box he came to on the way back to the flat. No one answered. He went to the flat and let himself in. No one was there.

Gregory Fairweather was quite sure there was some simple explanation. All the same, the next five hours were difficult to get through. He went out and came back several times, always hoping to be greeted by Elaine, but never being so greeted. Once, about mid-afternoon, he telephoned the office again, was put through to the design department, and once more got Penny-Fanny, who told him with a touch of stiffness that the information she had given him on his visit that morning was still correct and did not require to be updated.

It was after six when Elaine came home. She sank down on the sofa and kicked her shoes off, as if tired, but her eyes were very bright.

'Sorry I've been such an age getting home. Didn't get away from the office till twenty past five, and then the crowds were awful.'

'Big day?' he asked carefully.

'You can say that again. Fanny was away and I had to answer all her telephone calls as well as go to a design meeting. One of those that drag on and on with nobody putting forward an idea that anyone else can agree with.'

He handed her a gin-and-tonic, which was their usual drink together on returning from work. But he put his own down untasted, and when she was not looking he poured it down the sink.

That night Elaine slept deeply and in the morning he heard her singing softly in the bathroom. She told him, as they walked towards the tube station, that there was a design conference she would have to attend in a week or two.

'It'll be a matter of three or four days. I don't know yet whether it'll be mid-week or running across a weekend. Fred Fletcher's very keen we should all go. It's something to do with new techniques.'

'Well, of course,' he said, 'you'll be nowhere if you don't keep up with new techniques.'

'I knew you'd understand,' she said and gave him her little secretive smile.

He gave her the usual kiss when the train reached her station. Then he continued to his own, and went into the studio. Everything was exactly the same as when he had left it the day before, but somehow it looked different.

Gregory Fairweather glanced with distaste at his bars of silver, his furnace, his pliers and engraving tools. He knew he would not be able to work that day. But wait, perhaps there was one thing he would be able to work at.

On the bench lay Rod Barker's card with the telephone number of Glisters. Gregory picked it up. There was no telephone in the studio. He went downstairs to the coin-box in the hall. *Exire volo*, he said to himself as he heard the number begin to ring. That was rather a lot of letters. How would it be if he engraved them round the inside of the ring, and put just a plain design on the outside? Before the telephone had rung three times, he was already working on the idea. He was a brilliant young silversmith, and he had great things ahead of him.

PETER TINNISWOOD

At the Brasserie

My train arrived late at Waterloo station this day.

I am fifty-three. I live in Surrey. I do not love my wife.

The girl was already at work, when I entered the brasserie and ordered my cassis.

I sat at a table in a cool corner and watched her.

A French girl in London.

Exquisite.

She stuck out her tongue as she chalked on the blackboard.

'Today's Specialities.'

No doubt about my speciality.

Today, tomorrow and always the French girl in London.

Exquisite.

How old?

Sixteen I should guess.

She wore this day a white blouse.

It was loose.

Her breasts swung free beneath the cotton.

Plump breasts.

Her arms were bare.

Honeyed arms with a shimmer of down.

Her lips were wide. Her legs were firm. Her ankles were slim.

My wife said to me this day before I left her home:

'I love you, Charlie.'

I replied:

'Thank you.'

The girl looked up from the blackboard and caught my gaze.

She smiled.

In my arms she would smile even more.

A shuttered hotel room in a lazy town in Southern France.

Pollarded trees in the square.

Swifts screeching low over purring pantiles.

How she would smile in my arms.

How she would wriggle and writhe.

Slap of belly against belly. Swing of breasts. Shiver of tautening nipple.

They opened this brasserie three months ago.

How exquisite.

Every day I come to its coolness for my cassis.

Every day it is a refuge from loathing.

'I love you, Charlie.'

'Thank you.'

The girl arrived last week.

She smiled. She sang to herself. She swung her hips.

And every morning as she chalked at the blackboard her tongue worked cool runnels on her lower lip.

What work it would do on me.

A red-bricked cottage in a loamy village in Northern France.

Mist from the canal.

Hunched flap of heron.

Low moan from pit-head hooter.

Together locked in a downy bed, her tongue flickering and darting.

Motionless on my back as she quarters my limbs.

A long cry.

A shriek.

'I love you, Charlie.'

'Thank you.'

In my office there is no fresh air.

My secretary has troubles with her glands.

My personal assistant is an adulterer.

From my glass eyrie I can look out over the city.

Waterloo station and in its lee the brasserie and the girl with the firm legs and the white cotton blouse and the swing and lilt of her hips.

Walk in front of me, little one, across the mountain meadow.

The Alpine peaks glisten.

Ravens tumble.

Our chalet is over the brow, hidden by the larches.

Hand in hand we shall sit together on its Balkon.

Softly I shall lead you by the hand to our bedroom and its springy floor.

Fiercely I shall enter you.

'I love you, Charlie.'

'Thank you.'

Time for another cassis.

Only one more.

That is the rule.

The girl still chalked at the blackboard.

Tumble of dark brown hair.

Dark brown hair tumbled on the whiteness of my thighs.

My hands grasping tight at its roots.

My back bucking.

And outside the cries of the Algerian pedlars and the clicker-clacker of the whores on the boulevard.

'I love you, Charlie.'

'Thank you.'

The girl finished her work on the board.

She called to the waiter with the sickle-black moustache and the bullfinch-sleek hair.

He sidled over to her.

He placed his hand on her rump.

She smiled.

He rubbed his hand into the pit of her back.

Slowly she rubbed his loins with her rump.

She leaned back her head.

White neck.

Slim with a mole.

Tonight in his attic they will thrash and romp.

She will scratch and claw.

She will scream, and his smile will be cool.

I know it. I know it.

Tonight when I return home, my wife will say:

'I love you, Charlie.'

And I shall reply:

'Thank you.'

I know it. I know it.

I know it.

ANNE SPILLARD

Three, Three No Rivals

They walked along the path by the river. At last it had stopped raining, but their shoes still squelched and slipped in the mud, and heavy drops of water landed unexpectedly on their heads from the bowed branches of the alder saplings.

The river was as fat as a pig. It was brown and silent, there was no bubbling, no ripples. The weir and the stepping-stones had disappeared. The river was not a playful sinuous woman. It was a drain, whose task was to carry the floodwater away, to restore the earth-and-water balance of the land. And the cost the land paid for this service was in the colour of the river, as the alluvium moved on down to the sea.

'It's a good thing you had the pit dug for the silage. There'll be no hay this year,' Merle said. She was watching the muddy water make small whirlpools, a row of them over the place where the stepping-stones were. They had milked the cows, and had this rare free time outside, for it was still too wet and muddy to mow — the tractor was stuck in its own muddy ruts almost up to its axles in the Angle Field — no use trying to pull it out yet, for the fields were too hilly to work in this wetness. The lush grass was beginning to keel over in huge patches where the rain had pressed on it like a giant hand.

Tomorrow, hopefully, they would start to cut, to catch up after ten days' solid rain, when Bill had mooched around the farm, tinkering with the machinery, or standing in the kitchen, while she and Rachel baked, his shoulder leaning against the wall, looking impatiently out of the window, rubbing the steam off with his sleeve, to watch, swearing, as the rain continued to drip and drip over the lintel.

Now he put his arm round her, awkward, knocking down a

shower of drips on to her hair. She laughed, protesting, but they
came closer. They said nothing, edging their way along, unbalanced
now that they were twined together — Merle on the uneven grass
verge, while Bill sloshed in the middle, wettest part of the path.

Presently they reached the place where Crow Beck merged with
the river. Here the path turned at right angles back along the beck.
It was the end of their walk. They stood together, not wanting to
retrace their steps. They watched the two streams flowing together.
There was no fuss where they joined, just a small wave that formed
and re-formed, spinning brown froth off to circle round the
occasional leaves and twigs that floated down at surprising speed
with the current.

Bill bent and rested his face against her hair. 'You smell of
baking,' he said. His lips touched her hair. 'New-baked bread and
candied peel.'

'Scones. I made them while you were in the yard talking to Ed
Williams.'

He remembered when she had first come to the farm, how hopeless she had been with the cooking. Tins of beans and beefburgers,
that had been her style. He and Rachel had laughed at her delight
when the loaves, hot from the oven, stood on the cooling trays. 'Can
I? Can I do it next time?' As if it was a magic trick that Rachel had
performed.

'Of course. You can make them, and I'll watch. It'll be a change,
sitting in the rocker with my feet up, bossing someone about.'

But his wife bossed nobody, and in the months that followed,
Merle and she had worked together in the kitchen — Merle
laughing, singing, her cheeks becoming rosier, her skin bronzed by
the sun from working in the fields, bending over the table with her
arms floured to the elbow, while Rachel stood back from her,
smiling, her blue eyes set in the white wrinkles of her weathered
face. Bronzed smooth olive skin, fine, soft-petalled ageing skin. The
two heads bent together. Gleaming brown of a racing chestnut, and
the soft thick white of his wife's hair, neatly fashioned into a netted
bun. Buns, scones, loaves. His wife smiling, apart. Merle tossing the
dough across the kitchen suddenly for him to catch, making animals
from it — the cows. 'There's Blackberry, Bracken, Beatrice.'
Absorbed, her head on one side.

She worked on the farm too. At first she was frightened of the cows, but their black Jersey faces and their soft eyes disarmed her. He had taught her to milk. 'Like this,' he said, bending over her, his cheek tickled by the curls that crept from under the head scarf she had tied round them. He put his fingers round hers as they grasped the two teats. He pressed his head harder against Blackberry's flank as she bent comfortably towards them. He was afraid Merle would panic, lose her balance and fall backwards off the stool. Her fingers were stiff and nervous. 'They know if you're frightened; they don't like it. Be confident. Sing to them. They like a good tune.' She had sung almost in a whisper at first, embarrassed by his presence, then as she became more confident and the milk drummed into the pail, her voice became stronger and the tunes echoed round the farmyard and into the kitchen where Rachel bent over the Aga, smiling, stirring the evening's supper.

This was a time for confidences, as they worked together in the cowshed. Each day the flanks of the cows swelled further and Merle would exclaim as she felt the calf buffet against her forehead, moving inside its mother. The milk yield fell steadily as the time for calving came nearer.

He explained about his name. 'It's Wilhelm, you see, but I live here now, I belong here, so they call me Bill. I like that.'

Right at the end of the war, when he was seventeen, living in Bochum, he had been conscripted and sent straight to the Front. They had given him a rifle, with no instructions how to use it. He had stood there, on the waste ground, knowing nothing, panic-stricken.

He had run to a trench, 'Let me in, please find room for me.' But there had been no room. They had let him lie across the top of them, while they all cowered there and the fighting raged round them.

When it was dark, they slept, and when they woke, a Canadian tank was towering over them, and a Canadian voice was saying, 'Hi, you guys, out.'

So he had been sent as a prisoner to England. He had come to work on this farm. Rachel's father was alive then. In the evenings, he had studied English. His father had known how it would be, had made him join the Panzers. 'Then you will be sent to England if you are captured. There you can study. In Russia there is no studying for German prisoners.'

His parents were killed soon after he came to England. A crippled German bomber had jettisoned its bombs over the suburb where they lived above their shop. The whole area had been demolished. His parents' bodies were never found. He had felt as if his whole life in Germany had been wiped away, and after the war, when Rachel's father asked him to stay on and manage the farm, he had done so.

Rachel was thirty-eight when he first came to the farm. Her mother had died years before, and since then she and her father had lived alone. She seldom spoke unless spoken to. But she had the gentleness and humour of a contented person. She had looked after them both in her capable way, running the farmhouse, turning out to help them at the busy times. He had a strong baritone voice, and would be asked quite often to perform in the village. Then Rachel would come and sit in the audience at the village hall, smiling quietly to herself as he stood there on the platform receiving applause, bowing his stiff German bow.

He had many friends in the village. When he came home, a bit merry some nights, she would often be there, making him tea, smiling, buttering thick bread and handing it to him with a lump of cheese.

Then one evening in early autumn, her father died. Just stood there in the hayloft, where they were humping the straw, and put his hand to his chest. One cough and it was over.

Rachel had asked him to stay on. 'Dad would have wanted it,' she said.

So they had married, to make it respectable. Everyone knew how it was with them. They all understood about the farm, how important it was to keep it.

Ed was the only one who had come out with it, warned him against marrying her. 'What do you mean,' he'd asked, 'a woman twenty years older than you? You can't sleep with her, it's not right.'

He'd been aloof. 'I'm not going to sleep with her. We make a good team. Better than most couples. It's a partnership.'

'You're not a bloody Catholic priest. You're going to want it, sooner or later. What then? You're walking into a trap.'

'I don't have your needs, Ed. It will suit both of us.'

He was never bothered about women. His life at the farm satisfied him. Rachel was like an elder sister to him. The easy tolerance of her company, and the hard work needed to compensate for the loss of one pair of hands, filled his days with contentment.

So the seasons had gone by, till one day as they sat at the table eating their supper, Rachel said, 'You are thirty now. It is time you had a real woman, and a child perhaps. I am tired now. It would be good to have a young girl to help me. Brighten everything up.'

He had considered. He was not concerned for himself. But it would be a help to have someone else here. And Rachel was on her own so long. Perhaps it might work.

'So you came, our Merle, our blackbird,' he said, putting his arm round her. 'Bright orphan-bird, in from the storm,' he teased her. For she was indeed an orphan, and this was her first home.

She readily accepted their self-sufficiency, learnt about the generator, about their care with water in the dry weather. She tipped too much lime into the well the first time, and for days they teased her whenever they turned the tap on and the white water poured from it.'

Rachel mothered her shamelessly. 'She deserves a bit of fuss,' she justified herself to Bill. 'All those years with no love. We can make up for it a little.' She bit off a thread with her teeth, eased the material over the jeans she was patching for Merle. 'Anyway, I owe it to her. She makes me feel ten years younger, cheering the place up, always ready to give a hand.'

She papered Merle's room for her, choosing a paper covered in little yellow roses. 'It's selfish of me really, what I always wanted myself. Didn't seem worth it then — only Dad to look at it and he didn't care about things like that.'

Merle did the paintwork: white doors with yellow panels. When it was all finished, they let him see it. He stood at the door, his head bowed under the dark wood lintel, looking at the clean, bright room. The breeze lifted the light curtains away from the window, and he could see the apple tree in blossom outside. Each flower stood out clearly, five petals, with a fist of stamens in its centre. He looked at the bed with its white-painted iron ends, and Merle's pink cotton nightie folded neatly on the counterpane. A furry panda gazed at him from the pillow.

The women watched him, waiting for his approval. He drew in his breath. He felt ashamed. In this bright, innocent room, he saw himself lying close to her nakedness in the narrow bed. He saw her back, with her dark hair falling over her shoulders. The tips of his fingers tingled as he drew them over the smooth breasts, felt the hardening of the neat nipples.

'You've made a good job,' he said. 'You could go into business.' He could hardly look at either of them for the rest of the evening. Much later they lit the paraffin lamp and he went outside to switch off the generator.

In the silence that followed, he stood by the front porch looking across the lane. The tractor's shape showed dimly in the barn. Sheba got up off her sacking bed, sensing him standing there. She shook herself and came over to him. He bent down and stroked her head, as she nuzzled against him and sat on his feet. Through the glass of the porch, Rachel's geraniums looked like a shadowy forest. He noticed that the flowers looked darker than the leaves, that neither had colour. Everything seemed grey. Grey or black. A crisp yellow room, a pink nightie, rich warm skin. He went into the house and picked up the lamp which stood on the hall table where they had left it for him. He pushed his slippers off and climbed the creaking stairs in his stockinged feet.

Rachel called to him from her room, 'Did you shut the damper on the Aga?'

He reassured her, went to the door of his own room. He raised the lamp, and looked across the landing at Merle's door. A thin flicker of light showed under it. He heard her bed creak. She would be climbing into it now, the candle on the bedside table in the saucer with its broad gold and green border. The bed creaked again. Now she would be shrugging into the bedclothes, her hair spread over the pillow, the panda clutched under her chin. The light under her door went out.

Bill lay in bed thinking about his wife. Underneath his thoughts floated an apple tree, a bronzed vivacious face, and a delicious ache that grew and faded so that from time to time it washed over Rachel in waves. Until now he had never regretted his marriage. Yet it was

Rachel who had deliberately brought this situation about. She had made it clear to him that it was with her approval that Merle and he should, should . . . what? Become lovers? Have a child, she had said — 'There has to be someone to follow us.' He moved impatiently, found himself sitting on the edge of the bed. He was on the landing, his hand feeling for the smooth mahogany banister, his feet aware of the thinness of the strip carpet.

His hand found the cold brass handle. He opened her door slowly, quietly, stood peering into the darkness where he could just see the darkness on the pillow.

Merle sat up suddenly. 'Who is it?' she asked, frightened.

He soothed her, thought of a reason. 'It's only me. I'll take the calves into market myself tomorrow. I'll do the milking before I go. You can have a lie-in.'

Merle was surprised. 'I can't do that, I've got to help Rachel with the eggs.'

'Well, you and Rachel bring your stuff in the Mini. I'll see to the trailer and everything.' He realized how inconvenient he had made everything, how unconvincing it all sounded. He began to back out of the room. 'We'll work it out in the morning.'

'All right,' Merle said. She was thinking that Rachel had been right. 'Just have patience,' she would say when Merle protested, 'Of course he'll want you. Anybody would. We're lucky you came to us.'

Her heart beat faster, and deep from in her an instinct came to show that she knew, understood, why he was there.

'Is that all, shadowy knight?' she asked. She didn't wait for an answer. 'How pale your face looks in the moonlight.'

Bill closed the door. He felt his way back to his room. Lying on her back, Rachel listened. She smiled, turned over on her side pulling her feet up under the long winceyette night-dress, and settled down to sleep.

In the pub after the auction he leant against the bar drinking with Ed Williams. Ed talked prices, foodstuffs, and he tried to concentrate. He'd got a good price for the calves. He wanted to tell the women, see Merle's face light up. She didn't like it when the calves went, not when she'd fed and looked after them since they were born. Each time the door swung open, he turned from the bar.

Once, as he turned back, he caught Ed looking at him. He grinned, as if in apology.

Ed said, 'You're looking for her, aren't you? Missing her, I shouldn't wonder. A tidy piece like that, even you couldn't stay immune.'

For a moment Bill was silent. He was remembering their conversation so long ago now, how Ed had warned him. Now he turned and looked straight at him. He felt the need to defend himself. 'It *was* all right. For six years it has been.' Ed said nothing. The words came out quickly in the need to confide. 'What am I going to do? Rachel says it's all right, but it's not fair on either of them. Everyone talking. I can't leave Rachel, and I can't live there with both of them. And anyway, I don't know about Merle, what she feels about me.'

'Leave 'em both, Bill. There's trouble for you all there. Whoever heard of a house run by two women? There'd be no peace for you. Or them. Come in with me. We could get a loan and buy up Sherrin's farm when it comes on the market next month. That's right up against Foller's wood, and I've got half shares in that with old Smithson for pheasant breeding. We could clear that and our farm would go right through to the river at Brackenbury then. I'll easily buy Smithson out, he can't be bothered much longer going up that hill right away from his place. He's getting past it.'

It was carefully thought out. It flashed through Bill's mind that Ed had worked it out well beforehand, counting on him to come in on it.

Rachel came through the door, followed by Merle. He turned to beckon to them. 'You're a friend, Ed. Thanks. I'll think about it.'

Ed waved to the women. 'Let me know soon. You're not the only pebble on the beach, you know.'

Merle came through the crowd. She saw the men exchange looks. She half-understood their collusion. She felt the uneasiness that creeps into women, the two men looking at her, looking at each other, sizing her up. She felt her power, her attraction, the disturbance she was causing in them.

She put her arms round them both. 'You're talking about us,' she said.

Bill fished in his pocket. He brought out a red rosette. 'Here,' he said to Merle. 'Calf of the show.'

She laughed, delighted. 'Bluebell? I knew she was special.' She became sentimental, 'She did that for us, so's we wouldn't be sad for her.'

'Don't be daft. Come here.' He pinned the rosette to her sweater, feeling the softness of the wool under his fingers, aware of her pushing her breast against him.

Rachel squeezed her arm. 'That's lovely, dear. It's all because of you, looking after her that well.'

'Drinks all round,' said Ed. He turned to order them.

Merle looked at Bill and Rachel. 'No,' she said, 'not me. It's all of us. The Tuned-in Trio.'

Rachel laughed. 'Sounds like relatives of Noddy and Big Ears. Three's a bad number. Always an odd one out.'

'One is one and all alone and evermore shall be so,' Bill sang. It was one of the songs Merle sang to the cows when she was milking, one she had learnt sitting round the campfire on their treasured holidays from the orphanage.

'Three's supposed to be rivals,' said Merle. 'But we're not. I can't do without either of you.' She hugged them both. Bill eased himself out of the embrace gently, stiffly. He didn't look at Ed.

Rachel said quietly, 'And I can't do without either of you.'

Much later, they sat in the kitchen playing rummy. The room was warm and orange. A copper jam pan over the Aga reflected the orange curtains and the scrubbed wooden table. They sipped the mulled wine that Rachel had made to celebrate the calf's success, watching the slices of fruit bob about on the tops of their drinks.

Merle jumped up suddenly. 'Heavens! I forgot to shut the chickens up.' She put her wellies on, dragged Bill's mac over her head and shoulders, and went outside.

For a moment there was silence. Bill looked up to see Rachel smiling at him. He said, 'Ed asked me to go in with him, when I saw him today.'

Rachel laughed. 'You need all your time here. There's none to spare for him. He must be out of his mind.'

'He didn't mean that. It's time for me to leave here, Rachel. I think you've guessed what has happened.'

Rachel reached out and put her hand on his arm. 'I do know

what's happened. You love Merle. But that's right, isn't it? Isn't that what we wanted?'

Bill lifted her hand off his arm. He held it gently. 'It wouldn't work. The three of us. I am married to you. I don't know what to do. Perhaps she should go. Perhaps I should. Everything's my fault. I should never have let you talk me into having her here in the first place.'

'She loves it here. She is happy. She likes you a lot, Bill. We can all live here together. You know how well we get on.'

'No, Rachel. If I stay, everyone will be hurt.'

'And if you go, what will we do? Who will see to the farm? You want to leave two women to run it?' She moved closer to him. 'Of course you are attracted to Merle. And she to you. That's right and natural. Do you think I will interfere? It will be good for all of us. Soon enough you would have left here for another woman. A real one who would be good to you in bed. But you have her. There is no need for you to leave. And I will be happy, knowing the farm is going to be carried on, not living on my own. To me it is like having a son and a daughter with me. You can't go.'

He felt he had to make a decision. Here in the kitchen, with the warmth and familiar homeliness, Rachel's earnest face beseeching him, it was hard to get everything into perspective.

'No. It is not right. Imagine what everyone would say. They would never speak to us again.'

'Of course they will. They know about you and me, how we only married for the respect of it. They'll understand. And those who don't aren't worth bothering about. Besides, we're together. What does it matter what they think?'

But he stayed firm. 'No. We'll all grieve at first, but it's best in the end. You'll soon enough get someone to work here for you, and I'll help you out to start with. This way we can all stay friends.'

They heard Merle returning shaking his mac outside the door. Rachel looked at him with a warning. 'Don't tell her yet. Let me do it.'

He agreed with relief. He wondered how she would manage, hoped she would excuse him in some way. He wanted to disappear, dreaded seeing their reproachful faces in the morning. He knew he must go very soon. It would be unbearable here.

Merle came into the kitchen, shaking her hair. 'My, it's wet outside.' She walked over to the Aga to warm her hands.

He got up abruptly. 'I'm having an early night.' He pushed past her clumsily.

'Hey!' She was laughing, holding his elbow to balance herself. 'What's the rush? Anyone would think you were trying to escape.'

He looked down at her hand, then at her face. They looked at each other in a long silence. He saw her pupils darken and darken. She had stopped smiling. His eyes were so blue, like a sailor's.

'Is something wrong?' she asked finally, pulling away. But he had turned, begun to leave the room. He didn't answer.

He lay in bed. Downstairs he could hear the women talking. What were they saying? Plotting and planning. But they could do nothing. He had made his decision. He lay looking at the ceiling, feeling free now to think about Merle. He ached for her, longing to explain, to excuse himself. He heard them come upstairs. They said nothing to each other. He heard their doors close.

Half asleep, something brushed lightly across his forehead. Fingers traced his cheekbone, over his stubble, ran themselves lightly over his mouth. He opened his eyes, stayed still, tried to maintain the rhythm of his breathing. Darkness, with a misty white centre, moved closer to him. He felt the soft wetness of a tongue pressed in his ear.

He sucked in his breath, put his hand out suddenly, and grasped her wrist. 'Merle?'

'Wait,' she said. There was the flaring of a match, then a brighter glow as the candle was lit. Merle bent over him.

The top buttons of the pink nightie were undone. She pulled it to one side, exposing one breast, as if she was going to feed a baby. Gently she opened his lips with her fingers. She lifted the nipple to his mouth, supporting his head with her arm. She began to suckle him, rocking gently, soothing him into wakefulness.

Then she was in bed, the nightie a shadowy heap on the floor, and their hands and tongues moving and caressing.

She was a woman with instinctive sexuality, with no experience. She accepted this as she would accept birth, and, far away, death.

'It will hurt, won't it? But only the first time. Just be gentle, take a long time.'

He had eased himself into her so slowly, feeling the pressure against him, trying not to hurt, while she gasped, not wanting him to stop, fearing the pain, yet savouring it. He knew this was the special time, the time he would always remember. Then he was through, bursting into her, while she moved against him and he licked her tears, still inside her, held by her tightness, caressed by their fluids.

'I'll never leave you,' he said. And in the darkness of the pillow, she smiled.

They were appalled by the blood. She mopped it up with the nightie, pulled the sheet off. 'I'll wash them tomorrow,' she said, and until dawn they lay on the scrubby grey underblanket in warmth and crowded comfort.

Very early, even before the birds sang, he felt her move away from him, ease herself out of the bed. Still drowsy, he tried to hold her. 'Stay a little.'

But she dodged away from him. She picked up the nightie and crumpled sheet, and he saw the dim, naked shape of her as she opened the door and slipped out.

He could hear her in the bathroom, the water running, the rhythmic sound of clothes being pummelled in the basin. Later he heard her door open and close. Then silence.

His body tautened as he re-lived their love-making. He was disturbed momentarily by how little thought he had given to the fear of making her pregnant.

'Not the first time, surely. Not the very first time,' he reassured himself. Yet he remembered how totally they had immersed themselves in each other. A small frown stayed on his forehead until he drifted off to sleep.

He was first up in the morning. When he came back to the house for his breakfast, Rachel and Merle were both there. He could see them as he came past the kitchen window, their heads close together, one stirring porridge, while the other lifted bacon and eggs onto hot plates. They were both smiling, talking in low voices. He felt a moment of exclusion, of suspicion.

Then, as he opened the door and Merle looked up, shyly, doubtfully, at him, all thoughts except his need for her disappeared.

He went to the stove, took his plate from her. 'Watch out, it's hot,' she said, and the day slid into the pattern that it always had.

They pressed the pattern onto the thoughts that flickered and glowed in them all.

On her own, when they had gone out to begin the sowing, Rachel stood for a moment in the hall, feeling the cool silence of the house round her. She closed the door of the porch and put down the plastic watering-can that she had been using to water the geraniums.

Slowly she began to walk upstairs, rubbing fingerprints off the polished banister with her sleeve. At the top she paused. She walked towards Bill's room, easing the creases out of the scuffed landing carpet with her foot. His door was ajar. She pushed it open with her foot and stood looking in.

The bedclothes were pushed back untidily, partly on the floor. She went over to lift them up, noted the underblanket, the missing sheet. Mild voyeur's excitement, mixed with satisfaction, tingled through her.

She went to the bathroom for a clean sheet. In the airing cupboard the pink nightie hung from a wire hanger. She put out her hand and stroked the nearly-dry sheet that was draped over the tank, feeling the harsh crumples where Merle had rubbed it with detergent.

She looked at the bath, remembering the loss of her own virginity. She remembered lying there when she was sixteen and her father opening the door. He had just stood there, staring at her.

She had stood up slowly, stood in the bath, the water dripping from her, letting him see her, wanting him to.

That night he had come to her bed. Neither of them had spoken, nor had they ever referred to it. Three nights while they lived alone, he had come to her, and once when Bill lived with them. Four nights, and nothing ever said. But she had known she never wanted another man.

As if he were standing there now, she turned and said, half-aloud, 'Everything will be safe for us soon.'

Now they moved the big double bed from Rachel's room into Merle's room. Bill did not sleep there every night, or right through the night, being for the moment a surreptitious lover rather than a husband, half-persuading himself he was not committed here.

Merle tied a blue ribbon round the panda's neck and hung him on the side of the dressing-table mirror.

It was as if they were all waiting. As if they knew, without saying, that the final piece of the pattern had still to slip into place.

He saw Ed in the pub most Fridays. Ed didn't push him about the farm. Once he asked, 'Did you think about it, coming in with me?' but Bill had evaded him. 'Maybe, in a bit, Ed. Give me time. It's a big decision.' Ed sensed it was no good and left him alone.

One afternoon he came home from market to hear laughter and singing from the women. He walked into the kitchen, smiling, pleased to be with them. On the table was an opened bottle of dandelion wine.

'Have a drink, love,' Merle caught his arm, whisked him round in a circle.

'What are we celebrating?' he asked. He felt alone for a moment. They had started without him, knew something they were only now telling him about.

'Look!' Merle was sparkling, triumphant. She reached under the table and brought out a wicker basket. It was lined with soft blue cotton. A big blue bow was tied to its handle. Three tiny pairs of bootees were arranged in a circle at the bottom of the basket.

He looked, perplexed. 'Rachel did it. Isn't it lovely?' Merle said.

'Who's it for? What is it?'

Both the women laughed indulgently.

'Who do you think it's for?' Rachel said. 'Our baby, who else? Merle's pregnant.'

They both came over to him, and hugged him as if he had done something clever.

He pulled back, looked at Merle, shocked. 'Why didn't you tell me before?' He was hurt that she had not shared this with him, that Rachel knew before he did.

Merle soothed him. 'We didn't want to worry you. We wanted to be certain, make sure everything was all right.'

He was amazed. Everything was *not* all right, surely. And yet within this house everything seemed calm and happy and well-ordered.

In the weeks that followed, he came to accept the shift in the pattern. He slept every night with Merle. Kissed her impulsively when they were in the fields or with the animals. He began to see how they all had their essential part to play in the smooth running of the days.

Now, as he walked back with Merle, along the riverside to the farm, to Rachel sitting in the rocker, knitting for them, he put his arm round her till he could feel the thickening of her waist, the swelling of her, and the heaviness of her breasts.

'This is how it should be for everyone,' he said.

Merle felt the baby flutter inside her. 'Three's a lucky enough number, four coming after it.'

Grass bent by the flood of the river was beginning to show, pale green, as the level lowered. Soon the stepping-stones would link both banks again, and in a few seasons she would be bending over, holding a child's hands as he took his first steps over the water.

JO GILL

You Get What You Ask For

This year he'd get the cup, he was sure of it. Last year he had come second but that was because they had still thought of him as a newcomer — villages were like that. He had known it would take a long time, it was time he had needed and could use, but now, at last, he felt himself accepted as part of the place. After all, if he hadn't bought the Lodge it would have fallen down, rotten inside and out. He'd had the cash and the know-how to make it what it was today — a show place — and that sort of thing was respected. He'd taken a lot of trouble to make friends, solid friends. He'd played darts in the local, gone to church regularly, given and received cuttings, and tried to be all things to all men.

Sylvia was a handicap of course. When the Colonel thought of his wife he had to breathe slowly and unclench his teeth. There seemed to be something wrong with Sylvia; no doubt it was a woman's thing, her age and so on, but it wasn't getting any better. Long ago he had become resigned to the fact that Sylvia was one of those women who seemed unable to learn. Everyone made mistakes, but one didn't make the same mistake twice. As a young captain, that was one of the maxims he had impressed upon his men and had told his wife soon after the wedding, but apparently it was already too late. One would assume that a Rector's daughter would appreciate the importance of disciplined thought leading to controlled action, however he had been misled by her appearance. 'Demure' someone had called her. A homely girl, she had been bred in a decent family and reared in the fastness of Kent, a county seemingly of no particular interest, and he had expected inexperience, but was totally unprepared for latent sexuality. He had simply said, in a direct fashion so as to have no room for ambiguity: 'I can get a whore whenever I like. You are my wife, always remember that.' He didn't expect to have to repeat himself and she had understood, her docility was all he could have desired, but she never became what he called teachable.

For the next twenty-five years she had been dutiful, packing and unpacking as the regiment endlessly journeyed back and forth according to the rules of the game played by the War Office in peace time. Of course she had not fitted in with the other officers' wives, she had no gift for social intercourse and she had failed to produce children who might have eased her way. No matter how he had harangued her, she would not make the necessary efforts. 'You get what you ask for,' he had told her, 'and if you will not trouble to learn, you must take the consequences.' He was good at his job, his men respected him. He would never ask of them anything he was not prepared to do himself, so the peculiarities of his wife brought no lasting shame upon him and he was able to retire at the level to which he had aspired.

Sylvia had made one good use of all the time at her disposal; she had taken up gardening. Wherever they had gone, at home or abroad, she had created gardens of such distinction that she had been able to charge admittance and raise money for charity. He could remember one that had been all white, another that, all the year round, glowed with the richness of bronze, crimson and gold. Even her gardens had been strange, causing him embarrassment, but he freely admitted that all his present knowledge had stemmed from helping her. As his interest grew so hers waned. Now that he was an expert, keeping up with the latest on the scientific front, with a comprehensive library and a wide correspondence with other enthusiasts what, in the name of heaven, was she playing at?

The Lodge, their retirement home, had been carefully chosen so that they could each have their own space. Separate bedrooms, naturally. A study for him, a sewing room for her, though she didn't use it; even two bathrooms. The gardens were almost equal in area, so, quite simply, he had the front and she had the back.

In the front, order reigned. Tulips, followed by iris, marched four abreast beside the stone path, bordered by neat cushions of miniature pinks. In the tailored beds, standard roses under-planted with primula and viola, raised their gorgeous heads to survey massed banks of aubretia, arabis, cistus and saxifrage, while the hybrid teas, no less lovely, but by their nature gentler, grouped themselves in islands of gold, white and pink against the background of the impeccable lawn. Every tree in its season displayed itself proudly, secure in the careful pruning and spraying which ensured correct and contained growth. Almond, forsythia, ornamental cherry, magnolia, spruce, viburnum and witch hazel, each in its perfect shape, no one touching the other. Disease was rare and ruthlessly dealt with. Weeds necessarily appeared, but the combined efforts of the Colonel and the chemical industry made short work of them. As he leaned on his hoe, pipe in mouth, the Colonel knew that he had no rival.

The less said about the back the better. Sylvia had, in all senses of the words, gone to seed. It was essential the grass be cut, he had his own lawns to consider, and a man came in to keep it reasonable. On no account would the Colonel set foot there and neither was his wife allowed to wander round the side of the house carrying unnameable horrors on the soles of her shoes. There was a gate in the high brick wall which extended from the garage to the boundary fence, and that was kept locked. From the east wall of the house he had erected a trellis now completely covered with pyracantha, a majestic sight in all seasons. As far as he could manage it his defence was impregnable.

The only occasions on which the Colonel had to view his wife's deplorable handiwork was on his rare visits to the spare bedroom at the back of the house to check the condition of the window frames. Sometimes he forced himself to look out. Breathing slowly and clenching and unclenching his teeth, he would view the prospect with despairing rage. He would see Zepherine Drouhin, a riot of carmine careering crazily in all directions from what had once been a border, curling among cypress, crack willow and ilex, cascading down through poppy, forget-me-not and foxglove. Fru Dagmar Hastrup, twelve foot high and half as much across, was intertwined with common honeysuckle so thoroughly it would need an axe to cut it free.

The pond, once an elegant oval, was now dark green and thick with weed, barely visible through yellow iris and rampant nasturtium. Beyond, the old apple trees were shrouded in the misty blooms of Albertine and Wedding Day, dipping and twisting together like demented old women. He had once seen Sylvia, it was hardly possible to think of her as his wife, sitting on the mossy swing beneath the branches, her face pale as one of her own roses, grey hair lank to her shoulders, her tweed shirt and green jumper hardly visible. She was rocking gently to and fro, so much a part of the surrounding herbiage that, at first, he had not noticed her. She was gazing towards the house and he drew back in an unusual superstitious fear, unwilling to meet the eyes of what, for a horrid moment, looked very like a spirit of the woods.

The third Saturday in July was judgement day and the whole village was up and about in great excitement. The trophy, a large heavily-encrusted silver bowl, was awarded annually for the best flower garden. It was the most enviable prize for miles around and the competition was intense and quarrelsome. The weather for once had been kind; clear warm days and exactly the right amount of gentle rain at night. The Colonel had little doubt of the outcome, he had his rivals but he knew he outshone them. The judging began at nine-thirty and would take several hours, the outlying houses such as the Lodge being inspected in the afternoon by means of Lady Connie's Land Rover, she being one of the judges, together with Jack Bryden the publican; Gordon Hollingsworth, the manager of a local garden centre; and the Reverend Oliver Thorne, to see fair play.

Lady Connie had everything well in hand by mid-morning when the Colonel made his appearance outside the general stores. Slightly deaf herself, she made allowances for other people's hearing and her strident emphatic tones rose above the hedge of one of the cottages fifty yards away. 'I'm afraid sweet peas never do well in that corner, next year you should try a clematis. No? Oh well, it's your garden not mine. Come along, all of you, we're late for Mrs Ullivant and she's promised us a much needed cuppa.' Head up, tail in, Lady Connie emerged, saw the Colonel and shouted, 'We're coming to you last, about three ... can't wait to see ... heard so much ...' and headed purposefully down the lane followed by the others in single file, last out the vicar, hands fluttering in farewell. He turned and, finding the others gone, felt in his pocket for one of his boiled sweets, then, mopping his brow, he set off in pursuit.

The Colonel, beginning to feel the sort of excitement he hadn't experienced since the old days of field exercises, turned into the

King's Head for a snifter and then, unable to prevent a triumphal smile when anybody gave him the time of day, decided to drive into town to collect his shoes from the mender. Just as well to keep out of the way. He would lunch at the George, time enough to turn off the sprinkler if he was back by 1400 hours. Everything that could be done had been done, the tall wrought-iron gates closed against intruders and Sylvia commanded to keep to the house. She had one of her headaches anyway and was lying down.

Driving back to the Lodge at about five past two, the Colonel was aware of the heat and the silence. He had avoided the village and had seen no one; the judges were presumably making a wide circuit and would arrive from the south — out of the sun like attackers. They didn't worry him, though, he was waiting for them, fore-armed, impregnable, and they would surrender willingly to his undeniable superiority. His garden, like his regiment, was behind him, supporting and full of trust. He loved it as he had loved his men, it would not let him down, today of all days. At the bend before his house he braked and brought the car to a gentle halt by the high brick wall. As he got out to open the gates he was vaguely aware of something missing, a lack of a familiar shape in the corner of his eye. He was back at once in his field days with the army. 'Study the landscape', he would tell his men. 'Get to know the contours of the hills, the shape of the trees, the way the wildlife behaves. If anything unusual is going on, there'll be signs. You must know them like you know your own back yard.' He felt the signs now and the skin on the back of his neck prickled.

The sun beat down on the quiet garden as he pushed open the gates, and his eyes sent a message his brain refused to accept. It was all there, the grass, the flower beds, the curved stone path, the sundial, the bushes, the trees. The sprinkler was still turning. There was just one element missing — there were no flowers. Stalks rose bare-headed from the earth, branches extended like hands — empty hands. He realised confusedly that what was lacking as he came round the corner was the huge creamy mass of the low-spreading magnolia grandiflora by the wall. Every flower on that great tree had been cut off. Every rose had been removed from its bush. Every coloured head in beds and borders had gone and shaggy remains of rockery plants lay strewn on the glittering grass.

She had had four hours. The only growing thing she had been unable to decimate was the pyracantha, ten foot by eight of starlike blossom serene above the obscenity. Behind it a thin wisp of smoke.

BERYL BAINBRIDGE

People for Lunch

'We simply must,' said Margaret.

'Do we have to?' asked Richard.

'No,' said Margaret, 'but we will. We've been to them eight weekends on the trot. It looks awful.'

Thinking about it, Richard supposed she was right. Every Sunday throughout May and June they had motored down to Tunbridge Wells, arriving in time for lunch. They had left again at six o'clock, after Dora and Charles had made them a cup of Earl Grey tea. Apart from an obligatory inspection of the kiddies' new bicycles or skateboards, or being forced to listen to some long feeble jokes told by young Sarah, the hours spent in Dora's well-appointed house had been pleasant and restful. 'I don't think they expect to be asked back,' said Richard. 'They're not like that.'

'Not *expect*,' agreed Margaret. 'But I think we should.'

Dora and Charles were asked for the following Sunday. Richard and Charles had gone to university together, been articled together, and now worked for the same firm of lawyers, in the litigation department. 'Jolly nice of you,' said Charles, when he heard. 'We're looking forward to it.'

It had been a little tricky suggesting to Dora that she left the children behind. 'They'll be so bored here,' explained Margaret, when speaking to her on the phone. 'As you know we've only a backyard. There's no sun after eleven o'clock in the morning. And Malcolm won't be here.' She didn't feel too awkward about it because after all Dora had a marvellous woman who lived in, and Dora herself was frightfully keen once the penny had dropped.

'How did you put it?' asked Richard worriedly. 'I hope you didn't imply we ...'

'Don't be silly,' said Margaret crossly. 'You know me. I was the soul of tact.'

Two unfortunate events occurred on the morning of the luncheon party. The sky, which earlier had been clear and blue, filled with clouds, and Malcolm, who had promised faithfully he was going out, changed his mind. He said there was a programme he wanted to watch on TV at one o'clock.

'You can't,' wailed Margaret. 'We'll be sitting down for lunch.'

'I'm watching,' said Malcolm. He switched on the set and lay full-length on the wicker couch from Thailand, flicking cigarette ash on to the pine floor.

'Can't watch the telly, old chap,' said Richard bravely. 'Fraid not. We've people coming.'

'Piss off,' said Malcolm.

At midday Richard suggested Malcolm came with him to the pub to buy the beer. 'I'm not shifting,' said Malcolm. 'I don't want to miss my programme.'

While Richard was away, the clouds lifted and the sun shone. Margaret looked out of the window at the square of paving stones set with shrubs and bordered by a neat privet hedge. Although only seventeen, Malcolm was extremely tenacious of purpose. He would spend the entire lunch hour jumping up and switching on the telly after Richard had turned it off. The only slight chance of stopping him lay in hitting him over the head, and then there'd be a punch-up and it would undoubtedly spoil the atmosphere. She began to carry chairs through to the front door; if it were not for the privet hedge, they would be sitting practically on the pavement, but it couldn't be helped.

'What the hell are you doing?' asked Richard, when he returned with the drink.

'It's your fault,' cried Margaret shrilly. 'You shouldn't have boxed the television in. I'm not entertaining guests with the damn thing blazing away.' After several harsh words Richard strode into the house and began to manhandle the table into the hall.

'I will not ask you to help,' he called to Malcolm. 'I will not point out that your unreasonable behaviour is the cause of all this upheaval.' He swore as the table, wedged in the narrow passage, crushed his fingers against the jamb of the door.

'Stop muttering,' shouted Malcolm. 'If you've got anything to say, say it to my face.'

The table, once settled on flagstones, sloped only partially at one end. Covered with a tablecloth, a vase of roses placed in the centre, the effect was charming. 'I think it's better than indoors,' said Margaret. 'I really do.'

'I could have a heart attack,' said Richard. 'We both could. And that boy would trample over us to change channels.'

'Sssh!' said Margaret. 'Don't upset yourself.'

Dora and Charles arrived promptly at twelve-thirty. The moment they stepped out of the car the sun went behind a cloud.

'It's a little informal,' called Margaret gaily, 'but we thought you'd prefer to sit outside.'

'Rather,' said Charles, gazing at the row of bins behind the upright chairs. Richard kissed Dora and Margaret kissed Charles; the merest brush of lips against stubble and powder. 'I'm afraid I haven't shaved,' said Richard.

'Good God,' cried Charles, who had performed this ritual at seven-thirty. 'Who the hell shaves on Sunday?'

They went into the front room and had a drop of sherry, standing in a group at the window and eyeing the table outside as if it was a new car that had just been delivered.

'Lovely roses,' said Charles.

'Home grown?' asked Dora. They had to shout to be heard above the noise of the television.

'No,' said Margaret. 'We do have roses in the backyard, but the slightest hint of wind and they fall apart.'

'I know the feeling,' said Dora, who could be very dry on occasion.

They all laughed, particularly Dora.

'Belt up,' said Malcolm.

They trooped in and out, carrying the salad bowl and the condiments, the glasses for the wine. 'This is fun,' said Charles, stumbling over a geranium pot and kicking a milk bottle down the steps. He insisted on fetching the dustpan and brush. Malcolm was eating an orange and spitting pips at the skirting board. 'You're doing 'O' levels, I suppose,' said Charles. 'Or is it 'A's?'

'You what?' said Malcolm.

'Any idea what you want to do?' asked Charles, leaning on the handle of the brush.

'Nope,' said Malcolm.

'Plenty of time,' said Charles. He went outside and confided to Richard. 'Nice boy you've got there. Quiet but deep.'

'Possibly,' said Richard uneasily.

It was an enjoyable lunch. Margaret was a good cook and Richard refilled the glasses even before they were empty. It was quite secluded behind the hedge, until closing time. Then a stream of satisfied customers from the pub round the corner began to straggle past the house.

'What's so good about this area of London,' said Richard, after hastily dispatching a caught-short Irishman who had lurched through the privet unbuttoning his flies, 'is that it's not sickeningly middle class.'

'Absolutely,' agreed Charles, listening to the splattering of water on the pavement behind his chair.

Margaret was lacking spoons for the pudding. 'Please, Charles,' she appealed, touching him briefly on the shoulder. He ran inside the house glad to be of service. He looked in the drawers and on the draining board. After a moment Margaret too came indoors. There was no sign of Malcolm. 'Have you found them?' she shouted.

'Stop it,' said Charles.

'They're right in front of your eyes,' she bellowed.

'For God's sake,' he whispered. 'They'll see us.'

He backed away down the room. It was infuriating, he thought, the knack women had of behaving wantonly at the wrong moments. Had they been alone in some private place, depend upon it, Margaret would have been full of excuses and evasions. In all the twelve years he had known her, there had never been a private place. He had wanted there to be, but he hadn't liked to plan it. God knows, life was sordid enough as it was. He didn't know how old Richard stood it — his wife giving off signals the way she did. The amount of lipstick Margaret wore, the tints in her hair, the way everything wobbled when she moved. Dora was utterly different. You could tell just by looking at her that she wasn't continually thinking about men.

'Where's Malcolm?' asked Margaret.

'I've no idea,' he said. He found he was being manoeuvred between a wall cupboard and the cooker. He had never known her so determined. He glanced desperately at the window. All he could see was the back of his wife's head. 'All right, you little bitch,' he said hoarsely. The word excited him dreadfully. It was so offensive. He never called Dora a bitch, not unless they were arguing. 'You've asked for it,' he said. Eyes closed and breathing heavily, he held out his arms. Margaret, looking over her shoulder, was in time to see Richard rising from his chair. He waved. She fled soundlessly from the room.

Dora quite enjoyed reading in the front yard. It was handy being near the dustbins. When the weather was good they often lunched on the lawn in Tunbridge Wells, but there the grass was like a carpet to Charles and he grew livid if so much as a crumb fell to the ground.

'Where's Malcolm gone?' asked Margaret. Richard told her he was in the basement, probably listening to records. Actually he had seen Malcolm sloping off down the street a quarter of an hour ago, but he didn't want to worry her. Lately, Malcolm had taken to going out for hours at a stretch and coming home in an elated condition. They both knew it was due to pot-smoking, or worse. In a sense it was a relief to them he had at last found something which interested him.

'Do you know,' said Charles. 'I do wonder if we're doing the right thing, burying the children down in the country.'

'Oh, come on,' scoffed Margaret. 'All that space and fresh air . . . not to mention their ponies.'

'I know exactly what he means,' said Dora. 'They're very protected. When I think of Malcolm at Sarah's age, he was streets ahead of her.'

'Was he?' said Richard.

'Well, he was so assured,' Dora explained. 'Handing round the wine, joining in the conversation. I always remember that time we came for dinner with Bernard and Elsa, and Malcolm hid under the table.'

'I remember that,' said Charles thoughtfully. 'He crapped.' There was a moment's startled silence. 'It was your word,' Charles said hastily, looking at Richard. 'I remember clearly. I said to you, I think Malcolm's had a little accident, and you said to me, oh dear, he's done a crap. I thought it was marvellous of you. I really did.'

'Really he did,' said Dora.

'I wonder what happened to Elsa,' said Margaret.

When they had finished their coffee, Richard fetched a tray and began to gather the dishes together. It had grown chilly. 'Leave those,' said Margaret, shivering. Dora put on her old cardigan. It hung shapelessly from her neck to her thigh. Peering through the hedge she caught sight of the camellia in next door's garden. 'Isn't it a beauty,' she enthused, waving her woolly arms in excitement.

'I'll show it to you,' offered Richard. 'They won't mind you taking a dekko. They're a nice couple. He's something of a character. He wears Osh Goshes.'

'Charles,' said Dora. 'Please ring Mrs Antrim. Just to check if the kiddies are all right.'

Obediently Charles went into the house. He was followed by Margaret.

The telephone was on a shelf outside the bathroom door. He couldn't remember the code number. 'Doesn't he remember his little codey-wodey number?' said Margaret, who had been drinking quite heavily.

'Be careful,' he protested. 'The front door's open.'

'They've gone next door to look at the flowers,' she said.

'They might pop back at any moment.'

'Well, come in here then.' And with brute force she pushed him from the phone towards the bathroom. It was quite flattering in a way, the urgent manner in which she propelled him through the door. He wished her teeth would stop chattering; she was making the devil of a noise. Feeling a bit of an ass, he sat on the edge of the bath while she stood over him and rumpled his hair. 'Steady on,' he said. 'I haven't a comb on me.'

'Kiss me,' she urged. 'Kiss me.'

'Look here,' he said, wrenching her fingers out of his ears. 'This is neither the time nor the place. I can't relax in this kind of situation.'

'Oh, shut up,' she said, and shoved him quite viciously so that he lost his balance and lay half in and half out of the bath. At that instant she thought she heard someone coming up the hall.

'Christ,' she moaned, dropping to one knee and peering through the keyhole. There was no one there. 'Listen,' she told Charles, who was struggling to get out of the bath. 'If they come back, I'll go and you stay here. You can come out later.'

'What if Richard wants to use the lavatory?' he asked worriedly. Margaret said if that happened, he must nip down the steps into the yard and hide in the basement until the coast was clear.

'But what about Malcolm?' asked Charles. 'Malcolm's down there.' Margaret assured him Malcolm would be in the front room of the basement. Even if he did see Charles it wouldn't make much difference — Malcolm hardly said one articulate word from one week to the next.

'If you're sure,' breathed Charles. Half-heartedly he embraced her. He didn't quite know how far he should go. He felt a bit out of his depth. 'Are we ... is it .... should we?' he murmured.

'Play it by ear,' Margaret said mysteriously.

Charles was just unbuttoning his blazer when they both heard footsteps outside. In a flash Margaret was through the bathroom door and closing it behind her. He heard her calling, 'Cooee, I'm here.' Panic-stricken, he undid the bolt of the back door and crept on to the small veranda. Beneath him lay the yard, overgrown with weeds and littered with rose petals. A rambler, diseased and moulting, clung ferociously to the brick wall. Trembling, he descended the steps and inched his way towards the basement door. He stepped into Richard's study, gloomy as the black hole of Calcutta and bare of furniture save for a desk and a chair. Margaret had been right. Malcolm was in the front room playing records. Charles recognized some of the tunes from *Chorus Line*. He wasn't overfond of modern music but he couldn't help being impressed by the kind of enjoyment Malcolm seemed to be experiencing. There were distinct sighs and moans coming from beyond the wall. He eased himself into Richard's chair and waited for Margaret to send some sort of signal. The amount of paperwork Richard brought home was staggering. No wonder poor old Margaret behaved badly. Of course she didn't have any hobbies or attend evening classes. She wasn't like Dora, who was out several nights a week at French circles and history groups. He supposed things were different in the country. For some reason he felt terribly sleepy — probably nerves at being in such an absurd situation. He began to shake with weak and silent laughter and when it was over, fell into a peaceful doze.

He was awakened by a shower of spoons clattering on to the flagstones outside the window. The record in the next room had been turned off. Cautiously he advanced into the yard and peered upwards. Someone was standing at the kitchen window. Adopting what he hoped was a casual stride, he walked to the back wall and inspected the rambling rose. 'Green-fly,' he shouted knowledgeably, looking up at the window. 'Riddled with green-fly.' It was Margaret's face at the window. She beckoned him to come upstairs.

When he came down the hall, Richard was standing at the front door with Dora. He turned and looked at Charles with disgust.

'I've been pottering about in the garden,' stammered Charles. He thought he might faint.

'Isn't it sickening,' said Richard. 'Someone's pinched the table.'

Charles stood on the top step and looked distressed. 'Where are the dishes?' he said, at last. 'And the glasses?'

'Gone,' cried Margaret shrilly. 'Every damn thing.' She put the kettle on to boil while Richard phoned the police. When Richard came back, Charles offered to jump in the car and drive in all directions. 'They can't have got far,' he said.

'He's already driven round the block umpteen times,' snapped Margaret.

Just as the tea was being poured out Malcolm strolled in and helped himself to the cup intended for Dora. He leaned against the draining board, stirring his tea with the end of a biro.

'Where have you been?' asked Margaret. 'You've been out for hours.'

'The park,' said Malcolm.

'Use a spoon,' ordered Richard. Shrugging his shoulders, Malcolm ferreted in the kitchen drawer. 'There ain't no spoons,' he said. His father ran up and down stairs, looking to see if his camera had gone or his cufflinks, or the silver snuff box left him by his uncle.

Charles and Dora couldn't stay for the arrival of the police. Charles said he hoped they'd understand but he didn't want to risk running into heavy traffic. Driving home to Tunbridge Wells, he told Dora he thought it had been a bit silly of Margaret to put the table in the front yard. 'I'm the last person in the world,' he said, 'to laugh at other people's misfortunes, particularly Richard's, but it struck me as affected, you know. Damned affected. I was right up against a dust-bin. Come to think of it, it was bloody insulting.'

'Why?' asked Dora.

'Well, I think she was probably poking fun at us. You know, lunch on the lawn . . . that sort of thing.'

'Rubbish,' said Dora. 'She's just starved of sunshine.'

Charles felt awful. It was sheer worry that made him speak so spitefully of his friends. As soon as Malcolm had mentioned he had spent the afternoon in the park, he had realised how mistaken he himself had been about the noises in the basement. While he had sat at Richard's desk, the thieves had obviously been in the next room. He felt almost an accomplice. And those damned spoons lying in the yard — the police would think the thieves had dropped them. He could never tell Richard about it. Richard would be bound to ask what the hell he'd been doing in the basement. Even if it didn't occur to him for one moment he'd been after old Margaret, he'd still think it odd of him to have been snooping around his desk. Nor, thought Charles sadly, could he confide in old Dora.

She was leaning trustingly against his shoulder, tired after her pleasant day, humming the theme song from *Chorus Line*.

STAN BARSTOW

The Pity of it all

Wednesday afternoon, it was — as if she'd ever forget — half-day closing, and Nancy's mother was going on while she cleaned the house around Nancy, who was doing the week's wash. Since Nancy seldom went out in the evenings and couldn't watch television forever after she had put little June to bed, the house was near spotless before Nancy's mother started on it; but she had to occupy herself and Wednesday afternoon had become a ritual. Nancy's mother came and cleaned the house and went on about something.

What she was going on about now was what she had gone on about ever since Jim had been killed. Where was the sense, she asked, in Nancy tying herself to this house when there was a place for her at home, a garden for little June to play in instead of a short length of street and a death-trap of a through road at the end of it, and herself and Nancy's father to look after the child while Nancy went out and enjoyed herself?

Oh! and didn't she go on. Saying the same things, week after week. She had decided what she thought was best, and wouldn't leave it alone.

'I like my independence,' Nancy always told her. 'I like to have a life of my own.'

'You bring June to me on your way to the shop,' Nancy's mother said, 'and you collect her on your way home. You can't go out on a night because she's got to be looked after. If you call that having a life of your own. You never get out and see anybody.'

She saw enough people in the shop, during the day, Nancy always told her. She was happy enough in her own home when she'd done her day's work.

'A young woman like you, shutting yourself off,' her mother said. 'You'll never get anywhere if you don't get out and about.'

She would never find another husband, Nancy's mother meant. Jim
had been taken suddenly, and that was sad; but Nancy was a young
woman, with time to have another two or three bairns, but not if
she never went out and mixed with people socially.

It was the first week of the school holidays and children were
noisy in the street. Some young ones had been and fetched June
straight after dinner. June herself would be starting junior school in
the autumn. Then, with Nancy tied at the shop till six each evening,
Nancy's mother would accept the extra chore of collecting June in
the afternoon. All the more reason, Nancy could hear her mother
saying, why Nancy should listen to sense and sell this house and
move back home. But though Nancy had often spoken to Jim of
'popping round home' when visiting her parents' house, she no
longer thought of it as such. Here was home, the house she and Jim
had bought and done up together, talking of the day they would get
something better: a semi, they thought, with a lawn at the back to
sit out on and a vegetable patch where Jim could grow things. There
had been no rush.

Then they had come to tell her about Jim, baffled themselves by
the tragedy of it. In a safe pit with a low accident rate, and no
fatalities for years past, he had walked alone into a heading, where a
stone had fallen out of the roof, pinning him down and, so they told
her as a crumb of comfort, killing him instantly. She was carrying
the child and thought at first she would surely lose her. The doctors
told her she was tough. Her mother had been known to call her
hard. But Nancy had never paraded her feelings; she did not know
how to behave to impress others. Her duty was to hang on and
think of the new life growing inside her; a bit of Jim that he would
now never see. Perhaps she would re-marry one day; but she would
not go out and look for a chap, and he would have to be pretty
special for her to notice him. That, she had told her mother. It
seemed to Nancy that she told her every Wednesday, while her
mother went on.

Now she was telling Nancy that she'd had a reply from a guest
house in Bournemouth, whose address a friend had given her, and
they could have accommodation for the last two weeks in August.
Nancy's mother thought the south coast would be a pleasant
change, but if Nancy wanted to go elsewhere with a friend it would

be no trouble for her and Nancy's father to take little June with them. But no, there was nowhere else that Nancy wanted to go.

Afterwards, Nancy found she could remember that moment with vivid clarity, though its components were all familiar ones. There was the attitude of her mother's body as she held the vacuum cleaner while she wound the flex on to the hooks; the sudden rush of water in the automatic washer as it performed its last rinse; the sunlight on the step outside the scullery door. The voices of the children were no longer near.

'Just have a look out at June, will you,' she said, as she opened the washer and passed clothes over into the drying-compartment. 'They've gone quiet.'

Then a minute or so must have passed, but it seemed like no time at all before Nancy's mother was calling at the end of the yard: 'June! June, where are you? Ey, you two, bring June back here. Don't you know how busy that road is? No, keep hold of her! Don't let her—!' And Nancy was out and running across the flagstones and into the street, as though she knew before she heard that awful screech of tyres and saw the car slewed round the little legs in the blue-and-white Marks and Spencer socks, washed just once, and the stupid, stupid older girls who had led her into it, standing petrified, soundless, and she herself making no sound — not yet — while her mother set up an endless moaning chant beside her: 'Oh! oh! oh! oh! oh! . . .'

Nancy's father could not eat his food. Nancy had had nothing but cups of tea for over twenty-four hours. They talked behind her in low voices. 'It's the shock,' her father was saying. He couldn't take it in.

Nancy's mother was saying what she'd said ever since Jim died; that there had been no sense in Nancy living on her own with the bairn, when a good home had been waiting for them here. Nancy told her to shut up, let it drop.

'I don't care, Nancy. You could have come here and been as free as you liked. You can't stop living, just because—'

'Just because what?' Nancy challenged her. 'What are you talking about? I don't know how you can fashion to bring it all up. You never let things rest; you just go on and on. You were sick to

get me out of that house, and now you've got something you can
hold against me for the rest of your life.'

'Nancy!'

There might have been a row then, because if what Nancy
accused her mother of was not strictly true, her mother talking like
that would not help Nancy to stop thinking that if only she had
taken her advice little June would not have been in that road at the
moment that car came along, and . . . And if Jim had not walked
into that heading, or he had come out of the pit into a safer job, and
if she had never met him and she'd never had the child . . .

But the door bell rang.

Nancy's mother, on her feet, went to answer it, coming back a
few moments later to stand, curiously tongue-tied, inside the living-
room doorway.

'Who is it?' Nancy's father asked.

'It's a chap, to see our Nancy.'

Nancy's father began to get up from the table. 'She can't see
anybody now. Can't they leave her in peace? Some folk . . .'

'No, Cliff, wait a minute. It's the feller 'at . . .'

'Who?'

'He's come to see our Nancy.'

'Who is he?' Nancy asked.

'They call him Daymer. If you don't want to see him, just say
so.'

'No. If he's come we can't turn him away.'

'Look, Nancy,' her father said, 'there's no law says you've got to
see him.'

And she didn't want to, but he'd come and she must.

Her mother showed him in. 'This is a sorry house you've come
to.' That tongue. It could spare nobody.

In the one direct look she could manage, Nancy saw that he was
nicely dressed, still young. She wondered if his eyes always looked so
hurt, or if it was only because of what had happened. Of what, she
suddenly realised, had happened to him.

'Mrs Harper . . . I'm sorry to intrude on you at a time like this,
but I felt I had to come. There's nothing I could say that wouldn't
be hopelessly inadequate. You do understand that I hadn't a chance
of avoiding your little girl? It was over in a flash.'

'Nobody's blaming you,' Nancy said. 'It was an accident. They do happen.'

'It was an accident that took her husband,' her mother told him. 'In the pit.'

His voice was shocked. 'Oh, I'm ... It sounds worse than useless, Mrs Harper, but if there's anything I can do, anything at all.'

'You can't bring her back, can you?'

No mercy there. Her mother was, in fact, a good-hearted woman. But that tongue ...

'Have you any family, Mr Daymer?' Nancy asked.

'A boy, Peter. He's away at school.'

'I expect he'll be well looked after there.'

'Well ...'

'It wouldn't be easy for you to come. I think you for it.'

'If there's any way I can help, any way at all, please let me know. I'll give you a card and put my private address on the back.'

Her mother took the card. 'Oh, you work at Rose's, do you? I used to know Mr Finch's wife, before she died. We did charity work together.'

'He's my father-in-law. I married his daughter, Elizabeth.'

'A lovely woman, she was, Mrs Finch.'

'Yes, indeed. And now I must go. Goodnight, Mr Frost, Mrs Harper.'

'Is he in his car?' her father asked when her mother came back from showing Mr Daymer out.

'Yes.'

'I don't think I could drive a car again, if anything like that happened to me.'

But, Nancy thought, you'd got to keep going. There were times when you thought you couldn't. But you'd got to.

They sold cigarettes and tobacco and cigars, sweets, and newspapers and magazines in the shop. Some of the magazines Nancy was not keen on selling. They had pictures in them of women with their legs open, showing all they'd got. Sometimes the women had their hands down there, as if they were touching themselves up. Not that she was prudish herself, but it embarrassed her when men were embarrassed by buying them. Some of them were. Some were really brazen about it, eyeing her up and down as they threw the book on to the counter, as though she chose them all herself and guessed exactly what they would like. Still, they were dear and the owner said they made a good profit. Marjorie, the other girl, younger than Nancy and not married, thought they were a giggle, and when things were quiet she would pick one out and read the letters, which were all about sexual experiences.

'They must make them up, Nancy. Don't you think so? Honest. It's dreamland. Hey, listen to this one!' Well, they knew what men were like, didn't they? Marjorie would say.

Jim himself had not been averse to a look and a laugh, though when it came to the thing itself he'd been easily enough satisfied so long as he got what he called his 'nightcap' regular. He was always pretty tired and it didn't last long. It was all right. She'd loved him and couldn't complain, though just every now 'and then she'd find herself wishing for a bit of finesse, that they might linger, enjoy it for itself, not just for the end of it. And it had been a long time now . . .

Marjorie had a boyfriend, a cocky lad called Jeff, who sometimes called in to buy a packet of fags and make arrangements with Marjorie. When Marjorie couldn't resist telling Nancy what a smashing lover Jeff was she nearly always stopped at some place, cutting off the subject in a way which told Nancy she was sorry that she hadn't got anybody now. And Nancy wished she wouldn't, because she didn't want that kind of pity. It had been a long time . . . But she still missed Jim and could not bring herself to think of anyone taking his place.

Marjorie's big blue eyes brimmed with tears the morning Nancy returned to the shop. Nancy had to steel herself to accept this kind of sympathy. It was natural, but it threatened the defences she was building along the slow path to days in which there would be moments when her mind was not obsessed with what had happened. The nights were the worst, before she managed to sleep; then the mornings when she woke ready for a routine — the kisses, cuddles and chuckles, the dressing of a child's warm plump body — that was no longer there. It was why she was still with her parents: her own house had an atmosphere of expectancy, as though waiting for someone to come back from holiday, or a spell in hospital, and resume life as it had known it.

Sometimes Nancy took sandwiches to the shop — there was an electric kettle in the back room, where they could make tea or coffee — but it was nice to get out for a while around midday, and she went for a snack then to the Bluebird Café, a clean place run by a Cypriot family, a couple of streets away. This particular day she had gone in perhaps a few minutes later than usual to find it full, and she was standing looking for somewhere to sit when a man she hadn't so far noticed spoke to her.

'Mrs Harper . . .'

It was Mr Daymer, at a table for two, with one of the few empty seats in the place opposite him. She said, 'Oh, hello,' and he asked how she was.

'I was just going to order,' he said. 'Perhaps you'd . . .' There was a newspaper on the other seat, and one of those slim zip-up cases for papers, as though he'd been keeping the place for somebody. He reached over and moved them. 'Please,' he said. 'There's not much choice, anyway.'

She thanked him and sat down. As he said, there wasn't much choice, and she couldn't be rude.

'I haven't seen you in here before.'

'No. Do you come in much?'

'Yes, I suppose I'm a regular.' But he knew that. She somehow knew that he'd known. So what did he want with her that he had to pretend things and cap his pretence with a downright lie — she was sure he was lying — when he said, 'I had an appointment in town and just happened to spot this place.' He tried to smile, but it was a poor attempt. He wasn't easy. But how could he be? In his place she would have run a mile before meeting her face to face. So why was she so certain he'd been waiting for her, expecting her to come?

He handed her the menu. 'What kind of thing do you usually have?'

'Oh just a snack. Poached egg on toast. Something like that.'

'They've got what they claim is home-made steak-and-kidney pie, I see. What about joining me in that?'

She told him no, she wouldn't; that her mother would have a cooked meal waiting that evening. She didn't even want the snack now, just coffee, her stomach was all knotted, him sitting there bringing it all back so sharp and clear. But his eyes looked so hurt again that she couldn't bring herself to get up and leave him.

'Are you living with your parents now?'

'For a bit. My mother thinks I'll stay for good now. She was always on about it before. I've got a nice home though. I don't want to let it go.'

'I imagined you as an independent person.'

What did he know about her? He wasn't her class, though his voice was more careful than naturally posh. He was the head of a department coming down on to the shop floor in his nice suit and shirt and expensive tie, as at the firm she'd worked for before she married Jim. His fairish hair was just long enough, touching his collar, for fashion, but neatly cut. Like his fingernails. Neat hands — no oil, pit-dirt ingrained, work scars. A gold signet ring, heavy gold watch and strap. A Rolex. She'd seen them in shops, had once looked at some with Jim before he'd laughed and settled for something reliable at thirty quid with a face she'd thought rather smart. She had it in a drawer at home now. It was easy enough to look at his hands because it was too hard to look each other in the face.

He wouldn't have the steak-and-kidney pie when the waitress came for the order. No, he said, when Nancy said not to mind her, he wasn't really hungry and, like her, he would have a cooked meal this evening and he only ate a substantial lunch when he was entertaining firm's guests. And then, Nancy thought, he wouldn't bring them to the Bluebird, but somewhere like the Regent or the new motel. And when he had his meal tonight it would probaby be nearer eight than half-past six, with sherry or gin before it and a bottle of table wine to go with the food. Mr Daymer had married the boss's daughter — he had told them when he visited the house. Nancy's mother had looked up to the late Mrs Finch. Mr Finch apparently still lived in a big house on the other side of the park. She didn't know whether Mr Daymer was clever or not, but it probably didn't matter. He would be looked after in the firm because of who he'd married. He'd landed on his feet. He'd 'got it made', as Jim might have said. So what did he want with her? Oh, he'd done a terrible thing, but nobody was blaming him. Witnesses had said he hadn't a chance. June had been killed because silly young lasses had got her on to the wrong side of the road and then let her start to cross back on her own. They'd been taking care, had promised to take care, but their minds were too young to make them take care all the time. They knew, and they were sorry: everybody was sorry, but it was done. Mr Daymer was sorry, but as her mother said, he couldn't bring June back.

Because they had just coffee there was an excuse not to linger. Besides, Nancy thought the management didn't like people taking up tables for coffee when there were others wanting seats for lunch. Mr Daymer asked her one or two questions about her job; did she like it, and did her employer look after her. Then he collected his belongings and went out with her.

'Goodbye,' Nancy said. 'Thank you for the coffee.'

'Please,' he said, 'don't forget. If there's anything I can do. Anything at all.'

'That's all right,' she told him, and then again, 'Goodbye.'

She had an idea that he watched her to the corner, but she didn't like to look back to make sure.

He telephoned her at the shop a week later. As it happened she was on her own in the back room and answered herself.

'Could I speak to Mrs Harper, please.'

'Speaking.'

'Mrs Harper, this is Walter Daymer.'

'Oh, yes?'

'How are you?'

'Oh, pretty fair.'

'Is Wednesday your half-day?'

'Wednesday, yes.'

'Will you be doing anything then?'

A few weeks ago she could have answered him without hesitation: she would be doing the wash while her mother put the polish on a clean house around her.

'I don't know, really.'

'I wondered if you'd like to go for a drive with me.'

'Oh well . . . I don't know.'

'We could run out into the country. It'd be a change for you.'

'I suppose it would. But you don't have to. There's no need for it.'

'I'd like to. We could have lunch on the way.'

She said, 'Just a minute,' and laid the receiver down, stepping away from the telephone to think. She was standing like that when Marjorie came in from the shop.

'Are you still on the phone, Nancy?'

'Yes.'

'Are you all right? There's nothing wrong, is there?'

'No. I'm all right.'

The shop-bell rang. Marjorie left her. Nancy heard Mr Daymer's voice, small in the receiver. She took a deep breath and picked the receiver up.

They had said they would meet in the market car park, where Mr Daymer would arrive first and watch for her. Nancy hadn't wanted him to call for her at the shop — Marjorie might linger and, in any case, the proprietor always came in at the end of a working day. They were behaving, Nancy thought, like people with something to hide. But it was something better not talked about with others until it was over. Someone had told Nancy's mother that Nancy had sat with a man in the Bluebird. Nancy's mother had seemed pleased, probing for hints of a more than casual acquaintance, until Nancy told her it had been Mr Daymer. Apart from anything else, Nancy's mother had said then, Mr Daymer was a married man. Nancy asked her if she thought his buying her a cup of coffee constituted grounds for divorce. No, said her mother, but it wasn't a big town and people liked to talk. Nancy had told her mother she might fancy the pictures this afternoon and her mother had said that might do her good, help to take her out of herself. Marjorie had seen the film in question and talked about it in some detail.

Mr Daymer took her into a white pub on a hillside on the way. He wanted to buy her a good lunch, but all she would have was a ham-and-salad sandwich and a glass of lager. When she asked him how he had managed to take the afternoon off, he told her that he would be driving up to Newcastle when he left her. They were building a new factory there. She supposed he was important enough not to have to account for every hour of the day. He said he would also take the opportunity of calling to see his son, who was at a boarding-school in North Yorkshire. Peter had been writing home about bullying in the school. Mr Daymer's wife, who had experience of boarding-school, thought the lad was exaggerating; but Mr Daymer, who had not been away from home until university, felt that the boy was genuinely unhappy and wanted to get him transferred to a day school near home. He believed anyway, he said, that children should spend their formative years with their parents. Then he seemed to become embarrassed by talking about the boy, and changed the subject.

They drove on, arriving eventually at a hill top from where, Mr Daymer told her, you could look into three counties. Or you could, he said, before local government reorganisation had changed so many county boundaries. He wasn't sure where they were now officially. It was very beautiful, though, and they were lucky with the weather.

'I remember,' Mr Daymer said, 'when I was a boy and I got my first bike. A second-hand 'sit up and beg', it was. I attached myself to a local cycling club and they came up here one Sunday. It was a matter of pride with me to stay the course. Thirty miles here and thirty back. I slept for twenty-four hours solid after it. My parents thought I'd gone into a coma.' It sounded to Nancy as though Mr Daymer's parents had been no better off than her own. He was a poor boy who had married a rich girl, and there were things they didn't agree about. She wondered who most often had the last word. But now she had to get matters straight.

'Will you tell me something, Mr Daymer?'

'What?' he said. 'But look, I wish you'd call me Walter. Mr Daymer sounds so stiff and formal.'

She couldn't bring herself to do that, so she just said, 'Will you tell me why you wanted to see me again? Why you asked me to come out for a drive with you.'

'It's not an easy question to answer.'

'You must have a reason and I'd like to know what it is. It seems to me I ought to be somebody you'd be best off forgetting.'

'It can't do you much good seeing me, if it comes to that.'

'No.'

'It's just,' he said after a minute, 'that I feel so . . . so inadequate. And sorry for you.'

'I don't need your pity.'

'It's not pity. Not in the ordinary way. Anyway, why did you come? You could have refused easily enough.'

She thought about that before she answered. 'Perhaps I'm sorry for *you*. You can't stop thinking about it, can you?'

'No, I can't,' he said. 'I want to help you and I can't. There's nothing I can do. You know, even a simple thing like a holiday. If you wanted to, I could arrange it.'

'I don't want your money. And there's nowhere I want to go.'

'No. Forgive me. It was a foolish idea.'

'What does your wife think about it? You've told her you've seen me, I suppose?'

'She knows about the other time. I told her what I've told you — that I feel helpless. I thought that first time that you seeing me as a person might help you to get some kind of perspective on it. That it might help you to forget the stranger — the instrument almost — who knocked down your little girl.'

She found herself looking at the interior of the car she was sitting in as a thought turned her suddenly cold. Was it the same colour? 'This isn't the . . .?'

'No, no,' he said. 'I got rid of it.'

She let her breath go. 'But you made it in your way to see me that other time, didn't you?'

'Yes,' he admitted. 'Yes, I did. And I wondered afterwards, I wondered whether it had done either of us any good. Because' — his hands were trembling now; she felt that his whole body was trembling, and he was breathing like somebody who had just run up a flight of stairs — 'because,' he forced himself to say, 'when I think about you now I feel such an overwhelming tenderness and compassion, I can hardly hold it in.'

She began to cry then. He turned and shifted over in his seat as the tears came. 'Nancy . . .' He reached for her and pulled her close to him, his hand stroking her hair, and saying, 'Nancy, Nancy, please don't cry. I don't want to make you unhappy. That's the last thing I want. Please don't cry,' while, at last, she did cry. She cried and cried, as though her heart would finally break.

She cried because of what was past and because she saw with prophetic clarity what was to come. He needed her because of what he had done to her. He could not live with that without knowing her, and she could not turn him away until a time came, as it must, when he would have to go. She would move back into her own house and he would come to her there. Shyly, gently, with a romantic yearning, he would reach for her and she would take him into her bed. He would be gentle there, too, soft with a gratitude for the forgiveness of her body; and she would enjoy that, because it had been a long time for her. He would speak then of love, and the possibility of leaving his wife, disappointed at first, then grateful without knowing it, that she would not respond in kind. For something would happen. She did not know when, she did not know what. But something would happen and when it did she would tell him that he was not her man (he was not strong enough for her, though she would not tell him that). He need not be afraid she would cry for him; she had only ever cried for one man and he would never come back, and must he be hurt because she was not hurt again? Did he not want the peace of knowing that he had needed her for a time as she, she would say, had needed him, but that now it was done it was done? Was there no strength to be drawn from that, or was his heart one made for haunting? All this, she saw, would happen before she was alone again; though as she was the stronger and knew what was to come, she would in that way be alone all the time.

They sat apart again. Perhaps, after all, she thought, as he did not speak, he would find the strength to draw back now. Unnoticed, a darkening sky had piled up behind the car. Rain suddenly lashed the windows. Nancy shivered. Mr Daymer put his hand in her lap. She answered its pressure with the pressure of hers. Then, knowing full well how it must, must end, she waited for it to begin.

KEITH WATERHOUSE

Anybody's

I'll tell you one thing — if I had my time over again I'd be a teenager. They've got it all laid on. None of this will-she-won't-she rubbish in this day and age — can I have the last waltz, do you come here often, shall I walk you home, what are you doing on Friday, don't tell me let me guess: 'Staying in to wash my hair.' It's all discotheques and dolly birds now and you pick them like plums off a tree. On the pill, every one of them, so none of those phone calls out of the blue: 'Can Jacky Fordyce come to the telephone, please? Only it's urgent.' (Not that it ever happened.) And no waiting till Friday. Tonight's the night.

There was a letter in one of the auntie columns the other day — 'I am seventeen years old and have had a steady girlfriend for six months. My problem is that she is always on at me to make love to her. She has her own bedsitter so there is no lack of opportunity, but I do not know how to go about it. Worried Tom.' All I can say is, the world has turned upside down and inside out. *She* is always on at *him*! And *he* doesn't know how to go about it! Who cares? What's that got to do with it? Get in there, Worried Tom. Play it by ear, like we had to — when we got a look-in. *And* it wasn't single beds and popping gas fires — it was the corporation cemetery or nothing, winter and summer, rain or shine.

I blame the Welfare State, myself. They've got it soft. That and the population explosion. I don't have any actual figures, but the present-day world is definitely bulging with right ravers. Whereas when I had my chance — or rather, didn't — they were like all the other good things in life — in short supply. 'When the lights of London go up again, our mouth-watering selection of girlfriends will once again be in full production. Meanwhile, the present limited supply must be restricted to HM Forces and the Yanks.' Positively an under-the-counter commodity.

As for Worried Tom, if he'd been around in my day we'd have taken that problem right off his shoulders, because that girl of his, that right raver, would have been properly taken care of. *She* wants *him* to kip down with *her*! I've never heard anything like it! We'd have sorted her out all right, taken her off his hands, and I'll tell you how we'd have recognised her, Worried Tom. By the bracelet round her ankle.

That's what they wore, in those days. That's how you knew. A thin, copper bracelet — not a thick one, mind, a thick one meant she was on the game. But a thin copper bracelet round the left ankle, that singled her out as an amateur. It meant she was anybody's. And a bandage in the same position meant she was temporarily unavailable.

I only know one girl that fell into that category. To speak to, I mean. June Parkin. Seventeen, same age as me, engaged to a sailor, red hair piled up, orange lipstick, leg make-up, back seams painted on, platform shoes, and a thin copper bracelet round her ankle. Anybody's.

We used to go to the same youth club, Mondays and Thursdays. It was somewhere to go, better than hanging about round the air-raid shelter. Coffee, ping-pong, dancing to records — Glenn Miller, Whiteman, Guy Lombardo for the girls. The sweetest music this side of heaven comes to All Saviours Church Hall — no drape jackets, no jitterbugging, chewing gum must not be deposited on the dance floor, this means you. I was big mates with Ronnie Barrington and we went there looking for talent. Generations ago, when we were fifteen or sixteen, we'd done a fire-watching stint together in the tea warehouse where we worked. Nothing much to do all night except look at the stars and think about the mysteries of the universe. There was a little book we'd got hold of called *The Red Light*, and it cleared up most of those mysteries to our satisfaction. So we had the theory off pat and all we needed now was the practice.

There was a lad called Ray Sugden, big shoulders, wavy hair, looked like Danny Kaye. Known in our little circle as First-In Sugden. Whatever arrived in the way of talent, Ray Sugden was First In. The new talent always came in twos — you'd have thought it was Noah's Ark instead of a youth club, some nights — and First-In Sugden always got the right raver. The other one, the ugly one, the spare part, the one with the glasses, was yours. Thank you for nothing.

It was popularly supposed that First-In Sugden had been there as regards June Parkin, but one night at the dance he told me otherwise. A man with his experience didn't need to boast.

'No, never, youth. Walked her home once, though. I only wish I hadn't had to catch that last tram. She's panting for it.'

'How do you know?'

'Told you, youth — I walked her home.'

'Yes, but now do you *know*?'

'French kiss.'

What else was there to say? Bangle round the ankle, French kiss. Anybody's. And he's going on about his last tram. First-In Sugden — he could afford to be choosy, others couldn't.

But he did play fair, I'll say that, He gave me some valuable background information on June Parkin and he needn't have done that, he could have kept it to himself. She was engaged to this sailor, as I already knew, and had been since she was at school three years ago. What I didn't know was that the call-up had gone to his head, he'd taken to the navy in a big way and signed on for twelve years, and now he was in the Indian Ocean or Portsmouth or some such place and she hadn't set eyes on him for months. So, presumably by Forces' airmail letter, they had come to an agreement. Being a right raver, and wearing a copper bracelet round her ankle, she could hardly be expected to wait for him for ever. I mean she could, but not completely. So the arrangement was made that she would remain faithful to him from the waist down. Above and beyond that region, it was understood and agreed between them that she was anybody's. Or so I was given to understand by First-In Sugden, whose word I had no reason to doubt.

The conditions imposed by June didn't leave much to go on but what I meant to say was, half a loaf is better than no bread. Any port in a storm. Beggars can't be choosers. And other similar clichés.

Ronnie Barrington said I was wasting my time, but I couldn't see it that way at all. It was quite late on in the evening, two more records to go and then it'd be the Anniversary Waltz with Vera Lynn. First-In Sugden and his mates were out behind the church hall with some of the new talent; most of the others had chosen their snogging partners for the evening and were hard at it. That left me, Ronnie, June Parkin and a few spare parts. I was definitely in with a chance.

'You'll get nothing there, I'm telling you,' said Ronnie.

'Who says I won't?'

'I says you won't.'

'What do *you* know about it?'

'I *do* know. I'm telling you.'

'You could be wrong.'

'I could be right, as well.'

We talked a lot, Ronnie and I, but we didn't add much to the sum of human knowledge. 'Anyway,' I said, 'we can but try.' So I got her up for a quickstep and asked her straight out if she'd come to the pictures, and she said yes. Or at least, she didn't say no, which came to the same thing. The word 'yes' was not one frequently heard in our little group. What would usually happen, you'd ask for instance, 'Are you doing anything on Friday night?' and she'd say, 'Why, who wants to know?' and you'd say, 'Only there's a good picture on at the Paramount,' and she'd say, 'What am I supposed to do, come out in spots?' and you'd take it on from there. Are you listening, Worried Tom? You don't know you're born.

She was staying in to wash her hair on Friday but I got a firm promise that if I happened to be waiting outside the Paramount on Saturday night, she might come and she might not. She was only forty minutes late. Straight in the back row, straight to the double seats, arm round her shoulder before she'd even got her coat off, start as you mean to go on. It was Danny Kaye in *Up in Arms*. 'Do you know who he reminds me of?' said June. 'That Ray Sugden down at the club. They're ever so alike, don't you think so?' Two and threepence apiece I'd paid for those seats. For one and nine we could have been watching Mickey Rooney at the Regal.

But all was not lost. After a while she said she was too hot, and would I help her off with her coat. Never miss an opportunity. This time I got my arm round her waist and before long, through no conscious effort of mine, her head was on my shoulder. The exotic smell of face-powder is unknown to the present generation. Get in there, Jacky Fordyce. Danny Kaye was singing a skat song and the couples all around us were in close embrace.

'What do you think *you're* doing?' said June.

'Why, what's up?'

'Wandering hands. And if you pull that button off, you'll know about it.'

'How does it unfasten, then?'

'It doesn't. Not with that usherette watching us.'

She removed her head from my shoulder and sat bolt upright, but who cared? She had made in my opinion a very significant statement. Not, she had said, with that usherette watching us. Indicating that her only objection was to time and place. I could put no other construction on her words. So after that we watched the picture. It was implicit, I thought, that we would be taking the short cut through the cemetery on the way home.

'I don't call that a short cut,' June said. 'Anyway, it'll be closed, this time of night.'

'I know where the fence is broken down.'

'I bet you do. I bet I know who broke it down, as well.'

I was very pleased by that remark. Soon we were sitting in the little porch outside the crematorium. It was dark, no moonlight, no one else about, and I shouldn't have been feeling nervous but I was. I put my arm round the thick cloth of her coat and held it there stiffly. There was no response from June, but I thought I heard her breathing. Abruptly she said: 'If I ask you something, will you tell me?' Oh, God, she's going to ask me if it's my first time. Yes, June. I mean, go on, June.

'Do people talk about me?'

'How do you mean? What people?'

'*You* know what people. Ray Sugden, to name but one.'

'Why, what would Ray Sugden say about you?'

'I don't know, that's why I'm asking. You haven't such a thing as a ciggy, have you?'

I had one left. I was saving it for after.

'Is this your last one?'

'It's all right. We'll share it.'

We passed the cigarette between us. Our cold hands touched.

'Just so long as you don't believe all you hear,' said June. 'Because I'm not like that. I never have been and I never will be.'

'I never thought you were,' I said.

And that was that. Apart from Ronnie Barrington coming up to me at the club and saying, 'I could have told you you'd get nothing,' and me saying, 'What do *you* know about it?' and him saying, 'I *do* know,' and me saying, 'You weren't there, were you?' And apart from the news that leaked out the following week, that First-In Sugden had now been there as regards June Parkin.

'Too true, youth.'

'What? Straight up?'

'Straight up, youth? Lying down, you mean. Too true.'

What about the sailor, then? What about their arrangement — anybody's only from the waist up? And what about her not being that kind of girl after all? I was going to ask First-In Sugden about all this. I would have done, but he said:

'I say, youth, did you know she's got a crush on you?'

'Who — June Parkin?'

'No — Veronica Lake, who do you think? She cracks on she likes you.'

'Why, what did she say?'

'Just that you were a nice bloke. I mean, she kept going on about it, youth. She said you were one of the nicest blokes she'd ever met, and how she wished there were more like you. She said you were a really nice bloke.'

What a testimonial.

SID CHAPLIN

The Sea Rose

It was on a trip to the seaside that I first became aware of the two unfathomable mysteries of time and people. I was on holiday at my Grandma's, but Grandad wouldn't come. He was too busy building a cree or judging at a flower show. So Grandma said, 'Ah'll take the bairn — it'll be company for me and a treat for him.'

We were in position at the station an age before the train arrived. The place was swarming. There were hundreds of mothers carrying bags bulging with hard-boiled eggs and tea-cakes and bread and butter, a score or two of men moving stiffly in their blue Sunday suits, and a few thousand bairns. The tongues of the women went tappy-lappy in a festival of gossip that only paused to prevent the men from going down on their hunkers and having a canny bit crack. And the bairns shouted and laughed and refused to be told what was good for them and inevitably washed away with brief tears the back of the hand they'd been promised and deserved.

In the end the train swallowed the lot, settled on its springs, and went winding away through the fabulous mile of inky blackness that was our own tunnel to emerge into foreign territory and a brilliant blaze of sunshine. Out of the tunnel we took stock. I'd counted on window seats, but there we were, stuck in the middle of the carriage like a couple of cabbages.

The obstacle was an old man. I kept looking at him. I sent as hard as I could, but he didn't receive. He just sat there with his hands on his knees, back like a ramrod, eyes in front, absently playing with the bunch of medals on his watch chain and taking absolutely no interest in the scenery. He was a nice-looking old cove with a neat white moustache and a face that had known a lot of rain and whatever sunshine sixty or so summers had doled out. He was wearing a freshly-cut rose in his button-hole, a big white tea-rose.

After a time he caught me screwing my neck round to read his medals. 'Here, hev a look at them,' he said, unbuttoning his waistcoat and detaching the chain from the watch, then telling me about them — there was one for football, one for pigeon racing, another for first aid, and a real bobby-dazzler for running.

'By gum, that's a grand 'un, Mister,' I said.

'She's a beauty,' he admitted. 'But it wasn't a big race — only at a little village show.'

'But it's real gold.'

'It's the only gold Ah iver won.'

'My Grandad goes judging at shows. Maybe he judged you for this medal.'

'Ah doubt that,' he smiled. 'It's forty years come next show-day since Ah won *that* medal. Witton show it was.'

'My Grandma comes from Witton.'

It might have been a cue for Grandma, for just at that moment she chose to notice and say, 'He's not botherin' ye, is he?'

He leaned forward, 'Nowt to worry about, Missus. We're passin' away the time very nicely now.' She nodded with a pleasant smile and turned away. But the old man kept looking at her.

'Here's your chain back, Mister, and thanks,' I said.

'You're welcome, son.' He gave me a hard look, then dropped chain, medals and all into his waistcoat pocket. He gave my Grandma another look and muttered, 'Well, my sangs, it *could* be her.'

'It is, Mister,' I said. 'It's my Grandma.'

He laughed and rumpled my hair — a thing I never liked. Demonstrations weren't encouraged in my family. 'So your Grandma comes frae Witton, eh?' I said she did. 'Then you've got good stuff in ye,' he said firmly. 'Here, have a blackbullet.'

'I'd rather swap you seats,' I boldly answered.

'Well, by gum. And to think Ah've been wonderin' if Ah dare ask ye to swap me places — the sun's gittin' in my eyes.'

So we swapped places and somehow during the process I found the packet of bullets in my hand. Grandma came out of her trance, 'Now what's afoot — Ah hope he's not botherin' ye, Mister?'

'Niver worry about the bairn, Missus.' Keeping his eyes in front he added, 'He tells me you're a Witton woman.'

'He's a proper gossip.' But I could see she was pleased. 'D'you come from Witton?'

'Ye haven't changed much, Margaret,' he answered.

'Now how did you know my name?'

'Ah remembered your voice. Soon as you spoke Ah knew ye — and when the nipper said you came frae Witton — well, that clinched it.' For the first time since he'd changed places he looked directly at her. 'It's nice to meet you again . . . how long is it?' She looked down. 'It must be forty years come next show-day,' he said. 'Forty shows ago.'

The forty years repeated caught my ear. It seemed a long time, four times my life, time for four like me to grow through a procession of Christmas mornings, crawling from the cradle to infants school, four times ten of writing compositions, saying pieces at the Sunday School Anniversary, running, climbing, jumping in follow-my-leader, pugging nests of birds and bumblers, playing quoits, tip-cat, leap-frog, shouting 'Jack Shine and Maggie' along the long, dark streets, gathering brambles, going guising, sliding and sledging down the long white slopes so many times it made me dizzy to think of it. The many days and immense months stretching out into the great gap between one first-footing and another: all the ten of them multiplied by four reared in my mind.

I came out of my calculations to hear her say, 'It's Charlie, isn't it?' He nodded. 'How did ye manage to get on to *our* trip?' She demanded.

'Funny how these things happen, left the land — went on the railway — and in the end they shifted me down here.' He paused. 'Ah'm a foreman platelayer.'

'It's a painful thing to have to shift at our age,' said Grandma. 'But still — your family'll be all grown up now?'

'Ah've no family,' he said. 'No family at all.'

'So you never married?'

'No, niver married. But Ah've always been lucky in lodgings. And when ye've wandered a bit in your youth — and had it rough — you're thankful for plain food and a clean bed.'

To hide his face from her he turned to me: 'Look at them grit big eyes. By sangs, ye'll niver be dead as long as he's alive, Maggie.'

'He's my first grand-bairn,' she said. 'Ah've five daughters.'

'Ah'll warrant they'll niver match their mother.'

'Noo get-away wi' ye!' said my Grandma. Proud of his compliment, the old man settled back in his seat and so I caught a glimpse of the crimson tide taking imperial possession of her face and neck.

'So you didn't stick to Witton?' she asked.

'By gox Ah didn't,' he exclaimed. 'Ah up and cut loose, cut loose o' the leadin', the fork, the muckin' an' the turnip snaggin'. Remember the times we went snaggin' the low fields . . . so cold there was only your eyes to tell ye that ye'd hands.'

'Ah *hated* them low fields,' she said. 'Ah'm sure Ah shudder ivery time Ah see a turnip field to this day.'

'Ah, but it's a great thing to keep warm. Claes on your back, a spread table and a ready kettle — and bairns about the house. Them's the things that count.'

'It's funny how things come back,' said Grandma. 'Father always complained of the way you took up the fire.'

'Forty years back,' he mused. 'You wore a white dress and a big hat with flowers in it . . . Ah looked for ye after the race, but you'd gone. Ah remember Ah looked all over the field. But ye'd gone. Ah kicked me heels in the house that night and your family wouldn't say a word . . . .'

'Father had the fear of death in all of them.'

'When he landed back in the gig that night Ah asked him straight,' the old man continued. 'He just said, "She's where *you'll* niver find her, my lad. Ye'll niver lord it ower *my* land."'

'Alice's man took the farm,' said Grandma.

'Well, it's nice to know that somebody else didn't suit.'

'We managed without. Joe's a master of his trade and we never wanted for a thing.' She pondered a while. 'Did you win the race?' she finally asked.

For answer he took the chain from his waistcoat pocket. Watching him I now understood that it had been ready there for this very question.

'My, but it's bonny,' said Grandma.

'Funny, it was the first thing that bit lad of yours got his eye on. And to think it was won for you!'

Embarrassed, she fumbled with her gloves: 'He's quick to notice things. As full of questions as a judge.'

He nodded approvingly: 'Not afraid to put a question. Now me
— the more Ah wanted something the more struck dumb Ah
became.'

'Ye were a funny, quiet lad.' Struck with wonderment, I looked at
the lined, weather-beaten face and tried to imagine a time when it
had been smooth and he'd looked for a lass in white. Grandma in
white! It seemed impossible. Then the business of time struck me
again and I realized that four times my young life ago she'd been a
bonny lass and that four times my life again I'd be old.

A question hung between them that couldn't be answered. I
realised that when Grandma closed her eyes and pretended to sleep
— she never dozed.

So the old man talked to me. He told me of his travels over the
mountains to the Western Sea, his lonely walk along the Roman
Wall, his adventures with the shepherds of the Border Marches. Of
the time he ran for his life pursued by a giant goose, rode on a
haycock in a wild wind, wrestled with a wild billy-goat beyond the
Cheviot. I was almost sorry when the train arrived at the seaside.

Almost. For the moment we set foot on the platform I was mad to
get to the sea. But the old man walked with us and his pace was slow
and deliberate. Dancing with excitement I pointed out the giraffe
necks of cranes over the houses and leaning funnels at the end of a
narrow street. A seagull's cry set me tingling for sand and surf, but
it was of no use. 'Now just settle yourself,' she said. 'You've got all
the long day to look forward to.'

'It's only a minute or two away,' said the old man. He turned to
Grandma again. 'And you went and got yourself married, then?'

'Within a twelve-month. And niver regretted it.'

'Well, Ah'm glad,' he said.

'So you went on your travels.' Sensitive to every inflexion in her
voice I caught the faint note of indulgent contempt — a note the old
man seemed to miss.

'Ah travelled, yes Ah travelled. Ah must have hung around
dozens and dozens of farmhouse doors.'

'He tricked you with that bit about niver finding me,' she said,
and that note was back again. 'Ah was practically on your doorstep
all the time.'

He gave a little jerk. 'Ye mean ...?'

'Not a stone's throw from where ye got into the train this morning — at Lampley, a bare six miles from Witton.'

'Lampley ... it niver dawned on me!'

'That's where Ah was,' she said with a little shake of her head, 'for a twelve-month or more. It was worse than a gaol — at it from mornin' to night.'

'Well perhaps it was niver intended,' he said at last.

'No, you hadn't the compass,' she replied, and now the note was entirely indulgent.

And then, I remember, we reached the sea-front. Over the river, the yellow hulk of the Priory snipped a solitary cloud and, far below, the harbour walls reached out crablike for the infinity of sea and sky. There was the sound and white combs and the wide stretch of the sea. There was the noise of the breakers and some-thing apart and quite distinct — the great hum of people. The loveli-ness of it all crashed into all five senses, and without a word I ran helter-skelter into soft sand and never stopped until it was wet and level. There I turned. My grandma was waving. I waved back and watched. She shook hands with the old man. She turned away and he called her back. I could see her shaking her head. Then at last she left him and came over the sands towards me, but the old man remained just where he was.

'You shouldn't have run away like that,' she scolded. 'Without a word to that poor man.'

'He's waving at us.'

'Oh, for goodness' sake,' she said, waving back. 'Well, don't stand gawpin' — give him a wave back.' So we both waved. We were the first to stop. 'Come on,' she said, 'let's walk along and find a nice comfortable spot.'

'Let's walk to the pier.'

But, taking my hand, she turned the other way, and I knew there was to be no argument. We walked a while and she said, 'Is he still there?'

'He's still there.' And then I saw the rose hanging its head on her lapel. 'Why, Grandma, you're wearing his rose.'

'Oh, dear, Ah couldn't refuse it. What's he doin' now?'

'Standing like a sentry.'

'Ah wish he'd go. Look again — and don't turn round this time!'

'He's walking away.'

'*Which* way?'

'The other way — to the pier.'

'Well, thank goodness. Here, take my bag.' She unpinned the rose. 'He shouldn't be able to see us now, should he? Ah know it's daftness, but Ah couldn't wear it. Ah'll swear he's niver grown up in all these years.'

Like a girl she held the rose behind her back as she turned to look over the crowded sands. 'Aye, he's walkin' away, the poor man.' Then she moved over to the curling brim of the sea and threw away his gift with a stiff little motion of the arm — as if to hide the act. I remember it spinning in an eddy, then sailing away in the sea's buttonhole until a thundering wall of water swallowed it.

'That's finished it,' she said, and how was she to know another tide would bear it back in years to come? We waited but it had gone. 'Gone away,' she murmured, never knowng how often the sharp cry of a gull would return me to where her rose will always sail on the cruel, tender waste: the rose that went to sea.

ROBERT FURNIVAL

The Companions

Angus tied his dinghy loosely to one of the big boats moored at Roper's Ferry and got out his fishing-rod. The afternoon was unnaturally still. Even the boats were motionless on the water instead of tugging at their moorings, like horses jostling their heads against leading-reins. Each boat lay on its own perfect reflection, upside down as if resting on a sheet of brown glass. The only sound was the zizzing of Mr Roper's saw as he worked on a boat hauled up on the slipway. The glaring sun gave the sky a one-eyed, mutilated look. Angus avoided looking downstream to where his father's boat rode at the moorings. Every time he saw the boat he had certain thoughts which disturbed him in an exciting, interesting way.

He took out his jack-knife and prised the lid from his bait tin. Inside the tin the maggots heaved and squirmed, industriously burrowing through the peaty dirt in which they were preserved. Angus began to feel peaceful. The colours and shapes of the moored boats lulled him. He baited his hook and cast it into the brown glass, which reflected the orange float with complete fidelity. He fixed his eyes, trance-like, on the float. It was the wrong time to catch anything, the heat of the day. Occasionally a fat plop disturbed the river as a fish lazily lunged.

He took off his canvas shoes and lounged across the dinghy, dangling his heels in the water. Some way down the line a hatchway opened and the head and shoulders of a grey-bearded man thrust out, looked round, drew down again into the cool recesses of the boat. A white dog with a black-patched face scampered round the deck to the bows, looked with comical alertness across the river and yapped officiously.

Mr Roper laid down his saw, picked up his shirt and walked tenderly down to the big ferry skiff, as if the soles of his feet hurt

him. Angus watched him row the skiff across to the far bank where
a passenger waited by the steps in the shade of the willows. The oars
left barely a trace on the water, two lines of fading puddles. The skiff
laid no wake. It went across by instinct, habit. Angus envied Mr
Roper the muscles on his brown arms, flexing and letting go as he
eased forward and then drew back the heavy sweeps, persuading the
boat through the water.

Angus yawned and untied his dinghy. He left his rod trailing and
started to paddle up-stream to his private island. He did not know
why he had to go there but he recognized the moment to go.

He left the fishing-rod propped up in a forked stick and set out on
his usual leisurely exploration of his own domain. It was a muddy
little island densely covered by bushes, shrubs and trees. That was
why Angus had it all to himself. People could not land there for
picnics, or to relieve themselves, or make love. There was scarcely
room to sit down and spread a groundsheet.

He had made himself a small clearing at the water's edge, near
the inlet where he landed his dinghy. He also had, hidden away in
the lower branches of a tree, a few biscuits, and extra bait in case he
should ever be marooned by the floods which occasionally turned
the tamed, domesticated river into something wild, strong and of an
intoxicating, challenging excitement.

He climbed high into the branches of his look-out tree, having
collected a cigarette and a box of matches, wedged himself into the
crutch of two branches, lit a cigarette and surveyed the river. He
wanted time and silence in which to collect his thoughts. He was on
the point of doing something decisive but he did not know what.

Making a journey, perhaps. Something like that.

Or possibly saving one of the children who regularly fell into the
river, were caught by a current and swept into midstream. Angus
was doubtful about this. He was a very moderate swimmer. In fact,
to be honest about it, he could hardly swim at all. He swam best
when he was afraid of drowning.

Whatever it was it would call attention to himself, but not
clamantly. He did not feel neglected or ignored. It was more that he
knew he was changing, inwardly, and it was necessary to give some
outward sign of change so that everybody else would recognize him
for what he now was, acknowledge that he was a different person

from the boy who had come home at Christmas. He did not resent being described as a 'boy', but whenever he heard the word applied to himself he made some slight but important mental reservations. But he was powerless to describe the changes. They were to a certain extent driving him back into himself.

He stubbed out his cigarette carefully, anxious not to start a forest fire, and plucked a shred of tobacco from his tongue. The sun was in his eyes, dazzling him. He shaded them and looked downstream in the direction of Roper's Ferry.

Mr Roper was barely visible, like a large insect moving about with slow, deliberate motions. Angus caught the flash of his saw and watched the arm slide backwards and forwards like a piston. So familiar was the sight to him that he could feel the teeth of the saw nibbling patiently into the wood. Mr Roper had invented a secret mixture of sawdust and glue which was excellent for patching up gashes in the timbers of his boats. Even his father did not know Mr Roper's precise recipe.

It was like being perched high up in the mast of a big ship, up in the look-out tree. The island was roughly in the shape of a ship. When the stream was running strongly the bows of the island cleft it into two, and the stern streamed out a wake just like that trailed by his father's boat in a stiff breeze.

Angus could see the tall mast of his father's boat down at the Ferry, looking as slender as a tooth-pick at this distance. Nearer, it was so thick and heavy that his father could only just manage it single-handed even with the aid of a powerful block and tackle.

No. Stop it. He must not think about the boat. He would be drawn down to it. It had nearly happened before. Its presence was irresistible; but it must always be resisted. He was simply too small for the boat. He could not manage it. He could scarcely hold in a sailful of mild breeze, so large was the mainsail, and the tiller swung across the cockpit at the height of his chest. He had to acknowledge the painful truth. He might as well be a midget or a cripple. In a few years' time perhaps . . .

His mind refused to be turned. When he was on the boat with his father he was nearly always afraid, either when there was too much wind or not enough, so that the boat drifted on the tide, helpless. But it was an exciting sort of fear. When the boat heeled over and dipped one gunwale into the water his instinct was to throw himself into his father's arms. So far he had avoided this ignominious surrender. So far, fear had always produced the correct action.

Of course much of this was ancient history now. He was bigger, stronger. The change was developing rapidly. Every day he noticed something new about himself. No one else knew about it. Even his father did not know. Perhaps he was big enough to manage alone now?

His mother always avoided the boat except at calm weekends, when they ate sandwiches in the cockpit and sunned like lizards.

Angus jumped down, collected half a dozen flat pebbles and had skimmed three of them over the surface of the water when a thin blue snout came gliding into his circle of vision.

It was the girl in the canoe again.

He put down his three remaining pebbles, wiped his hands carefully on the seat of his jeans, and went to deal with her.

As usual she kept her canoe, as light as a floating melon-seed, just out of range of his outstretched arm, leaning back in her cockpit, into which she fitted as tightly as a cork in a bottle, and giving her double-ended paddle the slightest flick necessary to stay out of harm's way.

She derived intense pleasure from silently teasing him in this way. They no longer spoke. At first he had shouted to her to go away — this was a private island; there ought to be a notice saying no fishing, mooring or landing but it had been blown away in a gale — and she had shouted back at him and tried to nose her slim craft into the inlet. She had done this every day for three weeks. Now the terms of their warfare were well understood by both sides. Battle-cries were no longer necessary. They played out their game of challenge and repulse in concentrated silence.

She had no legs. That was his conclusion long since. The canoe grew from her waist in the same way that the double-tail curled grafted from a mermaid. She could not possibly get up and walk, but she was flippantly agile on the water, turning and skimming away faster than thought. He had to admit that she was more adroit on the water than he was in the dinghy. He dreaded being challenged to a race.

Erect, of course, she would be clumsy and unnatural, and crawl up the beach like a crab on all fours, sideways. She had brown skin, and hair bleached white by the sun. Her eyes were faded blue, very pale, almost exactly the same colour as the sky. She wore a curious singlet of black with a garish orange hoop round the middle, like a football jersey. It seemed to indicate that she belonged to some club or other, but Angus knew her to be, like himself, very much an alone sort of person.

He did not know why she had her mind set on invading his island; probably she had nothing better to do. Perhaps she was curious to explore the interior, or resented its privacy.

She used one of her favourite tricks — floating in to a part of the shore which was inaccessible to Angus because of the bushes, drawing him off in that direction, waiting until he was floundering in the thickest part of the shrub and then darting back to the unprotected inlet.

This time, Angus did not try to push through the bushes but waded straight into the water in her direction, a move which took both of them by surprise. They both hesitated, unsure of themselves. Angus felt the rich mud oozing up between his toes and beginning to form a slimy skin over his feet, then up to his ankles. He took a step backwards, carefully, surprised at the strong suction of the mud. The girl took advantage of his being momentarily off-balance, dug her paddle into the water and propelled the canoe like a dart straight at his legs.

Angus was taken so much by surprise that all he could do to save himself from ignobly sitting down in the water was to catch the prow of the canoe between his knees and hold onto it with his hands. Bending down to do this brought him closer to the girl's face than he had ever been before. Any expression she might have been wearing was totally eclipsed by her heavy pigmentation. If anything she looked bored. He could see two slight swelling bumps beneath her singlet.

She dug her paddle in again and thrust as hard as she could. Angus was forced to give ground. He felt the bank pressing into the backs of his knees. Deciding to turn defeat into victory he seized the cockpit coamings and dragged the canoe half out of the water, jumping up on to the bank as he did so, so that the canoe, shelved, had its snout poking up into the air at a ridiculous angle and its tail submerged. The girl sat midway, neither in the water nor upon dry land.

Angus was exhilarated. He felt boundlessly strong. Taking a fresh hand-hold he hauled his capture high and dry on to the beach and put his foot firmly on the snout. He looked triumphantly at the girl, who put her paddle neatly away, said 'Thanks', and stood up. She was wearing crumpled shorts. She did have legs. They were the same teak-brown colour as the rest of her body. She was a year or two older than Angus.

'At long last,' she said, looking about her. She brushed her hair back from her eyes. Angus went back to the place where he had left his flat stones and carefully skimmed the remaining three.

'You can't do that,' stated the girl, without challenge, simply asserting a fact. Angus picked up another stone and skated it with all his force. But she had confused him. The stone made one heavy bounce and then sank. The girl picked up a stone and flicked it without taking aim. Five skimming bounces. It almost reached the opposite shore. She did not even watch it after it had left her hand but turned and made a few steps towards the interior.

Angus said aggressively:

'Who said you could go in there?'

'I did. Who's going to stop me?'

'I am.'

'No, you're not. Nature's free, anyway.'

'Not this part.'

'It isn't yours.'

'I didn't say it was. But I know whose it is.'

'Whose?'

'My father's.'

It was a lie. Angus turned his head away as he spoke, and cleared his throat. The girl came up to him and caught him by the elbow, forcing him to look at her.

'What's your father, then? A lord or something?'

Angus shook his head.

'There you are then,' she squeezed her fingernails into his arm.

'Stop that,' said Angus, and rubbed his arm, which looked as if five white fingerprints had been scarred into it. The white marks faded almost instantly. She laughed.

'I'm older than you, anyway,' she said.

'Bet you're not,' replied Angus, but without enthusiasm. She made him feel uneasy. He did not know how to deal with her.

'Bet I am,' she said. He bent to pick up a stone.

'How old are you then?' she said. 'Ten?'

'Twelve,' said Angus, lying again. That was the second time she had made him lie. He felt angry with himself and flung the stone viciously at the canoe. 'I'll hole your canoe, then you'll have to swim back.'

'I don't care. I can swim that far. Can you?'

Angus narrowly avoided his third lie. He looked at her scornfully.

'I'm taller than you,' he said.

'I'm thirteen as a matter of fact,' said the girl.

'I don't care.'

She fished in the waist-band of her shorts, produced a large blue handkerchief, blew her nose, and neatly tucked the handkerchief away.

'Well, I'm going now,' she said, but instead of moving towards her canoe she took a sudden darting step towards the interior.

At once Angus flung himself bodily after her and grasped her hard by both ankles. She toppled over slowly, elaborately surprised. She came down on her face in a patch of coarse long grass with sharp edges. Angus pulled himself up on her back and pressed her cheek down into the grass. Suddenly he did not care how much he hurt her. There was a clump of nettles nearby. He took hold of her hair with one hand and tried to force her head towards the nettles.

Rather to his surprise she did not resist or make a sound. She might even have been smiling, unless it were simply that her mouth was forced sideways and apart by the pressure of his downward thrust. He dug his knees into her flanks. He saw what she was doing. She was daring him to put her face into the nettles.

He was reminded of being in the country, on holiday. He had gone out rabbit-shooting with a boy from the farm. The boy had wounded a rabbit. He let Angus hold it for a minute. The creature did not resist. It was soft and tense at the same time, lying trembling across his cupped hands. It gave off a strong odour. The blood welling from the corner of its mouth was winey in colour, rich ruby-black. It was the blood which stank.

The rabbit lay across his hands, indifferent to him, staring straight ahead with bulging eyes, quivering. Small pellets of excrement oozed from beneath its fluffy white tail. The farm-boy took it. They walked back along the road. At the first telegraph-pole the farm-boy casually banged its head until it lolled slackly down, hardly pausing in his stride to kill the creature, needing to bang it only two or three times.

Angus had the same feeling of sickening power, of an exaltation so strong that it produced physical nausea in him as he straddled the girl.

As he moved his legs he felt the soft downy hair on her calves. Her feet were bare. Her toes were arched tensely against his feet, pushing and gripping at the same time. He did not know what to do. He did not want to hurt her face. If he did, he knew that at once he would get up to hunt for dock-leaves to rub on the angry rash left by the nettles. He could almost feel the red blotches itching at his own cheek. He relaxed his grip on her hair.

The girl heaved her body upwards and over, flinging him off with an agile strength which a minute ago, in her limp and passive state, would have seemed unthinkable. Angus landed with a gasp on his hip-bone, jarred by the fall. She rolled over on all fours and crouched half over him, grinning, her white hair hanging down over her face almost brushing his forehead, as if waiting for him to make a move and then she would pounce.

She was playing with him, but with a serious purpose which fascinated, and in some parts of his mind, alarmed him. All his senses came alert. He watched her warily. His scalp crawled, there was a damp tingling sensation along the back of his legs, his fingers and toes clenched into the grass, hollowed out now by the rolling of their bodies into a heavily scented nest, cloyed with the odours of crushed grass bleeding green juices.

She was breathing deeply and steadily, not gulping for breath (the rabbit had breathed in the same way). At closer range he could see that her blanched hair had some darker streaks in it, making it tawny. He was surprised, agreeably, by her strength and dexterity. He stared at her insolently. She went on grinning.

He was not quite trapped.

Slowly at first he raised his legs, moving them upwards and sideways. Then with a sudden pounce he scissored them round her waist and held her there tightly. She did not react immediately or try to free herself, but crouched there for a moment summing up her new predicament.

Angus began to feel hot. He tried to brush the sweat away from his eyes but had to leave it as she took advantage of his distraction to lever his legs away with her hands. She succeeded in pushing them down a few inches, but in so doing his legs dragged down one side of her singlet. She was forced to crouch forward over him to prevent the shoulder-strap from tearing, but despite this the strap slipped off.

She was the same colour underneath the singlet as she was elsewhere. Angus wondered where she found the privacy to sunbathe with nothing on. The nipple on her bared breast was of palest pink, the colour of some small pebbles he had once found.

Cramp seized his calf-muscles. He released his scissor-grip, opened his legs wide and twined them round the back of her legs. She fell forward on to him. He pushed himself sideways and wormed out from beneath her, gripped by fear of suffocation. She held herself a few inches above him, propped up on her hands, and then let herself drop again. He moved his legs up and down, chafing her bare calves. He liked the feeling.

All at once he was parched, inwardly, not merely on the surfaces of his body but as if all the juices had stopped circulating, dried into salt-patches on the inside of his flesh. He felt an enormously overwhelming lassitude creeping over him inch by inch, lulling every tensed muscle into relaxation, finally invading his brain.

He felt drowsy but did not want to sleep. Despite himself, his eyelids began to droop. He was hardly aware of the girl. She pressed down on him with no more weight or purpose than the hot sky. He knew her only as an almost tangible smell which at first he could not recognize but after a few moments was able to identify: the bland smell of olive-oil.

They were no longer wrestling. The girl moved her body slowly and carefully above him. She took his unresisting hands and placed them where she wanted them. She shifted her legs into a more comfortable position. She closed her eyes. Time was measured by their breathing.

Angus anticipated each rise and fall of his chest, delaying and

advancing each breath to coincide with that of the girl. He had no
idea how long they lay there, scarcely stirring. The grass was cool to
the touch. All round about them was coolness. They themselves
generated a mounting heat which, strangely, was not uncomfortable
but safe and reassuring. Angus felt pleasantly dazed.

He moved his head from time to time and the girl's cheek moved
with him as if they were grafted together. Sometimes he felt the
flutter of her eyelashes on his forehead. Every time they moved she
gave a low murmur.

Then she began to drag herself over him. Angus felt his dozing
peace ebbing away rapidly. Startled, he opened his eyes. She was
straddling his chest now, her eyes screwed up tight shut, as if she
were in pain. Her singlet hung round her waist. She was pressing
the pink-nippled bumps together. He felt her buttocks tighten
against his ribs; saliva welled into his mouth. She gave a low moan
and slumped forward, limp, and feeling boneless as if she were
moulded from solid flesh and had no skeleton. Her breasts spread
over his nostrils and cheeks. He inhaled the suave oily perfume.
They were incredibly soft.

After perhaps ten minutes like this she heaved herself away from
him and sat down beside him. He sat up and bowed his head. She
selected a blade of grass and began to chew it, bored. She had not
bothered to put her singlet on again. Her back was criss-crossed
with marks made by the grass. Angus stroked it once as he would
have stroked a cat, idly, and then let his hand fall loose.

He was perplexed and began to feel a slowly rising melancholy
which, to him, was entirely new. He could find no cause for it. The
sun was hotter than ever. Light shimmered over the water. The blue
canoe hauled out onto the bank was now bone-dry. A wasp buzzed
indolently in the dinghy floating nearby. Angus felt tears pricking
his eyes and blinked several times to clear them.

He rose to his feet and brushed off the knees of his jeans. The girl
looked up at him, threw her chewed blade of grass to one side and
stood up next to him. She put on her singlet again. Angus avoided
looking at her. He felt so sad that he could have burst into tears.

She followed him to the water's edge and, as he untied his dinghy
and made ready the oars, deftly refloated her canoe and slithered
into it. He rowed rapidly, with a sense of purpose, down to Roper's

Ferry. He did not know what his purpose was. He only knew it was there.

She was able to keep pace with him easily but he still avoided meeting her eyes. There was something proprietary about her look which unsettled him. She had laid claim to him. He did not want to be possessed by her or by anyone else, even by his parents. He was his own.

A slight breeze sprang up, ruffling the water into a herring-bone pattern. Angus nosed the dinghy in amongst the craft moored at the Ferry and tied up alongside his father's boat. The girl hung back and watched. He climbed aboard and busied himself with the mooring warps. There was no one else about. His heart was pounding.

The girl watched for a few minutes and then paddled off swiftly downstream. He glanced up briefly and watched her out of sight round the next bend. Then he returned to his work. He did not even know her name.

The tide turned and began to ebb strongly.

ALUN RICHARDS

The Monument

Whenever Ethel Grail thought of her husband Oakleigh, she remained safely in her well-known role of the worshipping wife, paying tribute to the majesty of the man even in the solitude of her own mind. Thus, even privately when there was no possibility of her being overheard, she spoke of Oakie as Oakleigh, using his full name and not the common abbreviation heard along the dock.

Standing in the butcher's shop as she fingered a large lean pork chop, she might say, 'That'll do Oakleigh nicely,' or sometimes if there was a jumble sale to raise money for the Royal National Lifeboat Institution of whose local station Oakie was a prominent crew member, she would select an extra large, outsize workman's flannel shirt with the thought that it would be just the thing to cover the small of his massive back, always on offer to the weather. Other times, she'd walk to the headland of Ennal's Point, the little seaside village where they lived, and look the length of the bay to the neighbouring port of Sveynton and ask questions of the wind. 'I wonder where Oakleigh's got today?' It was always Oakleigh for in her mind she used his Christian name like a royal title.

It was not so with other people. If they thought her a quiet, mild little woman who seemed to have a duster forever in her hand, it was different with him.

'There he goes, that's Oakie Grail,' they said in lowered voices, pointing to the large barrel-chested figure. And indeed, his big-jawed, slightly lopsided, craggy face with its thick glowering eyebrows, quarrelsome flush and usually apoplectic wooden stare was a sight to behold, as was his immense girth. Despite his fifty-three years evidenced by the dense thatch of closely cropped grey hair dumped on his skull like a mound of cigarette ash, he retained a permanent air of physical threat which was always apt to confront those who came into reluctant contact with him, particularly the young, whose condition he seemed to regard as inexcusable. He was large, he was awkward, he was stubborn and so salty of tongue that he belonged in some people's eyes to that breed of yellow-oilskinned and sou'westered figures whose weatherbeaten faces stare out at you from the kipper packets, a breed long disappeared except for Oakie who, like his ancient trawler the *Ethel May*, wore a battered air of a remote and cheeseparing past.

'That's him,' the young lifeboatmen said when well out of earshot. 'That's Oakie, one eye on the gutter — you never know what you might pick up! And that's the *Ethel May* behind him. You wouldn't doubt it, would you? The wheelhouse is made out of driftwood and the winch fell off a lorry.'

But Oakie was skipper and owner of the last trawler sailing out of Sveynton. Others had bowed out in the face of foreign competition and poor catches, but not Ethel's Oakleigh. He was a man born to be a monument in Ethel's eyes, although when the time came for the second coxswain of the Ennal's Point lifeboat to retire, a position for which Oakie felt himself eminently suited, there was a moment when the monument shook.

Oakie's problem had always been that as a full-time fisherman who was often away at sea for several days on end, he was not available for many of the emergency calls which came for the lifeboatmen. All of them, like Jack Tustin the coxswain, lived within running distance of the lifeboat station and also within earshot of the secretary's house where the maroons were fired to summon them. In the old days, volunteer crews were composed almost entirely of fishermen who worked the oyster smacks from the village itself, but for years there had been no local fishermen and the crew nowadays was composed of men whose daily trade had no connection with the sea. They might be plasterers, painters, bank managers, school teachers or enterprising yachtsmen but they were not fishermen, as Oakie told Ethel after almost every launch. However, when the second coxswain retired through ill health, it was natural that Oakie should think of himself as the most likely candidate. He was not away from home as often as he used to be. He was never away at weekends when many of the calls came, as Ennal's Point, a fishing village turned commuter's paradise, was now a haven for yachtsmen.

These Oakie described to Ethel in no uncertain terms.

'Idjuts,' he called them, 'comedians who'd drown in a bottle.' She never contradicted him, perhaps because she knew that most of the casualties occurred at the weekends, particularly in the summer when visitors and trippers did what visitors and trippers always did — forget that the Bristol Channel and the Welsh coast had the second highest rise and fall of tide in the world.

'Tides is the villains, Eth,' Oakie explained once. 'Wind and tide together. Lee shore, d'you see?'

'Yes, Oakleigh,' Ethel said.

'And half the boats these days — matchboxes, plastic and paint! I wouldn't trust a dog in 'em.'

'Oakleigh knows,' Ethel would say to the neighbours. 'He really knows.'

'Yes, Mrs Grail,' the neighbours said. They wouldn't dream of contradicting him either.

But it so happened that Oakie's knowledge of the sea *was* expert. There was no one that Jack Tustin, the coxswain, relied on more. Put him on the wheel in a nasty tide race, he'd hassle the weather out of the course with hands and feet that could caress, twenty-five tons being just his dap. Put him on the bow with a manilla hawser in a Force Ten, you knew you had a man as good as two. He could not only tie knots, he could tie knots you could undo in a hurry, and he had a nose in a fog that was uncanny. He was a seaman through and through, a man who could read the sea by instinct: winds, currents, channels, rips, tide races. He knew them like the wallpaper on his bedroom ceiling — and that hadn't been changed for twenty years either.

'I don't know what I'd have done without him,' Jack Tustin said to Ethel many times and Ethel faithfully reported back. Oakleigh got on with the coxswain but he seldom praised any man.

'Tustin's all right as long as he's got me with him,' Oakie said.

In the past, he'd been away too often to be considered for any position above an ordinary crew member, but now he meant to do less on his own boat and more on the lifeboat. He'd a good bit put by and a new philosophy.

'If a man works as hard after fifty as he did before, he don't know what life's all about.'

'Yes, Oakleigh,' Ethel said.

'Second cox'n'll do me. There's a few there in that lifeboat house wants licking into shape. Bits of kids.'

'You always know your own mind, Oakleigh.'

'Hamatcheurs, I calls 'em, rank hamatcheurs.'

'They're not fishermen, Oakleigh. You've always said.'

'I have, I have,' Oakleigh said. Indeed, he had. It was his swansong, and the bright sparks in the village said that when he undressed, scales fell on the floor.

However, it was Ethel who remembered that one of the cardinal rules of the Lifeboat Institution was that both the coxswain and the second coxswain were not appointed by inspectors or the management committee, but by the crew members themselves. The officials could recommend, but ultimately, if you went to sea in a lifeboat, you had the choice of your own leaders. Ethel remembered the election when Jack Tustin was appointed, a sad affair because the previous lifeboat crew had all been drowned and there was some doubt whether a new lifeboat could be manned at all.

'Wasn't there an election?' she asked one night when Oakleigh, comfortably seated before the television with a half-crate of stout beside him, was watching a favourite cowboy in the saddle.

'Ah, that was different. They didn't think they'd even get a crew then.'

Ethel wasn't so sure. The problem was, there'd been no changes in the backbone of the crew for years. It was true that they'd recently had an inshore rubber rescue boat with a powerful outboard engine, manned by the younger members of the crew from which Oakleigh, being over forty-five, was excluded — it was because of the vibrations affecting your back, Oakleigh said. But she believed there'd been some fuss about that, and somewhere at the back of her mind she'd stored some information relating to the appointment of what they called the petty officers in the lifeboat. She was sure there had to be an election. She didn't know much about it, but she thought she'd better ask.

'Have you spoken to Jack Tustin about it?' she said casually, looking over her spectacles, her eyes opaque behind the lenses. She never raised her voice in the house even when Oakleigh had taken a drop too much. which he was inclined to do on occasions.

'I'm watching this by here,' Oakleigh said severely in his sand-and-gravel voice, nodding at the television screen. He was absorbed in his Western, and the noise of cattle on the hoof filled the little room.

She said no more.

The truth was, the appointment of the second coxswain was a foregone conclusion in Oakleigh's mind. ' ''Sperience,'' ' was how he put it: one word, ' ''Sperience.'' ' When he said it, shrugging his massive shoulders, it was as if a wave rose behind him and fell back — awed. He was already making changes in his mind. On high days and holidays when visiting dignitaries came to inspect the lifeboat station, the coxswain, mechanic and second coxswain wore white-topped peaked caps and reefer jackets instead of the simple blue jerseys with the red letters RNLI emblazoned on them as did the crew. Well, that would have to change. Smacked too much of the Navy, all bull and white paint. O. Grail would touch his forelock to no one, said Oakie to himself. No sir! Years ago he'd been expelled from the Sea Cadets for misconduct and then joined the army in a sulk. There had to be changes. He was the man for them, in a supervisory capacity, of course.

Ethel continued to study him out of the corner of her eye as she went on knitting. She was making a stole for their daughter May, who had long since left home, married and had children. May had very modern ideas, had wanted her mother to go out to work and make a new life for herself. 'I don't know how you put up with him,' May said when there were incidents like Oakleigh coming home from the club coach trip to Chepstow Races as full as an egg and wrenching the front door off its hinges when the lock jammed. There were other things, worse things, but May didn't understand. A king could do what he liked to the door of his own castle.

Ethel did not mention the matter again, but when she met Jack Tustin's wife when shopping in the village, she tried to bring the subject up casually. She spoke first of all of the man who'd retired, Harry Quayle.

'They'll miss Harry.'

'Of course,' the coxswain's wife said, but she made light of it. 'I'll be glad when Jack retires. There'll be plenty who'll want to take his place!'

'And Harry's place?' Ethel enquired timidly.

But the coxswain's wife did not seem to hear and they were immediately interrupted by the shopkeeper, so Ethel became no clearer on the subject. The following Sunday, when Oakleigh went down to the boathouse as was the custom, he returned with the news that Jack Tustin hadn't been there, but that some of the younger crew members were trying on his hat.

'Bits of kids,' Oakleigh said again. 'I told 'em to cut out the skylarkin'. Sharp, I told 'em. They know what's what when I'm about!'

She noticed he hadn't been to the Sailor's Safety for a drink with the lifeboat boys as he usually did on a Sunday. It was a custom which she knew he enjoyed and indeed, he always stayed until closing time, coming rolling home late to his Sunday joint but, by time-honoured practice, doing the washing-up on that day alone. She knew also that Jack Tustin never stayed long at these sessions and was much criticised by Oakleigh on that score. 'She don't let him out,' Oakleigh said of Mrs Tustin, adding darkly, 'Under her thumb!' with a shake of the head that implied a weakness of character which was pitiful. Ethel went out on Mondays and Fridays with Oakleigh, usually to the British Legion Club, and these were known as Ethel's nights. Oakleigh was thus a man of strict habits, which was why his Sunday rejection of the Sailor's Safety worried her. Perhaps he was taking a leaf out of Jack Tustin's book and remaining a little aloof already?

It was very odd, and the more she thought about it the more it worried her, so that her feeling of apprehension grew. Quite by chance, she happened to be in the village when she saw both the Tustins talking to the new lifeboat inspector who was staying in a nearby boarding house. He was a young-looking forty-odd with immaculate grey trousers and a neat hopsack blazer whose gleaming gold buttons contained raised silver crowns. Ethel had forgotten his name but she knew Oakleigh's opinion of him — 'Headquarters cowboy — gloves, visiting cards and scent!' He was a navigator of repute, but then Oakleigh's view of navigators was like his view of psychiatrists. They told you how to get to where you didn't want to

go, whereas Oakleigh smelt his way at sea, day or night, and on one
famous occasion when the lifeboat had been lost in a fog, Oakleigh
had heard the lightship siren miles away and brought them home.
'Ears like Jodrell Bank!' the boys said. But he knew, although they
added, 'If only Oakie'd go wrong — not the radar!'

The inspector's ears were neat like his blazer and, as Ethel passed
the little group on the other side of the road, she was aware that
they were looking after her and that she was being pointed out.
Then a minute later, another member of the lifeboat crew who was
known as Jigsie came along the road carrying a rolled-up chart and
was obviously going to meet the inspector. Jigsie was in his thirties,
a village boy who had gone to sea as an engineer, served his time,
and returned to join the lifeboat crew where his expertise with
outboard engines was much welcomed. He had mop of flaming
carrot hair, an eye for the girls, and was no respecter of tradition,
which locally meant Oakleigh alone.

Ethel carried away the image of him handing the navigation chart
over to the inspector and that night she thought of the shocks
Oakleigh had faced in his life: their daughter's sudden marriage, a
classic misunderstanding over leasehold, an occasion when he was
left out of a wealthy aunt's will, times when he would not speak for
days on end when his rage turned in on itself and eventually erupted
in a brutal destruction of inanimate objects which was fearful to
behold. If he understood the sea, people baffled him. They seemed to
breathe a different air. So sometimes he crushed doorknobs in a
dumb fury — even doorknobs seemed capable of answering back at
times.

One day he returned home from sea early and got himself
prepared for a meeting of the lifeboat crew in which the item
'Appointment of Second Coxswain' was one of several on the
Agenda. As Ethel watched him dress in his one good suit, she saw
his enormous hands knot his tie with a sense of alarm. Then he
paused to look for something quite unusual, a thoughtful expression
coming slowly over his usually blank face like a ripple on the water.

'What is it, Oakleigh?'

'Pencil.'

She hurried to give it to him. Pencil, she thought. They must be
voting after all. As usual, she'd had everything ready for him, tea on

the table the moment he entered the house, the specially baked date bread he had a fancy for — his mother would never have shop cake in the house, as he was fond of saying. Then she'd pressed his trousers and found the blue RNLI tie with its white-ensign motif and made sure that his last remaining collarless shirt was ready, together with the separate stiff collar — he was the last man in the village to wear such shirts and even the bank manager commented admiringly. Finally, somewhat taking away from the overall effect, he put on a pepper-and-salt tweed cloth cap — his best cap — the poke of which he pulled down flatly over his forehead and surveyed himself in the mirror. Despite his huge bulk, that enormous size-19 neck and the thick reddened hands whose thumbs seemed too close to his palms like a lobster's claws, he looked quite spruce, and indeed the sleeves of his jacket were so filled by his massive biceps that they might have been poured into the material. But Ethel, hovering about the hallway, searched for some word of warning as she had so many times, and indeed certain phrases returned: 'Leasehold is not the same as freehold, Oakleigh, you'll have to pay more.' Then there was another: 'It's May's getting married to him, Oakleigh, not us. They've just had a little accident, that's all.'

Oakleigh turned to her, jammed the pencil in his breast pocket.

'I shall probably have a few jars afterwards in the Sailor's. Don't you wait up.'

'Are you sure . . .' she began hesitantly but then stopped.

An eyebrow on his face lifted abruptly like the spring of a mousetrap.

'What?'

She said nothing in the end because she could think of no phrase that would do. Instead she remembered what she had said before: 'If your Aunt Nance wants to leave you out of her will, Oakleight, it just shows what sort of woman she is.' She meant ungrateful beyond words, but that had cost her the front door knocker. So she said nothing.

And down the street went Oakie, the poke of the cap leading like a visor, the lobster claws swaying below their sleeves, the booted feet punishing the pavement . . . down the street, along the sea front, that tree trunk of a neck writhing in the agony of the starched collar . . . along the sea front past the gift shops full of Welsh love spoons and imported woollens of dubious nationality . . . along past

the boat park where the yacht halliards whined in the wind — and
into the committee room of the Conservative Club, borrowed for
the occasion, where a browning portrait of Sir Winston Churchill
cocked a cigar directly at Oakleigh as he sat down upon two
protesting chairs and did not remove his cap. The lifeboat inspector
was present, the honorary secretary, the coxswain, the lifeboat
crews (first and second), the winchmen, and Harry Quayle bearded
and burly, eyeing a presentation electric kettle in its wrappings to
which Oakleigh like everyone else had contributed.

The meeting began, but first there was a respectful minute's
silence when all stood and bowed their heads to mark the loss of a
Scottish lifeboat crew, an unwelcome reminder of the seriousness of
their business. Oakleigh removed his cap and even Jigsie remained
unusually silent. There were also pencils and ballot slips for the crew
to vote, but Oakie said he had his own.

What followed is best related as Ethel finally found out about it.
She'd watched Oakleigh leave, his bulk filling the frame of the
doorway, then listened to his steel-tipped heels as they clinked on
the pathway and then, as she waited, it seemed to her that what she
admired most about Oakleigh was that he never changed. It was as if
the monument stood impervious to wind or weather, no matter how
the elements raged. As the minutes, then the hour, went by she,
sitting in her chair with her knitting needles clicking away, felt the
comfort of the utter predictability of his every action. The world
changed, so did people, but Oakleigh, ever since the day she first
met him bulging in thigh waders as he clambered up the foreshore
carrying a donkey that had been bitten by a rare poisonous fish —
Oakleigh remained the same. Even his expressions did not change.
When she — feeling the need to confess to him that she was illegiti-
mate, one of the world's casualties banded about from pillar to post
as a child, moved from one institution to another like an unwanted
parcel and crushed in the process — when she attempted to tell him
all this, the very reason for so much of her blank acceptance of all the
ills of fate — that face remained exactly the same. It glared at her
like a benign piece of granite: 'Marriage, I'm talking about, my girl,
got it?' The one thing he was quite right about was that she would
never have dreamt of saying anything but yes, and she had good
reason. There was nothing at all romantic about it; it was the plain

truth and a cardinal fact in her life. You knew where you were with Oakleigh.

But when he returned from the meeting, he was shaken. He did not remove his cap and wandered into the kitchen like a robot whose clockwork motor had begun to run down, saying only one word, 'Jigsie,' and the only thing she could do was what she had always done.

'I'll make you a cup of tea, Oakleigh.'

She was immediately aware of the difference in him. He sat down limply, not knowing where to put his hands. His paunch heaved, those massive thighs quivered. He was even pale underneath that burnt-oak complexion. She did not use a teabag as she usually did, but selected the packet of Earl Grey which their daughter had given them and brewed a special pot.

There followed a moment's heartbreak in monosyllables.

'Jigsie,' he said again. "Overwhelmin'."

'Perhaps it's the rubber boat?' she said meekly.

He did not seem to be aware of her lack of surprise.

'Bloody Jigsie. Ginger git . . . 'Bin divorced an' all.'

'They must have the youngsters for the rubber boat. It's the engines, Oakleigh.'

Oakie stared at the black-leaded fire grate. Like his stiff collars 'for best', it was the last black-leaded grate in the village, and the polished brass candlesticks above it were a legacy of his mother, who was in service when he was born and took the name of her employer's grand house for her only son, scorning her vanished husband. Now that glowering face was reflected in the polished brass and Ethel did not know what to say. She went out to pour the tea and when she returned, his hand went savagely to his tie and loosened it, the collar stud popping at the same time. She also heard the material of the tie tearing — his RNLI tie!

'I've finished with it,' he said hoarsely.

'The lifeboat?'

'Finished!'

'You've been in it since a boy.'

'Aye, fourteen. In the war I started. Mines there was then, all over the channel. Like confetti.'

'You can't give up, Oakleigh?'

'Finished with it, all of 'em.'

Behind her spectacles, Ethel's pale eyes stared at him. For once, she came within an ace of contradicting him.

'You can't, Oakleigh? Over this . . .'

His Adam's apple rose in a wave of flesh, swilled towards her. He glowered again. His eyebrows seemed to be closing right down over his eyes.

She gulped. It was more serious than the trouble with May. 'Not over this . . . somebody for the rubber boat, the engine?' She hesitated, swallowed, set down the cup of Earl Grey, found the courage, then came out with a precise sentence that went to the heart of the matter. 'I mean, it would make you look so small? *You*, Oakleigh?'

Somehow that registered. He spent a full ten minutes thinking about it, sitting there massively in the chair, the fists opening and closing as if washed by a tide of rare feeling. She knew, of course, that he could never give up the lifeboat. It was a part of him, as much a part of him as was the *Ethel May*, a character in her own right and named after all else that he valued in the world.

Later, she added a matador's thrust, the *coup de grâce*, 'How could they manage without you, Oakleigh?'

And that clinched it. Perhaps at that moment sitting there enthroned, his collar riven, tie askew, he could see into the future, could see with startling clarity — Jigsie, scarlet-faced, red hair sopping in the cockpit of the lifeboat, his engineer's hands on the wheel as they went astern without enough power in a nasty swell and bumped up against the concrete slip, Jigsie having forgotten to check that the rudder was lifted, and writing the rudder off in the process. Headquarters job that, and the boat off station for a weekend. Oakie would enjoy it like an aesthete, the rich orchestration of splintering timber, a symphony entitled 'I told you so' and the inspiration of a sentence of rare poetic eloquence: 'They'll have to have flag days and collecting boxes specially for you, Jigsie!'

Perhaps too, the memory of the way the voting had gone had already begun to fade — nineteen votes for Jigsie, one for Oakie Grail. But then, as they said in the village, there were only nineteen properly cast votes for one was spoiled. Upon that ballot slip there was a pencilled sentence written in a huge clumping hand that summed up a whole life as far as Ethel was concerned.

'*O. Grail,*' it said, '*the best man for the job in eny whether.*'

The monument had only shivered. Its foundations remained untouched.

JOAN BAKEWELL

A Walk Before Breakfast

I met them first in the spring. That is, I didn't meet them to speak
to or even acknowledge, nor was I ever to do so. I simply saw them
together. And that's how it would be. I was to be their witness,
their silent anonymous witness throughout the summer. We became
a trio — they providing the action, I endorsing it by observing
them. Unacknowledged.

The chestnuts were just bursting bud that April morning. A crisp
morning, early sunshine before breakfast. Time for me to walk
Scamp in the park. I did it every day. Friends of mine went
swimming or jogging; some played tennis. I walked the dog.

I noticed *her* first — or rather her dogs. Two beautiful red setters,
bounding into the park from the rear door of a large blue estate car
parked on the perimeter road. I was always on the lookout for other
dogs on Scamp's walk. He was no longer young and agile, and could
be snappish. Usually I was pleased when other dogs avoided him,
but on this occasion as the red setters fled away from us I had a
sense of disappointment, for their owner was striding after them,
long-legged, auburn hair tossed back, the same breeding as her dogs.
I had hoped, had we passed, to give her greater scrutiny. I stayed
watching them all — the dogs circling and racing, she striding
purposefully up the sloping path. And I stared long enough to see
him join her.

Suddenly she broke into a little tripping run and he appeared from
nowhere at the brow of the hill, his arms wide to embrace her with
such ecstatic abandon that I looked away, blushing. I called Scamp,
dug my hands deeper into my pockets and walked on briskly. I went
some ten paces further before allowing myself, on the pretext of
finding a stick to throw, to turn and watch them. They were
walking now, arms around each other, gaze to gaze. He, dark and

broad, a head of black curls, heavy browed, intense. A golden labrador was prancing among the red setters. His dog. What, I wondered, was the explanation of this encounter.

I didn't mention it when I got home. Why should I? My domestic affairs were themselves not particularly orthodox. Or, for that matter, satisfactory. It seemed that wherever I turned for affection — and I turned often — the need was rarely gratified. And indeed what had I now witnessed — meeting after long parting, old acquaintances, family reunion? I knew it was none of these things. Lovers: the air breathed it. Had other walkers noticed, I wondered, or just myself. We were a glum lot, the park walkers — exchanging sullen nods, no words. Perhaps I was the only one to see, to appreciate, to enjoy the moment. I kept mum and hoped my lovers would be back another time.

In fact, they were there the very next day. They had arrived ahead of me this time and their dogs were already cavorting together along the broadwalk under the lime trees. They were sitting on a bench. I spotted them as I nosed my way across the early traffic and, once inside the gate, stooped to let Scamp off the lead. 'This way, this way, boy.' I took the direction towards their bench. I set my pace slower than usual to allow myself more time within the orbit of their enchanted circle. But I didn't try to hear what they were saying. Indeed, I made a conscious effort, by a discreet humming, to avert that possibility. I treasured their privacy for them. And if I was trespassing a little within its precincts I excused myself on the ground that they didn't seem to notice.

The next day they were there again. And I, too, watching. This time her arms circled his waist, his upraised hand stroking her head. This awkward tenderness slowed their pace considerably and I, approaching head on, was able to examine them more closely. They were both older than I had at first supposed. His head of black curls was well touched with grey. There were deep lines at the corners of his eyes. Her eyes were pale, but the depth of the sockets gave her a gaunt look, curiously poignant. They couldn't be much younger than myself. They looked up briefly away from each other as the labrador approached to sniff at Scamp. I was all readiness to nod and smile. They ignored me, or rather simply didn't see me.

They were there most mornings throughout May and June.

Sometimes they strolled, apart from each other, holding hands and laughing easily and often. Sometimes they were intense and silent, hugging close as though they were cold, although the sun was warmer and earlier each day. Just once I saw a tiff between them. I was at a distance across the grass when it began. I heard sharp and brittle cries. They had stopped walking and faced each other. Suddenly she ran off in a sulk towards a large chestnut tree now in full leaf and burdened with blossom. She leant forward against it, her brow against the bark, sulking and teasing. I passed by. Ten minutes later on my return to the park gate I passed the tree again. She had her back against it now. He held her face in both hands.

It was difficult sometimes to contain my excitement about them when I returned home. I was so committed to them, that stepping out each morning was like keeping some secret tryst of my own. And whatever transpired in the park between the two of them cast its shadow of elation or anxiety forward across my day. I said little on my return to disguise the curious variety of my own excitements. Conversations at home were now strained — informative rather than confiding. My reticence wasn't noted. Indeed, as things deteriorated in my own life, an open rift at home became a distinct possibility. I faced the prospect of being entirely on my own again. Without even the most grudging affection. The dread made me more and more dependent on my morning lovers for assurance. They gave my days a naive optimism. They came to represent my ideals, my only joy, my sense of hope. My green rendezvous with them under the trees, our windy encounters on the brow of the hill, my furtive glances passing the park bench — all these brief moments nourished my spirits. A corner of my word was still young.

In early July I had to take a holiday. The break-up I had been anticipating had become inevitable. I don't enjoy going abroad much, but friends had inveigled me into sharing a villa in Tuscany for two weeks. A neighbour took over Scamp and his visits to the park. I was pleased to see Scamp again on my return and as I quietened his eager leaps and lickings I referred enquiringly to the success of the walks. A few showers, an aggressive Pekinese — no further details were volunteered. Alone, I patted Scamp fondly: 'How are they boy, still there?'

They were. Their tone and mood had mellowed, it seemed to me, in the full blooming of their love. The eager expectation of her arrival was no longer quite so keen. She knew he would come and was satisfied. They no longer clung and clutched so frantically to each other. And as the grass yellowed for want of summer rain and the trees got dusty in the heat, they loitered beside the regimented and brilliant flowerbeds. Content.

Then one day I noticed them more hesitant, more absorbed again, walking, turning, stopping. I sensed a new development and, cutting across the laid-out paths, drew nearer to verify my suspicions. She was crying quietly and openly. He was making no effort to console her. But he looked desolate.

All was back to normal the next day, however, and my spirits rose for them. Throughout August the children in the neighbourhood were home from school and out early, rattling bicycles and shouting to each other from the swings. My lovers never seemed to notice. It was as though the park was as quiet as ever. They were oblivious and absorbed. It was I that was irritated at not having them and the park for ourselves. The three of us.

It was early September, as the first brown touched the leaves, that I saw him hit her. His hand struck her flat across the face, its force throwing her off-balance. They had been standing talking as I came in by the far gate. If there had been an argument there were no raised voices. It was the smack of the blow, its actual sound that shook me. I was too far off to register their expressions; nonetheless, I was surprised when they walked on together and he casually put his arm around her shoulder, drawing her towards him. That day he saw her into her car; usually they went their separate ways within the park. This time, as she drove off, he stood a long time watching after her.

I was deeply distressed. That day I found it hard to concentrate. On several occasions I forgot to answer when spoken to. Someone asked if anything was wrong. 'Yes,' I said, 'I've had bad news,' and left it at that. All night I lay awake, anxious and fearful. Towards dawn I fell into a fitful sleep and dreamt of a strange house: removal men were emptying it of furniture. My furniture. I was helpless to stop them.

Next morning I set out early for the park, so early that I knew I

would be well ahead of them. I took the morning paper with me to
pass the time and sat on the bench, reading. He arrived first, the
golden labrador edging off towards familiar smells. He circled their
usual meeting place, casually at first, then looking at his watch,
walking up and down the same stretch of path. She never came.

Next day was as I feared. He turned up alone. This time he didn't
hover expectantly but strode purposefully up and down the paths. I
contrived to pass him and, aching for him and for myself, forced a
'good morning'. He nodded, surprised.

Another week and she still had not come. He turned up for a
brisk stroll with the labrador. No more than that. He knew she
wouldn't come again. I concurred with his attitude and tried to ape
his unconcern, his matter-of-factness. Someone at work, knowing I
was in need of sympathy, invited me to a dinner party. They were
the sort who entertained regularly, stylish people with a smart
home. I took trouble to look my best. The effort cheered me up a
little.

It was a fatal move. She arrived with a tall grey-haired man, much
older than herself, very solicitous, fatherly even. He was, of the two
of them, obviously the one best known to my hosts. She was
introduced as his wife. I shook hands with each of them. Her hand
was tense, small in mine, nervous. It was the first time I had been
close enough to look directly into her eyes. I saw no sign of recog-
nition. She was looking quite beautiful. Others noticed too and
appraised her golden limbs and shoulders almost brazenly. They had
been to Sicily for two weeks, her husband explained. She'd needed a
rest, run down. Not working too hard, someone said, and silence fell
on embarrassed laughter.

We did not sit near each other at dinner, but her voice chimed
clearly to my end of the table. As she drank more wine, she began to
laugh loudly, a rippling affected laugh. Everyone else laughed too.
She was obviously amusing them. But while their attention and
approval pleased her, she glanced frequently towards her husband.
He nodded gently in answer. Her dependence on him was total.

He was, it turned out, a doctor with some sort of stake in a
therapeutic unit. I couldn't make out of what kind. He chose to
dismiss all reference to his work. The conversation roamed instead
around the interests of other guests. I even spoke of my own work,

diffidently enough, although my hosts politely exaggerated its importance.

The meal was rich, and what with the strangeness of dining out, the sheer shock of actually meeting her, and the pace at which everyone was eating, I began to feel quite ill. In the bathroom I fought down dizziness, steadied myself and decided I could hold out. If I could simply sit tight for half an hour or so, I'd be fine.

They were the first to leave. Among bird-like cries of farewell, I merely nodded to each of them, my eyes consuming her every move, loath to let her go. But convulsed inside by her presence, her departure, that part of her which I alone in the room knew about. My part of her.

They were scarcely gone when the gossip began. More drinks circulated. I refused, straining as I was to force a recovery of my digestion and nerves. From the tittle-tattle, it appeared she was an out-of-work actress, much given to scenes and tantrums, suicide attempts. Her beauty had won her what few parts she'd played. There was much crude laughter about casting couches and a woman's traditional way to the top. 'But surely not true in her case?' It sounded priggish and, eager to snub any censoriousness on my part, they turned on me with glee. 'What! And how! Sleeps her way round every director in the film business . . . coils them round her little finger. Callous, that's what. He's her great prop, of course. Always ready to pick up the pieces whenever things go wrong, when someone takes her seriously, thinks it's them she wants and not just the starring role. It happens you know. Happened quite recently in fact.'

I stumbled out into the early autumn night. What bitches! What callous bitches! And yet I knew there was truth in what they said. I knew she deceived men. I knew she had deceived me. I walked through the darkened path on my way home. I was in no hurry. I sat briefly on a bench, walked beneath plane trees, climbed to the hilltop. There I sat down on tufted grass and surveyed the twinkling lights of the city spread out below. As I headed for home, the first rain of a coming storm splashed my face.

MARGARET SEYMOUR

Coming Home on the Bus

I could spend the rest of my life on this bus, meandering round the villages, getting nowhere fast, doing nothing, not even reading the book on my lap, the autographed work of the Geordie poet, *Hadaway Hinny*. I bought it for the photograph on the cover, a pit called Eden where my father worked; but all that is far from my thoughts just now.

I sit near the front behind the driver and can see my reflection in his back, but for once don't find it distracting. I look beyond it, feeling lethargic yet wide-awake. The breeze is blowing my hair about. Everything else seems perfectly still. It's afternoon and the middle of summer, not the most memorable time of year; it hasn't the flavour of spring or autumn. An important time if you're busy with harvest, but fairly meaningless if you're not.

This country is nothing to do with me, although I've lived here half my life. When I first came, the stretches of greenness seemed uniform, but now I can tell whether they're sugar beet, straw-berries, peas or wheat. Today, in the heat, nothing seems green; the land is sun-bleached, the trees dark and heavy. I know the land-marks: pylons, silos, water towers, churches and derelict mills, but not as I knew the pitheads at home.

It must seem strange to the boy from Wisbech, this sudden emptiness and space. Worse for him. Wisbech is neither here nor there. In the season, he tells me, everyone stays off school to pick things. What do *you* pick? Just my nose.

I've driven through Wisbech. Nice old waterfront, Georgian buildings. Wisbech has the same crime rate as Birmingham, in proportion to its population. Where did you find that statistic, I wondered. Made it up, didn't I. Comes in useful for conversation.

Who does he find to talk to in Wisbech? What does he do? Does he go out? Does he lie and watch telly from his grandparents' sofa? We never talked about where we lived. That seemed to be the last thing that mattered. But I know that he spent most of his life in London. When I heard his accent I thought he was one of the overspill people. He is, in a way. Overspilt. Squeezed out. No, it's not true. He made the decision. That's what I admire him for.

Everyone thought him a bit of a lout. It was unfortunate, on the first evening, that he should be sitting with the senior schools inspector and the Arts Council man. It wasn't showing off, he was going mad with boredom at their mealy-mouthed dialogue, when he brought up the subject of female circumcision. At least they began to notice he was there. He told them quite a lot about liver-flukes too. He becomes transformed when he starts to talk. He's really interested in these odd subjects, that's why I don't call it showing off. Then, at the pub, he hardly said a word. The Geordie poet was holding forth. He drank lemonade and played Space Invaders. He told me that during 'A' levels he got through twenty quid on slot machines.

Where does he get money to spend? He isn't working. His mother in London — is she feeling guilty? He must have a father somewhere, too. I remember I asked him, what does your father do. He vacuum-packs bacon. Does that make you rich? The boy from Wisbech wants to be rich; it's his only ambition, or the only one he likes boasting about, at least to poets and white-haired ladies. I like the way he boasts. I don't think he knows I enjoy his behaviour, I try to ignore it, but secretly I have to admit that is how *I* would like to behave. I am very bored with genteel people, their mild conversation — 'A pity the rhododendrons are over' — their unquestioning, gracious sense of regret.

He doesn't bother to get up for breakfast. When people are drinking coffee and talking, he'll be in the library reading. He's always either still or active; he never contrives to be soft and polite. Sometimes he'd rush out into the grounds with the Geordie poet, chasing each other and jumping and yelling, or leaping about in the swimming pool. I believe he is a very good swimmer. He always sat on his own in lectures, slumped in an armchair or on the floor, with his legs stretched out and a cowboy hat half over his face. He sat so still that people ignored him, but he seemed to know what was going

on. I liked to watch him get up from the floor. The bones of boys
and the joints of their limbs seem to be made differently from
women's. One day he sat on the windowsill with his feet up and his
arms on his knees, in silhouette. The light at the edge of his face was
blurred. Perhaps he doesn't even shave . . . .

When I stayed in the Quiet Room one evening he came in to ask
me if I knew what was wrong with the telly. I said I didn't. He said
neither did he. He started looking at the second-hand devotional
books which are stored in that room. I went on reading. He began to
talk about the Second World War and his grandfather in North
Africa and petrol being more common than water, and brothels in
Cairo, scorpion fights and unpleasant diseases. I thought I would tell
him about my son, who's now halfway round the world on an oil
tanker, but it didn't fit in to the conversation. We talked about
death and films we had seen. I mentioned my husband, but he
thought a solicitor sounded boring and wasn't impressed that his
spare time is spent voluntarily guarding the Bird Reserve.

We talked quite a lot, in between sessions. He knows I'm a
teacher. He asked me what kind of teacher I was. I said I was the
kind who has pets. Usually they were eager boys whose best work
got read out to the class. I don't see many of those nowadays. He
said *he'd* had an essay read out. I asked him what his essay was on,
thinking of what my kids like to write: *The Incredible Monster,
The Unknown Planet*. 'Coleridge,' he said. All I could say was,
'Coleridge?'

His name is Stephen. Saying his name suddenly makes him seem
further away.

After supper they used to suggest 'we adjourn to a neighbouring
hostelry'. Once I sat next to the Geordie poet. He comes from the
same part of Durham as I do. I told him the name of the colliery
village where my parents live in an NCB prefab. He thinks I've
betrayed my origins because my accent has disappeared. I think he's
betrayed the working class by glamorising their way of life. He soon
got drunk and drowned his opinions. He got the white-haired ladies
to sing, told them jokes and had them in fits. I talked CSE to the
schools inspector. The boy from Wisbech was watching me. We
went back in the inspector's car.

I've been to this sort of course before. The party on the last night is awful, A Celebration of Words and Music with frozen pizza and violent wine. I told him what it was like last year. Why do you come if you know it's like that? Because I haven't much else to do. Was I right, I said when the evening came, isn't it just as I described it? No, the boy from Wisbech said. When you described it it was funny.

After the Celebration was over and everybody had gone to the pub, we went outside to look at the Ice House. It's hidden by trees, quite a distance away. Something so civilised is a surprise in such a remote and rural setting. It's very deep and made of brick. They filled it with ice from the lake every winter and used it for storing food and wine. All that bounty preserved for so long under the ground, just waiting for the master to make his demand. Now of course it's empty, but the brick is still in good condition.

We went down the steps and stood together in the small arched doorway, trying to see into the chamber. He leaned forward, resting his hand against the side. He seems to have the sort of eyes that penetrate darkness. He held on to my shoulder, forcing me to look closer too. It smelt of dead leaves. He said, let's go down — there must be a ladder. But the grid across the entrance was fastened. There are ways and means of opening padlocks. I didn't say anything. Do you want me to? I had to say no. I didn't like it. I didn't want to go there in the dark.

We walked through the woods to the back of the farm. Last year I saw a badger there, but last year I walked round on my own. I told him I'd seen a badger there. He didn't know they were very rare.

We came back by road. It was dark and cold. He let me wear his Arran sweater. Did your mother knit this? My grandmother did. I thought he must be the eldest grandchild.

When we got back we drank stuff out of the coffee machine. The others came in fairly noisily, then slumped into chairs and sat around as if paralysed. We sat on the floor and read yesterday's paper. There wasn't much point in going to bed. The Geordie poet came in with some beer and his arm around a perfumed widow. He started a row with the boy from Wisbech, who seemed to know more about politics than he did. That's when the others went to bed. I stayed up to see what would happen. After they stopped going on at each other, the poet said, howay, man, let's have a game of snooker. I gave Stephen his jumper back and said cheerio. That's when I thought I wouldn't see him again.

I shared a room with the perfumed widow. This morning I carried her cases downstairs. She wore a different dress every day. She thinks I'm dashing back home to my family, to mountains of washing and unmade beds, and wishes she were. Last night she got weepy in front of the mirror and told me about her wonderful husband and the twenty minutes it took him to die.

I enjoyed saying goodbye to those people. They rushed out of breakfast, offering each other lifts to the station; getting off early was so important. I stayed there cheerfully and ate all the toast and hadn't even started to pack.

Lend me ten pence, I've got to ring home. Stephen was there looking just the same as the night before. Did he beat you? I asked. Only at snooker. He came back and sat at the end of the table. Are your parents picking you up? My grandfather. When he's fed the hens. He sat there with his legs stretched out, looking at me and not making a move. Then he said, what are you grinning at. Nothing. Just you. He waited till the smile wore away. He tried to outstare me. I started moving things on the table. There's heaps of food. Look. I lifted the lids of the stoneware dishes — they stay hot for ages. Sausages, bacon, tomatoes and beans. He said that's the only kind of food he likes. He got up from his chair and went round the room collecting bottles of sauce and ketchup. He stood them on the table between us. I fetched all the partly-empty teapots. We had enough tea to last us all morning.

He didn't look up or talk while he ate. I found myself treating him like my son, pouring his tea and waiting for him to tell his adventures. He left a lot of food on his plate. I said something stupid about his mother. He said nothing. He pushed away the plate. I poured some more tea but he ignored it. He suddenly said, she's more concerned about her boyfriend. Then he told me about what happened. This scruffy bloke. He came to the flat when the younger brother got into trouble. He's actually the brother's social worker. He moved in with them. He's half her age. He shoots his mouth off all the time. He looks a bit like the Geordie poet but he can't tell jokes, he's an idiot. Stephen couldn't stand him living with them so

he went home early one afternoon, took his stuff to Kings Cross
Station, got on a train and that was it.

The bus on which I'm travelling stops. A woman is standing beside
the road. There's nothing to indicate it's a stop. She leaves her bike
in the ditch and gets on. She's the one whose son has the market
garden. She doesn't know me. Either my face looks different today
or else my expression is forbidding. I'm glad I don't have to speak to
her. Today I'm travelling incognito. I'm nobody's neighbour,
nobody's form-mistress, spouse or mum. I'm the person who talks
to Stephen.

He came to the bus stop to wait with me. He carried the case he
had watched me pack. He sat on the perfumed widow's bed and I
told him about my grandfather who volunteered in the First World
War because it got him away from the pit. He looked up the times
of the buses for me. He seems familiar with women's habits, at least
he doesn't find them distracting. His mother's flat in London was
small. He had no room to do his homework.

What is she like? How does she feel? Does he intend to go back to
her?

Don't have to, do I? I'm going to Cambridge. You're going to
Cambridge? In October. What does your mother think about that? I
haven't told her. Maybe not, but I bet his doting grandmother has.
He doesn't like the thought of an all-male college. Poor boy. How
sad. But I don't think it's an insuperable problem.

I expect I'll be back with the non-exam stream in the so-called
Remedial Mobile. There seems no point in giving up teaching. I
have no earth-shattering decisions to make; I've always settled for
what I've got. I think of all the genteel ladies regretting the
rhododendrons were over, and feel detached and happy and glad and
look out of the window at sunny fields.

I suppose that this is being mature.

PAUL ALLEN

Alice Out Loud

Fred stepped heavily inside and let the front door swing shut, unaware of the glass rattling in the porch which he'd glazed himself. Made a beautiful job, though he said it himself. 'Home, love.' He put his cap on the hook and watched it slide down his mac on to the floor. No reply. Still sulking, sulky cow. Well, let her. He wasn't bothered. He sucked the middle knuckle on his right hand where he'd skinned it, worse than skinned it, trying to get that sod of a clutch back into one of the reps' Cortinas. It still tasted of blood, and axle grease. Better clean it up, get a plaster. She'd feel sorry about that, be forced to, then they could patch up their little do from the night before without referring to it any more. Anything but dredge the whole thing up again. 'Alice! Can you fetch out the plasters?' Still no reply. 'Alice!'

It took fully three minutes for him to realise that he was home and she wasn't, for the first time in thirty years, except when she'd been in the Infirmary with her gall bladder and then he'd mostly gone up to her sister's for his tea. Yes, and what about his tea? 'Shan't get it misen!' he told the kitchen, belligerently. He went into the lounge, switched the cricket on; 'rain stopped play'. He sat in his armchair, feet on the stool as she wasn't there to stop him, and spread out *The Star*. 'Chuffing *Star*!' It was always full o' nowt, he thought, casting his eye over news of record unemployment figures. It was *The Star* that started this little do off.

'Beats me why tha can't read papers same time as other folk,' he'd said, gazing gloomily at the fitted shelves he'd made out of the chipboard his pal in the supply department had let him have cheap, as it was surplus to requirements. 'I'm done wi' it be time *Cross-*

roads is finished. Full of nowt, any road. Give it up if it weren't for
Mark the Ball. Give it up, any road, if I don't win it soon. Les in
Cold Stores has won three times in five years. I know for a fact it's
fixed.' And all she'd done for an answer was to rattle the paper in
that meaningful way she had; meaning, 'Why won't you stop your
rattle and let me get on with my reading?' He'd never known
anybody for doing things meaningfully like Alice. She could scratch
her ear meaningfully, could Alice; and worse.

Trouble with chipboard, it never looked really finished, somehow,
not even with that veneer on the doors. 'I've got work in the
morning, love. The onward march of industry. I shall miss it if I
don't get some kip.' This time the paper was re-folded. Meaningfully, of course. He couldn't bear it any longer. 'What're you
reading, any road?' That's what she'd meant him to ask all the
time, of course. But she didn't haul in the rod and line straight
away. Instead she dropped the paper on the floor. 'All right, Fred. I
give in. Shall I switch off or you?' 'Nay, tha can switch it off. It
were thee kept it on.' And she got out of bed clumsily, padded
across to the doorway and switched the light off, tripping over his
slippers by the end of the bed, on purpose so he'd feel guilty about
leaving them there and about not having replaced the fitting in the
bedside light yet.

He felt the bed sink and billow back as she got in; a comfortable,
companionable mood took over. He'd get his eight hours. She
didn't want to discuss something in the paper after all. 'G'night,
love.'

'Since you ask, Fred, it was all these women who've written in,
about their marriages, after that article last week: "Does Your
Marriage Really Work?" Sex lives and everything. There's one
woman from up in Laird Drive, gave her name and address ...
she'll get some talk if she goes to Hillsborough shops.'

'Laird Drive? There was a house in there, in last Saturday's
paper, twenty-five thousand. Only a semi.'

'Yes, but it had a flat built on, over the garage.'

'Still, what d'you reckon ours is worth now? We probably
couldn't afford it if we had to buy it now.'

'Fred, I'm not talking about the price of houses. I'd be ashamed
to put in the paper what she said.'

'Course, we're not as grand as Laird Drive down here. Near enough opposite the club, is that.'

'But it wasn't what the women had put in. It was what the, well, editor, I suppose, had put in underneath. Bits of advice. Little gems. Beautifully written.'

Fred looked at his watch. Still only twenty past five. He wouldn't actually expect to be eating his tea for another twenty minutes in the normal way. They always sat down to it to coincide with the early evening news, not that there was ever anything on it worth hearing. The thing was, why was he so extra hungry on this particular day? Anxiety? Rubbish. What had he got to worry about? He'd said he loved her, hadn't he? Anyway, she'd be back soon, forced to be. Maybe he'd just have a little something, a biting-on to keep him going till she arrived. She'd never know about that, unless she'd taken to counting the bread slices.

Only there weren't any bread slices. No bread in the bin. No biscuits in the biscuit tin except one rather soft old digestive, and he hated digestives even when they weren't soft. 'It isn't right, it isn't fair,' he told the fridge. 'I haven't done anything. Nobody can say I have. I shall have to eat something, though.' He ate the soggy digestive and discovered there was a repeat of *Father, Dear Father* on ITV. Load of rubbish, but he might as well . . .

'Are you awake, Fred? He had given himself away by immediately starting to breathe in long, measured breaths. He should have just done nothing, kept quiet, no tricks. But Alice seized her chance. 'Only I was thinking, you know, "Does Your Marriage Really Work?" What it was saying, it was often the little things that broke up a marriage, especially in later life. Little personal things, like . . .'

Fred snorted. 'Like cold feet and cold hands? Or like keeping the ruddy light on and reading when your husband wants his kip? And then worriting away at summat or nowt all night when he has to get up int' morning to go to work? Aye, I can imagine. Tell you what, I'll put up wi' yer for a while longer on condition you go to sleep. Now.'

There was a silence. Fred breathed out and crossed his fingers on the left side, away from Alice. Then she said: 'So you feel it, too.'

Another silence. 'What d'you *mean*, too?' A shorter, tighter silence, then Alice, quietly and slowly and unstoppably: 'You feel our marriage is on the rocks, Fred. Lots of little irritations on which the ship of matrimony may founder. That's what you feel.'

Fred felt his shoulders tensing and realised he was clenching his toes as well. 'I do not feel that. We rub along. Get some sleep.'

'Fred . . . Fred, do you love me?' It was as if she had unsheathed a sword he'd never known she had. 'What sort of a question is that after thirty years?'

This time Alice snorted. 'Quite an easy one, I should think. You've had thirty years to think about it.' And when he didn't answer: 'Well? You were saying?' Fred let go with a painful wrench. 'Of course I love yer.' And then: 'Now will you go to sleep?' But Alice was up on her elbows, her face reflecting the dull orange from the street lamp filtering through the curtains. He had an incongruous image of himself as a rabbit caught by a ferret. He lay still, rigid, seized.

Alice wasn't looking at him, though, not at anything he could see. She was still talking. 'Only it is about twenty years since you last said so. After my sister's wedding, if I remember right, and you were the worse for drink at the time.'

'Light ale.' Fred latched on to the only specific object on his mental horizon. It gave him strength of a sort. 'I must have said it since. I'm always saying it. Get some sleep.'

'You're always saying get some sleep. But I suppose if you mean it, it might save us yet.'

'Save us . . .' Fred started to interrupt, but Alice didn't hear.

'We haven't kept the romance alive. We haven't been aware of each other as people. The little sparks that must be forever fanned to keep the warmth glowing in our hearts. The little candle whose flickering flame lightens the dark corners of a relationship grown old and stale through years of unquestioning custom.'

That's soft, thought Fred. Aloud he said, 'That's what's written in *The Star*?'

'It's beautiful, isn't it? Beautiful and sharp and dangerous. There were things in it you could put on calendars.' The sudden shift brought Fred up on to his elbows too. They looked like a pair of figures on a church tombstone, suddenly galvanised by some

Frankenstein into startled life. 'What calendars?' he cried, grabbing at the chance of a diversion.

'The sort of calendars that have things on. Mottoes, proverbs. Words of wisdom. Little gems.'

'Oh aye. Like, an hour before midnight is worth two after?'

'Or hell hath no fury like a woman scorned.'

Maybe calendar mottoes weren't a diversion. Fred tried once more. 'Intellectual passion drives out sensuality.'

It had made her pause, that. He pressed his temporary advantage: 'On the calendar at work. We've got one, in the garage. A gem for every day of the year. Load of rubbish.' There was a silence again. Alice lay back, head clumping into the pillow. Fred lay back too, but with a deliberately more controlled movement. If only he'd left it there. But something he didn't know about in the quality-control department of his mind made him ask: 'What about thee, then? Does tha love me?'

'Ha!' Alice made a short, hard noise that you couldn't call a laugh. 'So you see fit to ask. That article's achieved something, then.' Well? Why didn't she answer? He wasn't going to ask again, no matter what. 'There's things about you I don't love.' He wasn't going to ask what; it was absurd, a middle-aged couple having to have this sort of conversation. If his mates in the transport department ever got to hear . . . but he couldn't stop himself. This awful, never-to-be-repeated confrontation had acquired a momentum of its own, like that runaway bus in Wadsley Lane; you just had to hang on and hope. He asked, 'What sort of things?' and made it sound injured. At least he thought so. 'Like what? Come on.'

'Like not letting me have *The Star* delivered, just so's you can pick it up on the way home, and I can't read it while I'm getting your tea so I never get a chance till bedtime, and then you complain. And I don't like the way you blow your nose.'

'But everyone blows their nose.'

'Everyone doesn't look in their hankie afterwards to see what they've managed, like a dog sniffing its own business.'

'There's nowt wrong wi't' way I blow my nose.'

'And putting on that thick Sheffield accent to show me up. Like Walter Gabriel with clogs on.'

'I come from Sheffield. What's wrong wi' that? Any road, just because your dad had a newsagent's out at Worrall dun't make thee landed gentry.' His voice was rising to match hers, both in volume and pitch. Good job they knew how to build walls in the old days.

'And I don't like the way you won't wash under your arms before you come to bed.' There'd been a half-sob in Alice's voice on this and he couldn't speak for the way his own voice would come out. He swallowed, took a breath and tried to divert her again. 'I . . . er, I thought male sweat were supposed to be an aphrodisiac.'

'Oh yes? Oh yes? And what would you do about it if it was?' That, he thought. That. The way any woman could always, in any circumstances, produce a knock-out punch which no man could withstand. He was beaten. 'Alice, tha's been saving this up. It's getting very embarrassing.'

'It *is* embarrassing. It *is* embarrassing.' Alice's voice was near a shriek now. In triumph or pain? Hard to tell, hard to know at this precise moment whether they were different anyway. 'I've been taken for granted, and unloved, and starved of romance, and put up with nasty habits for near on thirty years and it's more than embarrassing. It's rotten tragic!'

Six o'clock. Christ, he was getting hungry. He looked out of the window: hail, coming down like stair-rods and you only saw the stones individually as they bounced back off the lawn, leaping in the air as if shocked. He hoped, vindictively, that she was out in it wherever she was. He'd have to eat, have to cook. 'Cook summat,' he said to the curtain rail in tones of great wonder. The curtain rail was coming away at one end. Loose plaster, trouble with these old places. Still, that could wait. He went into the kitchen, and started to look through the cupboards with the feeling of nervous awe he got when Alice made him go in a museum or art gallery on holiday. 'Rice pudding. Cling peaches — what's Cling? Apricot halves in syrup. Pilchards. What does she get them for? Tomato purée, whatever that is. It's a vendetta. She's left me wi' nowt to keep body and soul . . . tomato soup! Magic! Good old Heinz.'

Now then. He approached the wall tin-opener warily, regretting that he'd ever agreed to chuck the old one out. Still, he'd fitted it to the wall; he ought to be able to use it. He opened it out. The house was silent but for his heavy-breathing concentration. He edged the

tin, noting its A2 size with the professional eye of a man who had
worked twenty-seven years for a food giant, up against the business
end of the opener. Nothing seemed to be happening. He told himself
not to panic and tried again. Nothing. Perhaps it would be all right
to panic a bit? No, be sensible — tin openers couldn't be in league
with troublesome wives who didn't know when they were well off.
He tried again and, without noticing what happened precisely, was
overjoyed to find the opener gripping the tin, albeit rather shakily.
He turned the handle slowly. The tin began to circle on the opener,
a clean cleft appearing in its rim and then an orange-red bubble
of the world's favourite soup plopped disfiguringly, temptingly
through. He could have cried with simple pleasure and relief. Then
the tin-opener dropped the tin on his carpet-slippered toe.

The little storm of his swearing blew itself out. His toe wasn't
broken, only bruised; but badly bruised, and she'd be sorry about
that. Soup covered the kitchen floor with its shallow, viscous film,
cutting him off from the kitchen door — as he realised when the
doorbell rang.

'That's right! Come home when I'm at me lowest ebb. Well, tha
can wait while I clean up.' The doorbell rang again. 'Oh, can't wait
then? All right, if that's what tha wants.' And he deliberately
padded through the slurping lake and trailed grotesque orange
footsteps down the hall. Such a tasteful colour Alice had thought the
off-white rug inside the front door.

The third, impatient ring of the doorbell as he was about to open
it stirred his righteous anger. 'All right, I'm coming, you daft cow.
You Judas. You Quisling. What have you got to say for yourself
. . .' He found himself facing a bewildered young man with a fresh
face, corduroy jacket, slightly too-long fair hair and an infant pot-
belly. 'You're not Alice.' The hail had yielded to a steady all-
permeating drizzle.

'Well, no. I have to admit that. Whatever else I may be, I am not
Alice.'

'Who are you?' This with a bit of aggression to cover his feeling
foolish.

'Mr Cooper? I'm from *The Star*. I've got . . .' Fred slammed the
door in his face, and felt better at once.

'*The Star*? Sod off, then, bloody rag. Just lost me wife, thanks to you.' He tried to make it final but he didn't move away from the door. The young man's voice fluted back to him, strained through the letter box.

'But I've got something to tell you.' Silence. 'You'll be interested, I promise you. Good news.' Further silence. 'I can't shout it out. We're not supposed to tell the whole neighbourhood straight off. Oh ...' and he muttered something Fred couldn't hear, then: 'Look, I'm writing a note. This is bloody ridiculous. I'm writing a note and I'll push it through the letter box.' And a few furtive, scrabbled seconds later a torn-off sheet of Reporters' Notebook appeared, fluttering to the tip of Fred's soupily squelching slipper. He picked it up suspiciously by the corner, and read: 'You have won a thousand quid on Mark the Ball — best near-miss.' He fumbled with the catch and opened the door. 'By 'eck,' he said. 'Well, by 'eck ... tha'd better come in.'

It was an awkward encounter for Fred. You can't shout at a man who's trying to give you a thousand quid, even if *The Star* did owe you something for that daft article. And you can't be at your best when you've got a reporter sniffing the air like a pointer because there are tomato soup-coloured footsteps all down your hall and a thin red tide seeping out from under your kitchen door. It all came out in the end because the reporter wanted to know what the money was going to be spent on, and Fred couldn't answer without Alice.

'Usually a car, holiday, new furniture, anything like that,' the man — couldn't have been a day above twenty, thought Fred — waited expectantly. 'Doesn't have to be true, doesn't commit you to anything,' he added when Fred failed to respond. 'Only we have to say something. Then more people enter next week and my wages, miserable as they are, keep getting paid.'

Fred blurted it all out, a mixture of anger, shame, relief and guilt. The reporter was mildly interested. 'Good grief,' he said. 'So people actually read all the gunge. Must tell the lady in question. Make her day — oh, not your little problem of course. Sorry about that. Still, not a bad angle, Mrs Cooper was away from home last night and unaware of her good fortune etc etc.'

'You can't tell everyone about that.' Fred was outraged, but the reporter jolly well could tell everyone and would unless Fred gave him a few decent quotes soon. Fred, plaintive and hungry, only said: 'I want my tea.'

The reporter, who probably couldn't fit clutches on Cortinas, could work a wall tin-opener. He found some beefburgers and mushy peas, found a plate and cutlery, nagged Fred into washing his hands and waved aside a complaint about mushy peas with the pertinent observation that Fred could eat them or leave them and go hungry. 'Tha'll make somebody a wonderful wife,' said Fred, turning sour again.

'And that's more than can be said for you,' said the reporter, who'd also cleaned the kitchen floor and was now only interested in Fred's age, occupation and short-term financial ambitions.

And then, the interview half-complete, Fred saw her coming, out of the lounge window where he supposed he'd been looking all the time. Bell-shaped, but like a bell made of sponge, not metal-hard, she was plodding, no other word, up the long wet hill from the suburb's busy heart in the valley. She had a silly polythene square tied over her head and under her chin and it reflected the grey of the stone-fronted houses that lined the road. She waved at a police panda car, a Chevette, as it went past, but awkwardly because she was carrying some shopping and the bag was pulling her arm down. A gust of wind swept more rain into her face and her head went down for a moment, her glasses slipping forward on her nose. She raised her head again and shook the glasses back in a dogged, clumsy movement, loosening her hair, as grey and wet as the rest of the summer.

'I'll make an excuse and leave,' said the reporter. 'Back with a photographer later, OK?'

'Aye, make it up, say what you want,' said Fred, watching Alice come slow and determined up the front path, letting the gate swing to behind her.

'We never admit to that,' said the reporter, letting himself out.

She sat in his big armchair. 'Just this once, Fred,' she'd said. He'd been going to offer it to her anyway, of course he had. She looked damp, but not wet. She hadn't spoken, except about the chair. What now? 'Alice?' It came out as a whine, which he hadn't meant. 'Yes,

Fred?' 'Well . . . I mean . . .' he tailed off, unable simply to ask her where she'd been, what she wanted, where they were both up to.

'I see you've cleaned the kitchen floor, Fred. Thank you. And made your tea. That was well done.'

'Alice, I've been worried sick.' Oh dear, that old trick, he thought. How he despised her when she'd said it to make him feel guilty about staying out the extra hour at night. She was smiling at him now. She knew. And then she started talking, as if she'd decided not to let him stew any longer. She was having mercy.

'I went out this morning.' Well, he could've guessed that but he managed not to say so. 'We'd run out of a few things.' Ha! Yes — bread, eggs, biscuits! 'And I got some television stamps. Then . . . well, I just carried on. It was fine this morning, remember? Clear, that just-washed look after rain in the night. We never walk now, do we Fred? I walked. Past them — those — flats, Regent Court. Past the dog track. Over the river. Over the railway. There's a foot-bridge. And then up. It's a long haul up the other side, Fred, but from the top you can see right over Sheffield. Used to be houses, that hill. Slums, they said. We never knew anybody who lived there. Now, well it looks so green from away on this side. When you get there it's just, well, a bit dirty. A few wild lupins, poppies, dark red, dock leaves, thistles. Some unmentionable rubbish. A bit of a quarry. A bit of concrete on top, fenced off.'

'Where the helicopters land,' said Fred, eager to have something to say which wouldn't get him in deeper. 'Next to Shirecliffe College.' He couldn't tell if Alice was interested in his topographical contributions.

She carried on. 'Scruffy. Barren. But it's like the roof of the city. Seems you can see it all. Not the river, because that's hidden. Them — those — gasometers of course, and all the flats, the big blocks, Kelvin, Hyde Park. They look barren too. A church on the hill opposite. Would it be Walkley or Crookes? Then two grander ones in the middle, in the shadow. One black, one clean and white.' Cathedral and the Catholic place, thought Fred. Weren't they calling that a cathedral too, now? He said nothing. 'So big, all of it. Spreading over the folds and into the little dips, like when you spread a blanket on the grass and don't smooth it out. I looked over to here, where we are, and couldn't tell which was our house exactly.

One tiny speck in a row of tiny specks and me and Fred even tinier specks inside it.' And Fred looked at her and she was back on that scruffy hillside in her mind, looking down on herself and him in the ant-heap.

'I can get above it all here. Look down on it, see its good points, its bad points. Get above it.' Alice went silent. Fred couldn't tell if he was meant to speak. He didn't.

Eventually she sighed. 'It's difficult . . . d'you think it's the same with life, Fred?'

'Eh? Are we back to them calendars?'

'It was a silly argument, about silly little things. Though I did mean all of it.' All of it? 'I do run around after you, wait on you hand and foot. That's true, but I don't blame you for it. You . . . you know everything about me, where I am all day, what I do. Until today, anyway. I'm well-known territory, familiar ground. That's true, but it's not your fault.'

'Well, love, it's not as though I'm doing exciting things at work all day. Working on other men's cars I could never afford. No company car for a garage foreman. Same routines, same noises, same bloody jokes,' and Fred's voice almost broke as he said it.

'I know,' Alice began, gently.

He went on: 'I'd get out if there were owt else. I've always said that. Ever since Albert were crushed by the fork-lift, fourteen year since, come August. I'm just hanging on till it's done wi' in another ten year, unless they lay us off.' He paused. 'What about . . . tha knows?'

'I'm sorry, Fred. I was just picking up anything within reach to hit you with. Oh, but it's true enough. I hadn't noticed it, or not said so out loud to myself. But you've got like all the other old men. Neck thickened, your face is always red now. You've got that great pot on you. You cough something rotten in the mornings. I know I'm no oil painting. I look at myself sometimes. Dumpy, sagging. We never were Clark Gable and Carole Lombard, even at the start, but we used to pretend a bit. Remember them — those — dances? The last waltzes? Holding on in desperate silence. I knew what was in your head. ''She's not the best-looking piece in the hall but at least I've got me 'ands on 'er.'' Eh?'

'Alice! I never knocked you about. I were never unfaithful to yer.

Yer've never gone short, not really short.'

'No.'

'I know you wanted to live somewhere a bit grander.'

'And you wanted a council house so you could spend what you earned.'

'We could've lived on Wisewood, Alice, we still could. It's the best estate in town, they all say that.'

'And still handy for Dial House Club, eh Fred? I don't begrudge it you. We think we're settling for second best for the time being, something better later. Then you're ten years off retiring and you realise: this is it. Surviving. Between the washing machine and the Hoover and tea on the table when he gets home . . .'

'Time clock and grease gun and overtime in the pea season so you can pay for a fortnight in Sidmouth. Alice! Bugger me if I didn't nearly forget! You'll not believe this, but I've won a thousand quid on Mark the Ball. Best near-miss. You can have what you like! Within reason.'

'I shall have to think about that. Hey, but they owed you a thousand quid for that daft article, didn't they? Still, I'm glad I didn't chuck myself in after all.'

'Alice! Chuck yourself in where?'

'The Don, this morning. I thought about it. Only it didn't look deep enough, and I didn't fancy polluting myself to death.' Fred stopped himself, just, from telling her it was deeper if she'd gone down to the weirs by Neepsend Lane. Instead he said, '*The Star* giveth and *The Star* taketh away. And they never even know who we are. A circulation figure, a name on a coupon.'

'That's what I mean, Fred. You've got to be able to look down on it.' They sat for a while, an easy silence broken by the theme from *Charlie's Angels* coming faintly through the wall from next door's television.

'How did tha get back, Alice? Not walked all the way again, surely.'

'Police car brought me. Sent a panda to see who the mad old woman crying in the rain was.'

'Crying?'

'I didn't know I was. The rain was hurting.'

'Police, though, Alice. Did anyone see . . . ?'

'Nobody as knows us, Fred, don't worry. I made them drop me at the bottom of the road. Nobody'll connect it with you.'

'Nay, but I'm glad tha's come back. I'm a babe in arms wi'out thee.'

'No, just a helpless old man, Fred. It's a bit less appealing. But it's true, isn't it?'

'I had a horrible thought when I was, when I was waiting for you to come home; what'll I do when tha dies?'

'Look on the bright side, Fred. Any luck you'll die first.'

'Alice!'

But they managed quite a cosy pose when the reporter came back with a photographer. The caption said they couldn't believe their luck.

ELIZABETH NORTH

Juice

In order to carry on her adulterous affair with Julian, Joanna had a
list of what she called her feigned activities. One of these was
raspberry picking, and on this day she drove in her fast, low sports
car with her short fair hair blowing out behind her in the breeze, to
the local raspberry field. She arrived just before ten o'clock and
picked like mad. The man who owned the raspberry field had never
seen such a rush job on his well-tended rows of fruit: 'You've hardly
been half an hour,' he said, weighing the four punnets on his scales
in the shed at the bottom of the slope. Beyond him stretched his
property of canes, and further up the hill, his strawberries. 'You
broke existing records last month with the strawberries, I seem to
remember,' he said.

So he had noticed her before. She looked at her watch. If Julian
had fallen in with her plan he would be waiting in the lay-by two
miles up the road. She did push him around a bit, expecting him to
meet her in a peculiar assortment of places. Sometimes the
arrangements gave her quite a headache, but you expected that.

'Seven pounds exactly,' said the man. 'How very accurate. I'm
afraid they will be over by next week.'

'No, school will have broken up by then,' said Joanna.

'Children like picking,' said the man, who was a recently
redundant business executive trying to supplement the income from
the investment of his golden handshake.

She was about to sling the bright blue plastic punnets on the back
seat of the open car, but hesitated on noticing her folded tartan rug.
It stayed there always these days, and the raspberries must go elsewhere.

'Shall I put them in the boot for you?' He rather fancied her long-
legged thoroughbred looks, although he was a faithful loving

husband who had seldom strayed. His gesture was a compliment —
part of the service in a way — plus a mild but by no means
uncontrollable desire to look for a few moments longer at the way
her unbrassiered breasts swung under the loose T-shirt that she
wore.

Joanna had noticed that far more men dwelt desirously on her
figure since she had been in love with Julian, and she wondered if
this raspberry man guessed what she was up to, rushing through the
picking in the way she had. It all must show: her ardent sexuality of
these last two months, her sharply planning mind and her
consuming need for Julian. It had been easy so far in the warmish
dryish summer. Not a lot of sun they'd had, but still, there had been
grass, mostly dry, upon which to spread the tartan rug in the geo-
graphical area which lay between her town and Julian's. How wise
to choose a lover from a different town. Or lucky to have found this
man who came from one.

She looked around the field and noticed a few other pickers
dawdling, and remembered the pleasure of time taken back in her
more leisurely days. Partly she noted the details of the place so that
she could tell Mike, her husband, what the raspberry fields were like
today. She rehearsed in her mind how she'd describe her day: 'Well,
when I'd dropped the children off at school, I popped up to that
raspberry place. That bloke — you know — the ex-director from
wherever it was ... gave me a look.' By dropping in this mention
of her appeal to another man, Mike would, she hoped, be given the
impression that she could not be dissembling. It was hard work, this
planning and dissembling, but was, without question, worth it for
the feel of Julian's lean arms, smooth chest, his head under her chin
and his overwhelming fantasies about a future they would plan
together but would presumably never have. She did not like to see
too far ahead, but she had to listen to his dreams and sigh: 'Oh yes,
my love,' while keeping in mind that it would never happen and
might not work out happily even if it did.

Which is why she had to hang on carefully to Mike. The plan was
not to leave him or to cause him to leave her. Whether she wanted
him or not was not the question. The plan was the plan was the plan
was the plan, she told herself, much wishing she could bring herself
to discuss it with at least one other person who was not involved.

Giles, the owner of the raspberry field, a round-faced man in his fifties with thinning but still well-cut hair, lifted the boot of the car and saw that, apart from a wheeljack and some well-wrapped tools, it only contained a small child's sandal — a single shoe, sandy from some seaside trip. It reminded him of his own sons, now at expensive boarding schools. The raspberries had begun to help to pay the fees and the boys returned in time to help with the end of the picking season and the cutting-back of the canes and the dividing-up of strawberry plants.

Joanna stood beside him holding a punnet in either hand, noticing how she'd even picked a lot of stalks in her hurry: he would think her very careless, which she must not be. Then she saw him looking at the tiny sandal, saw him pick it up and move it to one side as if it were an important piece of goods to be handled reverently. As well, she saw it as a gesture which reminded her that she was a mother who held everyone's fate in her hands at this time. Tread carefully, Joanna, Giles seemed to be saying, as some sand trickled out on to the black rubber matting of the sun-warmed boot.

'Have you far to go home?' said Giles.

'No ... only just ... no, really not too far,' she gabbled, not really listening, thinking of the beloved foot that went into that sandal, thinking also of Julian's long thin feet in a hayfield two days ago entwined with hers.

'They might get hot. Might be too hot for them in there,' he said.

'Oh, the raspberries, yes. See what you mean. It doesn't really matter.'

Tightness in her neck as she felt the moments ticking on and saw in her mind Julian sitting in that lay-by. He was not the sort of man who sat in lay-bys, and she must in future not choose lay-bys. Even if he waited, which he surely would, the agony of thinking of him waiting there was giving her this tightness in her neck. He'd sit there smoking, with the window of his estate car open, possibly reading, looking at his watch from time to time, and doing ordinary things he did when she was not beside him, doing things that were another part of his life. Like the sandal was another part of hers.

Giles was in no hurry and it was early and still quiet in the raspberry field, and his only other duty at this time was to stack up the punnets and wait for his wife to walk along the track from the house with the news of what other raspberry fields locally were charging per pound today. Then he would write this on the notice board. Meanwhile, in this pause, this sunny pause with a few clouds, white clouds, banking up behind the dry earthy rolling hills, he could dawdle, wondering at this woman's bony shoulders and tight neck muscles. She was, say, ten years younger than his wife, whose neck had coarsened in their years abroad and who had been through many nervy phases at about Joanna's age.

Sometimes he watched a hawk in the sky dive down. He'd got to know much more about the birds and the significance of heights of clouds and the way the grass blew and the sound it made, and wondered if he would become a contemplative in his old age. More often still, he hoped that people like Joanna — people with her seeming intelligence and style would come to the field and find him more interesting than they might have expected.

'Well, if it isn't far,' he said.

'Not far,' said Joanna, not daring to look at her watch again, but feeling a pulse throb in her temple. Perhaps the strain of this, the whole gorgeous thrill and strain of it all would suddenly kill her. She might die from the tension of it right here, on the earthy dusty patch outside the shelter where the man had weighed the fruit. And Julian would think that she had let him down and not dare to come along and look for her. Had she indeed even told him about the raspberry expedition?

'If it's not far,' said Giles, taking the punnets from her to put them in the boot, 'the heat won't get to them.' He stood and waited for her to fetch two more for him to line up on the flat floor of the boot. But she stood there, staring at him, not, it seemed, in such a hurry any more.

'Are you making jam,' he said, 'or freezing them?'

One day she had told Mike she was going to the hairdresser, had taken rollers in a bag and sat in the car after Julian had driven off, rolling up her hair in a style which was anathema to her. 'They did it very badly,' she had told Mike, 'appalling, isn't it? I hate these waves.'

'Not quite your best,' he had said, so agreeably that she had hated him for it.

Giles strolled to fetch the two remaining punnets, since she seemed to make no move herself. 'All part of the service,' he said as she stood still, frozen to the spot. What did she expect from him? What did she see when staring at him? Coming closer, he smelt that she wore an expensive scent, reminding him of some he'd bought his wife once, guiltily on coming home from a conference.

For Joanna, it seemed that even as she looked into the boot, the raspberries became juicier. Translucent globules of this juice surrounding them, they swam in it, and were nearly jam already. Jam for Mike and for the children. 'Yes, I'm making jam' she said, although she had a large deep freeze and always froze soft fruit.

'Perhaps some newspaper beneath them,' Giles suggested, 'or they'll drip.' The blue plastic punnets, bright blue, had holes in the bottom. He held one up to show her. 'Oh yes, newspaper,' she looked wildly around, her eyes almost as startlingly blue as the punnets themselves.

'I'll get you some,' he turned towards the shed.

'No, really, honestly . . .'

He stopped and stood there with his hands in the pockets of his baggy linen trousers. He was a nice shape for an oldish man, with his check shirt open at the neck, not unappealing, and the sort of man one could collapse on if one wanted to collapse. Which she would never do, because collapsing was not going to be the way this stage of her life came to an end.

The floor of the boot was corded rubber and she saw a trickle of juice seep out and run an inch or two from one of the punnets. Maybe she should have newspaper there in case by noon when she had left the car, had gone with Julian and found a leafy lane . . . 'That's very kind of you,' she heard herself say. The *modus operandi* of her present life must be to maintain all functions, not let things leak out through any weakness in façade.

He seemed to dawdle in the shed, stalling her by his niceties. She could slam down the boot and drive off in a puff of smoke. She'd paid him for the fruit and had no need to wait for him. Already she was feeling less than perfectly prepared for Julian, was sticky and a little sweaty even. This week was the last before the holidays, and when they said goodbye in two hours' time, there'd be a month-long gap, and who knew what might become of love unstructured by shared jam?

A skylark began to dart and swoop in the sky above his head as Giles, returning from the shed with folded copy of the *Financial Times* in hand, saw her leaning, looking in the boot, gripping its hot metal edge. The shining car, the angle of the leaning woman's hip: so easy to say something, pay a compliment perhaps, with no intention of pursuing it, and with his wife about to walk up from the house. 'Pink newspaper,' he said and held the paper out, almost as if it were a handkerchief to soak up tears. 'Is there anything . . .?'

'No, nothing thanks.' Joanna, marshalling her resolution and her years of being pleasant in exchanges with all kinds of men who sold her things, stood up, drew breath, felt tall again, helped by seeming to enjoy the air, the skylark and the puffy clouds. In the leafy lane Julian would push the hair back from her face and she would reach for the buttons of his shirt. The folded rug would be unfolded, lain, spread out. 'No nothing further, thanks very much,' she said as Giles spread the *Financial Times*, having pushed the punnets to one side and noticed how the juice was already spilling, inching along the rubber runnels towards the sandal, mixing with the grains of sand.

'How very kind,' Joanna said. The skylark dipped and flapped, twittered and soared and had to work with frantic wings maintaining balance. She, Joanna, had recovered now. Perhaps she'd been a bit dismissive in a way, but one had to wait, hang on, grit teeth and trust in practised habits of communication. A little effort only was required, a little sacrifice. That way one could retain one's polished surface in the ordinary and not give way what was extraordinary. Oh, I can do it, thought Joanna. Giles moved his head out of the way as she slammed the boot.

His wife, on coming along the track, was passed by the car in a cloud of dust. She walked in denim skirt and canvas shoes and came towards him by the shed.

'So you've already had a customer?' she said.

'Yes,' he answered shortly, sounding more intemperate than he had been for years.

RACHEL BILLINGTON

Pastoral

'What an energetic sky!' Anna lay on her back looking upwards. She thought that the sky was like a huge cinema screen tipped horizontally over her. Earlier it had been a basic blue, streaked with ladders and hills of purplish grey moving fairly slowly from end to end of her vision. But in the last few minutes the clouds had begun to bunch and bustle, causing great white mountains to be followed by vast aquamarine lagoons.

Martin, who had enjoyed deck-chairs ever since he'd realised that putting them up was a celebration of mind over matter, looked at Anna with exasperation. He registered exasperation but his face as he considered hers, upside down and wide-eyed, showed affection. 'You couldn't say that about you!'

'What?' Anna, more star-fish than ever, had forgotten she had spoken. Now she felt as if she lay in a high wind. The sky rushing over her flattened her into the grass.

'Energetic. You don't look very energetic.'

It was after lunch on Sunday. They had eaten roast lamb with mint sauce and rice pudding. Now they sat or lay on the lawn. Later they must drive back to London.

Further down the lawn Martin's mother, who had cooked the lamb and picked and chopped the mint, was weeding, bottom up, inside her herbaceous flower bed. She looked more like a shrub than some of the shrubs. Whenever Martin thought of his mother, which was fairly often since he was fond of her, he imagined her like a duck fishing, bottom up.

'Look at Anna! Don't you think she's the laziest sight you've ever seen?' Martin called to her. The only response was a tassel of withy winde thrown on to the grass behind her.

Anna, however, bunching up her limbs as if they had suddenly changed texture and shape, shot upright. 'What do you mean! I could take on the world!' She began to run on the spot, feet flexing, elbows tight. Afraid she might collapse again like one of those wooden animals jointed on string, Martin got up from his deck-chair quickly and took her arm. 'How about a walk?'

Anna stopped running and looked into his eyes. 'Why does it make you anxious when I take a rest?'

'You do it so thoroughly,' he said. The truth was it reminded him of her in bed, naked and soft and one hundred per cent willing. Her willingness both attracted and unnerved him. He supposed he had been brought up in a tradition that suggested women should be a little reluctant.

Anna said nothing but he knew from her eyes that she understood. 'We'll walk,' she cried, giving a look to the cloudy mountains, 'up hill and down dale and if I fade you can put me on your back.'

'When will you be back?' said a voice, accompanied by a hail of prickly dead-heads.

'Soon, mother, soon.'

They left the garden, sometimes bright now, bathed in the blue lagoons, and sometimes shaded by the mountains. They went through the house, which was much darker than either. Black, almost, to Anna's sky-dazed eyes.

There they found Martin's father gloomily facing a table-full of examination papers. Anna was shocked and took his arm. 'You can't stay inside all afternoon. We're going for a walk.'

Martin frowned in case his father should decide to accompany them. But the gloom was more the solemnity appropriate to the schoolmaster's task and he was really enjoying himself. 'No, no. I shall mow the lawn when I've finished.'

'Is domesticity a horticultural habit?' cried Anna as they passed through the house and struck on to the lane which led up to the hills.

Not knowing if she was being critical, Martin didn't answer. He understood nothing about Anna's character, despite having known her for nearly two years and been her lover for at least half of that time. They lived in London, they lived apart, they both enjoyed

working hard. There was never time for something as unpro-
grammed, as labour intensive, as getting to know each other.

He could see what she looked like. Although that changed extraordinarily with her mood. At the moment with her T-shirt, full
skirt, gym shoes and hair hanging down her back, she reminded him
of an illustration from a thirties' school annual. Even her face,
which was often quite small and pointed, had softened into teenage
contours.

Actually she was in her mid-twenties, or perhaps more. Martin
remembered her telling him that she had done the same job for six
years. It was extraordinary, too, that someone as restless and
changeable as her should have done the same job for so long. It
wasn't even a good job. Assistant to an estate agent. Once he had
picked her up from her office and her face had been tiny. Her legs,
however, had been delectable, long and shiny in high-heeled shoes.
When she was with him she generally wore sandals. Now she
scuffed her gym shoes up the dusty track.

The hill was steep, giving an excuse for lagging. 'We get the
climb over early,' said Martin encouragingly.

'I know. I was looking for snails.'

'Do you like snails?'

'I used to collect them when I was young.' She bent sideways and
took from a low twig a round striped object. 'I liked these best
because I pretended they were humbugs. I loved humbugs.' She bent
again and held up between finger and thumb a tiny pale yellow shell.
'I called these lemon drops, and the pale brown ones were butter-
scotch.'

'I hope you didn't eat them.'

'Only when I was very small. I played games with them. I owned
a sweetshop. I was the customer too. I was a very solitary only child.
The problem was when they walked off the counter.'

Martin laughed. But he was puzzled. Anna a solitary imaginative
child loving the countryside? The only link with her past he knew
was her mother, a matter-of-fact widow living in Dorking. Perhaps
she hadn't always lived in the suburban south as he'd assumed,
though he supposed snails might like suburbia as well as anyone. She
was finding more now, attached like Christmas decorations to the
hedgerow.

'It's all the rain,' he said, showing his country lore. He had been born and bred in this greenness. Ridden his bike up this lane even when it was deep with mud. But he'd never noticed the snails before. At least not so many. 'Come on, or we'll never do the circuit before tea.'

'Ah, it's a route march, is it?' Anna carefully replaced the humbug and the lemon drop on appropriate leaves.

They began to walk up briskly. Anna twisted her hair behind her ears and dropped it inside her collar. Her face narrowed and became paler. Perhaps it was the reflection of the green leaves which closed in a tunnel above their heads.

Martin had brought Anna to stay with his parents two or three times before. They had walked. Even up the same hill. But she had never seemed so individual before. She had been part of a pattern started in his adolescence. Nice girls brought home. Liked by his mother as much as him. He had not wondered about her. No questions. They did not know each other.

'I like the tunnel. But I liked the sky best.' Almost as she spoke, they burst out on to the top of the hill. Four paths met. But from the point of one field the whole village and valley in which it lay could be seen. Martin turned there automatically and stared down, just as automatically, for his own house.

'Do you like your house?' Anna said at his side. It had not crossed his mind she might not want to stand fixedly gazing from this viewpoint.

He turned to her, surprised. 'I don't know. I know it too well. I can't see it anymore.'

'But if you had a house, would you want it to be like that?'

'I suppose I will have the house some day. Do you like it?'

'I like the garden. The house is too dark for me. The windows are too small. I like looking at it from outside.'

'But your flat is almost underground!' Martin thought he sounded too vehement, as if he'd been upset by her remarks. But she replied even more passionately.

'I hate my flat! Hate it! But if I looked for somewhere better it would be like looking in forever to the life I have now. I'd hate that even more!'

'But you've had it years. And your job — years.'

'Oh yes. But it'll change. Sometime.' She raised her eyes from the calm roof-tops to the wild sky, now almost at eye level. 'Look. The clouds are racing us.'

They turned together and again took a brisk pace. Now they had reached a plateau, the track was flat, wide, bounded only by hedges laced with elderberry. They bordered wide fields. To the left a golden cornfield swept up and away. To the right, short-cropped green grass.

Soon there was a soft scuffling sound and a huge flock of sheep spread towards them. Almost without sound, except for two or three black-and-white dogs, chivvying them with a yap, they flowed into a gate a hundred yards further on. They were still pouring through, blocking the track, when Martin and Anna reached them.

'Look at the way they tread on each other's toes!' exclaimed Anna.

'No worse than commuters,' Martin could see two men beyond the flow. One he knew. He waved, causing the woolly grey mass to scatter temporarily. 'I used to go fishing with him,' Martin explained. 'He always caught something. I never did.'

'So you weren't always a winner!' Anna laughed.

'It depends whether you're after big fish.' Martin was a successful solicitor specialising mostly in conveyancing. That was how he'd met Anna in the first place. He knew he suffered from over-importance. It was a bachelor's failing, he forgave himself. Only temporary. He remembered the name of the man now, Jack Shepley. Once they had been good friends. Now, as they came face to face over the bobbing rear ends of two hundred sheep, they had nothing to say.

'Hello, Jack.'

'Hello, Mart.'

A pause.

'You look well.' Actually Martin thought he looked old, weather-beaten and pot-bellied.

'Down for the weekend?' Into this Jack, perhaps unconsciously, put a wealth of the true countryman's contempt for the town dweller who thinks a pair of wellingtons and a long stride puts him on a level.

When they passed on, Anna picked a long stem of bay willow

herb and waved it over his head. 'If I was a fairy godmother and changed you into a country solicitor with tweeds and a pipe and roses as red as your cheeks, would you be happy?'

Martin looked at the pink flowers shaking over him. He realised he had never even considered such a question. He had simply gone to London after university because London was where the jobs were. 'I suppose I could come back here now I'm established,' he said, following his own train of thought.

'But would you like it?'

'No,' he wondered whether to be honest.

'Go on,' Anna threw away her wand. 'I won't sneak.'

'The fish aren't big enough.'

'It's all right,' said Anna, smiling and taking his arm as if he needed comforting after such an admission. 'I like ambitious men. In fact,' she danced away from him again though looking over her shoulder, 'I love ambitious men.'

Love. Love was not a word in Martin's vocabulary. It had never been used between them before. Now she had thrown it down. Or up into the air, perhaps. Lightly, like a bauble. She looked at him still, as if wondering what he would do with it.

'I love the countryside,' he said marching soberly on. But even so he had used the word. It left an unaccustomed shape in his mouth. She seemed satisfied, at least not disappointed.

They walked again and soon, reaching the end of the track, met another cross-roads. 'Right to the railway track, left to the Ladies' Mile or straight on to the Enchanted Village?' asked Martin.

'Enchanted Village,' replied Anna promptly. The road down to the Enchanted Village had once been paved, but tilted down at such a slope that winter rains had turned it to a river and washed the surface into gullies. At the bottom, the water oozed onto a flat round pond on which the fattest geese and the largest ducks sat lazily. Beyond, the little village, like an illustration out of Hans Andersen, boasted two fat black-and-white pigs, a stableyard with cobbles, a comfortable stone house with a swing on the lawn, a row of little cottages, a small yellow church, a square rectory, a row of gigantic chestnut trees laden with brilliant green chestnuts about to split out their shiny brown conkers and a very old, romantically dishevelled water mill. There was no human being in sight.

Anna stood in the middle of it all with a complacent grin. 'Life should be like this,' she said.

'And four children tugging at your skirt.' Martin watched her admiringly. He had meant it theoretically but it came out rather more personally. He saw Anna considering the picture and found he was interested in her reply.

'Despite being an only child,' she said, 'I'm not against four. I'm not against one either. Nor ten. Though I would be against none. I don't think the act of creation should be packaged.'

Martin, being practical in his instant reactions, thought of Durex Featherlite. But then he thought he liked her dream of the act of creation, so he reserved a vulgar joke.

'My sister's two are perfectly acceptable human beings,' he announced instead. 'They play in sandpits, laugh when tickled and encourage the provision of huge teas which are mainly eaten by grown-ups.' He was pleased with this little speech, even surprised by his own perspicuity.

But Anna laughed almost derisively, 'At least you don't hate children. Which way now?'

Disconcertingly close to the Enchanted Village was a road. Not a road that more than one car every ten minutes passed along. But a road nevertheless. As they neared its smooth grey surface, Anna felt a drop of rain tickle the top of her nose. She saw one fall on Martin's pale high forehead. For all his love of the country he would never look a countryman. 'Rain!' he shouted, preparing to bend double and run.

A tree, or rather a great spire of overgrown hedge, was the nearest substantial growth. They ran. But the rain beat them to it, hissing down on to the road like tiny silver snakes and rebounding up again.

They reached the spire, but its shelter was mainly illusory. 'Like religion?' Anna thought to herself. She peered at Martin. Had he noticed the shape of the tree? She never thought of him as someone who wore glasses, but he did. And now they were steamed over, making his large hazel eyes look like fish swimming in deep water. His usually pale cheeks were quite flushed from all the running. The rain ran down the spire, sliding gracefully from leaf to leaf, until it settled on their clothes.

'We're getting wetter under here than outside,' said Anna, losing her nerve over the matter of the shelter of the church being illusory. She so wanted to believe. Sometimes she thought what she needed in her religious life, her almost non-existent religious life, was a strong leader.

'It's only a shower!' Martin bravely stood out on the road. He looked up. 'Our tree's just like the spire of Sherborne Abbey.'

It was like him to be so precise. She was excited, nevertheless, that they saw the same shape. 'Did you ever go to church there, as a child?'

'As a child I went to church constantly. There as well as other places. My parents went through a religious revival when I was four. It had nearly passed when I was fifteen and now they barely show the scars. I bear the scars.'

Anna and Martin had only once been to church together and that was at a friend's wedding. They had not sat together. But afterwards Martin had squeezed her arm, saying jovially, 'There's nothing like a good church ceremony, I always say.' It had struck her as unlike him, then. But now she understood. He had an untapped church background. Waiting. Like her.

She ran out to join him, for the rain had stopped. She swirled her dripping skirt about her knees and cried, 'So cooling after a strenuous walk.'

They marched on. The road was hard on the feet but the views opened out in field after field of ripe corn, divided by circlets of dark woods. The rain cloud had almost gone, sweeping the sky into a new blue brilliance. Here on this more open ground they could feel the wind again.

Anna ran, opening her arms wide. Her clothes flapped. She felt as if she was hanging herself on a clothes line. She knew Martin wouldn't run. He only ran for a purpose. She liked that. When she sat in her estate agents she dreamed of flying. Sometimes on hot summer afternoons she actually fell asleep.

'Left!' Martin shouted behind her. 'The gate!' To Martin she was a bird. He had liked birds. Once he had filled in books about them. But he had left that behind him with university. He had worked so hard.

'Shall I climb over it?' Anna looked at the gate doubtfully. Only two or three bars remained, tied up with string resembling straw.

'Piece touched. Piece played.' They jumped, touching the top gingerly like cats. Martin looked so pleased with his spring that Anna kissed him quickly on the cheek.

He put his hand there and stared at her. Her hair was wet, her eyes shiny. As shiny as the green grass on this new track. The word love came into his mind and went.

They walked on. Anna was pleased with the effect of her kiss. Really, she liked sudden touching more than pre-ordained love-making. Bed was so boring. Well, not exactly boring. She thought of lying with her arms pinned above her head by Martin. Of his weight and his heavy body on her. She blushed.

'Now over this gate. Right turn for a hundred yards along this lane and then straight across the fields. Do you think I should encourage my parents to build a bomb shelter?'

Anna tried to collect herself. Was this an appeal to her intellect? Even a test? She remembered a programme she had watched saying three airtight weeks was all that you needed. 'Three weeks underground would be worse than death to me.'

'This area would be pretty safe from the blast.'

What Martin enjoyed was practical theory, Anna decided. Martin had decided much the same thing.

The volley of conversation was quite satisfactory to both, when they were interrupted in the game by a gigantic animal being led out of a gate ahead of them.

'It's a bull,' whispered Anna.

This was unnecessary. The three men worshipful around it, the gold ring through its nose, the Neanderthal colossal stupidity of its every movement made it obvious.

'How pathetic!' whispered Anna.

Martin took a step of disagreement away from her but said nothing. They watched. The bull was being led towards the field in which a herd of mottled cows grazed. One of the men opened the gate. The others pushed and pulled. The bull entered. Strange squeaks of, perhaps, ecstasy came from its mouth. It rocked up and down.

'How silly!' said Anna. Then, rethinking, 'How disgusting!'

The cows put their heads up, with a very casual show of interest. Trying not to hurt his feelings, Anna thought. The bull moved slowly, then faster. Every part of its absurd over-developed body swayed and bounced. 'So humiliating for the poor old thing,' said Anna finally as the cows found just enough energy to blink and shift their pattern.

Martin said nothing and they walked on, saying good-afternoon to the bull's keepers as they passed. They leant on the gate, watching.

Anna saw that she had offended Martin. His masculine solidarity. Bulls were not silly, even if their role had been usurped by a bottle of refrigerated semen. She strove to find the right note.

'I think I appreciate the theory of a bull more than the reality,' she said. 'I used to have erotic dreams about bulls.'

'Oh, really,' said Martin, suddenly finding her deeply unattractive. 'We turn left here.'

They turned left. They became part of a wave of golden corn. Acres and acres of it. Anna decided that bulls and sexuality were best kept for dreams and allowed herself to be swept into the late summer fertility. That was a much more acceptable image. More general.

Martin too relaxed, 'I've never been on this path before,' he said, 'though I've often meant to.' Ahead of them a semi-circle of dark trees crowned the gradual sloping hill. Anna looked back at the road. She had thought so. The slope of the road was crowned by a semi-circle of old stone-built houses. Art imitating nature. Or nature art? The idea and the sight made her extraordinarily happy.

She pointed it out to Martin who looked and loved it too. She saw him happy and the love in his mind shaping in his mouth.

The clouds were collecting again. Not heavy but low and close — forming like a velvet cap. It seemed warmer. They picked ripe heads of corn and chewed the seed. The darker air made the colours richer, the textures heavier. Anna felt a heaviness in her limbs and went close to Martin.

'Give us an arm!'

Arm in arm, they walked, contented, chewing, exclaiming at the beauty. It was the middle of their walk. And then they were on their way back.

Despite the heaviness, they seemed to cover ground more quickly,

as if the homeward turning made them quicken like horses. But they
didn't want to be back.

Martin stopped at a barn. It was set exactly in the middle of a
field. The corn had been cut round it so that sharp stubble edged its
walls. 'I've always thought there should be a house here,' he said.
He took Anna in his arms and kissed her. She felt dry now, except
for her hair which was thick and held the damp. He kissed her
gently.

'And who do you think should live in it?'

'A beautiful maiden with damp hair the colour of a raven's
wing.'

'And would she have a prince?'

'On occasions.' He laughed and let her go.

'When the 6.05 from Waterloo was running on time,' said Anna
knowingly. But she stayed close to him. She loved him.

They passed out of that field and into another as smoothly green
as the other was prickly. A vast empty sweep of green. 'I bet the
sheep came from here,' said Anna. She thought nostalgically of the
beginning of the walk. As they reached the corner of it, Martin
kicked out piles of stone from under the grass. 'Do you know, we've
been from Dorset to Somerset and in a moment we'll be back in
Dorset again.'

Another gate. Another climb. Another hill. And below it as
before, though now it was far to the left, the village again. Anna
could even see Martin's parents' house again. It took little imagination to see his mother imitating a hibiscus.

Suddenly tears filled her eyes. Why was life always so disappoint-
ing? Always. Ever since she'd been a little girl and found snails
didn't taste like humbugs.

'What's the matter?' Martin took her hand.

'Nothing. Nothing.' Anna dashed his hand away and ran over
the crest of the hill. It was so steep that she disappeared immediately
and spectacularly. Martin stood still for a moment, admiring the
view. The sky the other side of the valley was beginning to streak
with the evening sun in a multitude of colours. He tried to count
them but it was impossible. Besides, he knew he must follow Anna
over the edge, slipping and sliding over grass and thistle and nettle.

He had never been very sure-footed.

'I never thought you'd catch me up,' Anna rested, panting, at the bottom of the steepest incline. From then on it sloped gradually through a field reclaimed from a dozen marshy streams. They stood together under a large oak tree.

'I'm a very determined man,' said Martin, pushing his glasses which had fallen to his cheeks back up his nose. Nevertheless he knew he wasn't the least bit ridiculous. He'd tumbled down that slope for her.

'I'm not,' she said, staying a little way from him. 'Very determined, I mean. Not very organised or anything, really. Just myself.'

Martin put his hand on the trunk of the oak as if to steady himself. 'I love you,' he said in a loud voice.

'Oh!' Anna laughed. Anna blushed. She felt something more was expected. 'Oh, good!'

Martin still stared, fixed against the tree. It only then occurred to her that she'd never actually said she loved him. She'd thought it so often that she assumed he would have heard. 'And of course I love you too.'

He became unfixed from the trunk then, and came towards her. But they didn't kiss. Hand in hand they walked down the long, sloping, once-marshy field. The evening sun dispelled the streaks and cast long shadows at their feet. She leant her head on his shoulder. She was taller than him and it was easy. Who would ever want a great beefy hulk, she thought vaguely to herself.

As they neared the village a dog barked and Martin tried to remember if it was Saturday or Sunday. On Monday something very important was happening. Something very important to do with work. On Sunday nights he worked till two or three in the morning. He decided it was Saturday.

They strolled through the village, nodding benignly to Mrs Jessup, who had three dogs who regularly fouled Martin's parents' lawn. They wandered up the hill to the house, murmuring satisfactory things like, 'Lovely cup of tea,' and, 'Won't we be stiff tomorrow.'

They only stopped short, perfectly stunned when they entered the house and found Martin's father still at the table covered with exam papers. It was lit now by a somewhat devilish red streak of sun, but otherwise the scene was unchanged. They stared, round-eyed. He put his head up.

'Had a good walk, did you, er, um?' His head went down again.

They went out on to the lawn. Here, things had moved from one bed to another. A flourish of excavated dandelions greeted their arrival. This time Martin was not put off.

He stood with his arm round Anna and said in his convinced and convincing lawyer's bellow, 'Anna and I have got engaged. We're going to be married!'

His mother's head pushed its way out of a tangle of clattering honesty. 'Oh, darling, I am pleased. You must have had a good walk!'

LIANE AUKIN

The Train

It was eight o'clock on Tuesday the third of May in Westcliffe-on-Sea and the rain was bucketing down. Heilpurns Tropical Outfitters was a lock-up shop. The work room and offices were on the ground floor, and above were the three rooms that Bron and Lilah had lived in since they came to Westcliffe twenty-six years ago. Lilah, sipping tea in the kitchen, had been waiting for the postman. Now she reached for the pot to pour a second cup, and carried them both into the bedroom.

'Tea, Bron.'

'Wassa time?'

'Eight o'clock. Not that it matters to you what the time is. It matters to me but that doesn't matter to you, so who am I talking to and why do I bother? Here.' She put the cup down beside him. He didn't move.

Lilah sat at the dressing-table. On either side of the mirror stood a framed photograph. One was of Bron and Lilah on their wedding day, the other was of their grand-daughter, Polly. Polly had been to art school; she had wonderful taste, the figure of a film star and a great future. She could be a buyer at Liberty's, everyone said, no question. She was living in a flat in Paddington with a fellow called Doug. They had been living together for over a year. Lilah hadn't met Doug but she reckoned that if he was good enough for Polly he was good enough for her. She wasn't going to interfere. She had tried with Polly's mother and look what happened. The crazy girl had run off with a Hungarian circus performer, leaving Polly behind, and had never been heard of again. The trouble was that ever since Polly had confessed on an afternoon visit back in November that she was potty about this Doug, Lilah had been waiting for the summons — Gran. Come. We're going to get married! — but weeks had passed and there were no more visits, no letters and no mention of any date. Last night she had suddenly wondered if they were planning to sneak off and have a registry office job. The idea had kept her awake for hours. All this made her very agitated. She started to brush her hair.

'There was no letter again.'

Bron didn't respond. Lilah put on a little powder and was about to apply lipstick when she remembered the nature of her first appointment this morning. 'I said, there was no letter.' More silence. 'And Hardiman Brothers are expecting delivery Thursday. It's going to be a busy day and I have to go out.' She parted the curtains to see if it was still raining. Out in the yard a line of sodden underwear flapped in the wetness. She turned in a fury. 'You didn't bring in your thermals. Didn't I tell you yesterday to be sure and bring them in? Look!'

Bron turned slowly to look at his wife. A year ago the doctor had told him he had a slight heart condition, so now he always moved very carefully and very slowly. If they ever lose the lion, they'll ask you to do the petrol ads, Lilah was given to say.

'I must've forgot. The Goldmanns were here, I told you.'

'What's that got to do with the washing?'

'They were having an argument about whether or not Chairman Mao was still alive.'

'Chairman Mao?'

'The Chinese fellow. And she started to shout and then she felt faint and he said she ought to have a cup of tea and have a sit down, you know the Goldmanns. I was stuck in the shop for hours.'

'All you had to do was say he was dead. Finish!'

'I don't like to interfere.'

'That's what they said about Hitler.' Bron shrugged and closed his eyes. Lilah got dressed. 'Now listen, Bron. You get those things in and put them through the mangle. You'll do it slowly but you'll do it. I'll see you half-eleven.'

She pulled the collar of her coat high about her ears and set off down the road. As she walked, she ran her tongue around the familiar gap in her top jaw where the new tooth was to be fitted at nine-fifteen. If it wasn't for Polly she wouldn't have bothered, not after all these years, but, as she said to Bron way back in January when she made the first appointment, 'I only have one grand-daughter and if I can't have a full mouth of teeth for her wedding, then what has it all been for?' She turned the corner into the high street, walked past the Co-op and the Express Dairy, crossed at the zebra crossing and stood outside number thirty-two. Knock and Naylor, Dental Surgeons. Mr Naylor had the letters BDS after his name. They sound more like undertakers than dentists, thought Lilah. She went in.

Mr Knock, his drill poised for action, was waiting for her.

'Try and relax, Mrs Heilpurn.'

Lilah wondered why a man like Knock, dedicated to the care of others' teeth should not do anything about his own halitosis. Miss Samuels, his assistant, all pink and white like a Cindy Doll, twittered in the background with her little aluminium dishes.

'When's the wedding, Mrs Heilpurn,' asked Miss Samuels.

'Not now,' said Knock crossly. 'You must forgive her, Mrs Heilpurn, but Miss Samuels' prince has also come.'

Lilah, who had been holding her breath ever since Knock started bending over her, smiled and nodded. 'He comes to all of us.' Knock started in with the drill.

'Your teeth must have moved, Mrs Heilpurn. I'm sure they weren't so close together last time. It's going to be a tight squeeze. Yes ... definitely shifted.' Lilah grunted. 'Hang on while I drill a bit off the one next door. Be brave and remember you'll want to give a big smile when they take the wedding photos.' Miss Samuels giggled. Knock continued. 'Yes, definitely closer. Shame to lose a bit off a perfectly good one but I can't send this back to the technician, it'd break his heart. Get the amalgam ready, nurse.'

How could teeth shift? Lilah opened her eyes. Knock, blinking behind his pebble lenses, looked like a stunned pterodactyl.

'How can teeth shift?' she asked. Her mouth was full of swabs, and Knock assumed she was grunting again. 'I've never come across such an *extreme* case of shifting. Now, brace yourself. This is going to hurt. Wider please.' He jabbed a syringe sharp into Lilah's upper gum and she gave a shriek.

Knock and Samuels soon had a really good rhythm going, and metal dishes, syringes and spikes passed briskly back and forth between them. After a while, Knock straightened up and Lilah was able to take her first deep breath.

'Miss Samuels, pass Mrs Heilpurn a mirror.' He pressed a pedal and Lilah sat upright and looked at herself. 'What do you think?'

'I think I've still got a swab in my mouth.'

'Then spit it out, Mrs Heilpurn, spit it out.'

Lilah spat. She looked. The new tooth was considerably greyer than those on either side. Mr Knock beamed at her. 'No food or drink for three hours, fill in the forms before you leave and try and take a few hours off if you can.'

'The shop doesn't run itself, Mr Knock.'

'How's your husband?'

'He suffers from a rare disease called ''I'm tired, Lilah'', otherwise he's fine.'

Lilah left the surgery, signed her name several times, and Miss Samuels twittered her out into the wet street. It was coming up to ten o'clock. She was due to give Mrs Leroi a fitting at ten-thirty. She caught a bus.

There wasn't the call for Tropical Outfitting these days. In the beginning, when they first started in business, there were so many people going out to do service in India and Africa and all the ladies had to have the right dresses, and safaris had been a popular honeymoon idea, but now, although there was work for the doctors and nurses going out to the Arab countries, orders had been falling off. Lilah had started her own side of the business — holiday clothes for hot climates and the larger lady. Mrs Leroi was off to Benidorm. She wasn't asking for silk pyjama suits or organza shifts but still, a cotton dress now and again made a nice change from shirts and shorts and surgical gowns.

The bus dropped her off at the corner of Shanklin Avenue and a few minutes later an arthritic maid-of-all-work showed her into the Leroi three-piece sitting-room. Lilah strapped a pin-cushion to her wrist and got down on her knees to make the final adjustments to the hem.

'Try not to bend, Mrs Leroi,' she said, 'I'm trying to get this hem even.'

'I'm not bending, Lilah. It's my build.' Bloody mansion block, thought Lilah.

'When's the wedding?' whined Mrs Leroi.

'June,' she lied.

'June? Last time I asked you said May.'

'May, June, what's the difference with a life-time ahead of you?'

'Lilah, what's the matter with your voice? You sound as though your mouth is full of cotton wool.'

'I've been to the dentist. My lips feel like blubber.'

'What did you have done?'

'Bridge.'

Mrs Leroi gave Lilah a smarmy smile. 'For the wedding, I suppose.'

'I only have one grand-daughter.'

The massive Leroi gazed at her reflection in the mirror. 'She'll be doing her own cold buffet, I suppose.' When her son, Maurice, had married Harry Hackleman's lump of a daughter, Pearl, the reception had been at the Esplanade Hotel.

'We haven't decided,' said Lilah, 'Polly'll want something simple. She's like me. Nothing ostentatious.'

Mrs Leroi clapped her fat little hands together. 'That reminds me, Lilah. I thought gold buttons instead of the white. They'll go better with my pendant.'

'If you insist. Now please try not to fidget. Every time you move, remember I am down on my knees with a mouth full of pins trying to follow you.' There was a long silence.

'You haven't mentioned the carpet, Lilah.'

Lilah, who had been kneeling on it for half an hour, looked at the emerald-green pile. 'Oh, I noticed as soon as I came in. It's beautiful. Such a lovely green and a wonderful quality.'

Mrs Leroi heaved her fat shoulders and sighed deeply, 'It's a green carpet.'

Eleven twenty-five. Bron, in slippers and rolled shirt-sleeves, was at the kitchen table drinking tea and reading the paper. He had some kind of bandage wrapped around his right-hand index finger. Lilah came in. She could tell at once he'd only been up a half-hour or so.

'Have a cup.' He indicated the pot.

'No, thank you.'

'Biscuit?'

'Bron. I have just had a bridge fitted and Mr Knock said I wasn't
to eat or drink for three hours.' A pause. 'At least.'

'This Knock's a dentist?'

'No, he's a quantity surveyor.'

Bron looked up. 'Let's see, then.'

She bared her teeth at her husband. He peered at her over the top
of the paper. 'I'll miss that gap,' he said, 'It gave your smiles a
particular charm.'

'If you only miss it when I smile then you aren't going to miss it
much.' She hung her coat up on the hook and came to collect the
dirty crocks. 'Pass your cup.'

Lilah carried the dirty dishes to the sink. She slammed them down
on the draining board. Over the sink hung a mirror, but the glass
was misted over and when she looked to catch a glimpse of the new
tooth it was like trying to see her reflection in grease-proof paper.
The rain pelted down onto the little sky-light and Bron's inter-
mittent, nervous cough was driving her mad. Suddenly she let out a
howl. It was so shrill and horrifying that Bron forgot all about his
poorly heart and leapt to his feet, thinking she was hurt. Lilah stood,
her hands over her mouth, staring at the pile of wet thermals lying
in a puddle of water on the floor. She turned, howled again and
pointed an accusing finger at him. He, in retaliation, held out his
bandaged one to her. She slapped his hand away . . . Bron sat down
defeated. Lilah, gasping in her rage, went to a cupboard and pulled
out a black polythene bag. She started to stuff the wet clothes
into it, pounding with her fists to squeeze them all in. She dragged
the bag over to the kitchen door, opened it, dumped it on the steps
and slammed the door. Then she came across to the table, sat down
and began to cry.

Bron coughed. 'I tried with the mangle but then my finger got
caught . . . .' he trailed off hopelessly, 'I'm sorry.' He coughed
again and waited a moment. 'Tell you what, why don't I pop out
and buy us some fresh fish? You'll enjoy a bit of fried fish, we
haven't had it in a month of Sundays.' Lilah sniffed, and he felt
encouraged and leant over and tried to pat her cheek.

'That's my injection!' she shrieked out, clutching at her face.

'That's what's getting you down, isn't it?'

'It's getting so I can hardly hold my head up in Westcliffe any more. Everywhere I go it's, when's the wedding, when's the wedding?'

Bron relaxed. They were back on familiar territory. 'Who asked you to tell everyone in the first place?'

'When I have a little happiness in my life why shouldn't I want to share it? Didn't she say to me, Gran, she said, this, what's-his-name, this Doug, is the real thing. Isn't that what she said?'

'She never mentioned getting married.'

'Two and two, Bron.'

'Makes four.' And for Lilah one and one had to make a marriage. 'They wouldn't want a white wedding, anyway,' he went on, 'probably turn up in denims and sweat shirts. Lilah, why don't you accept that Polly lives another life. She's different to us. How often does she come to see us? Once in a blue moon.'

'Can you blame her? Westcliffe! Living here is about as interesting as watching a plank warp.'

'But she doesn't want her grandma hanging about. She wants to be independent.'

'What a thing to say. I'm all she's got, unless you want to count yourself.'

Bron mouthed 'one' and stabbed his chest with his bandaged finger. This made him cough again.

'She's in an emotional state,' said Lilah, her voice cracked with tears, 'and at times like that you need someone close, like I am to her. You remember our wedding?'

'I have a faint memory.'

'You'd never have got through it without me.'

'Lilah, it was our wedding. Without you there would have been no wedding.'

'Precisely. What dreams I had. What promises you made. Yes, yes, a salon in South Audley Street, button-back chairs, Wilton carpets. How come Minnie and Lewis had a West-End salon? Did they have more than us when they started?'

'Minnie has a wholesale business in Mortimer Street, not a salon. And coming here was your idea, not mine.'

'You like the sea.'

Bron could feel his heart starting to beat rather hard. 'Anyway, look what happened to Lewis.'

'All right, so he died. But it's better than living in a dump like this.

He reached for his jacket. 'I'll go for the fish.'

'Bron!' Lilah was on her feet. 'We are going up to London.' The jacket fell from his hand. 'I want to see Polly. I've had enough of this not knowing.'

'I don't want to go to London. Everyone smokes up there and it makes my eyes water.'

'I want you to go and buy yourself a shirt.'

'I've got one.'

'So there's some law says you can't have two shirts? I'll pay. Mrs Leroi gave me cash. Here.' She reached for her bag. 'Take a tenner and buy yourself a new look.' Bron didn't move. 'If you don't get a shirt I'm not going with you.'

'I'm very tired, Lilah.'

'A day out is what we both need. Bit of a lift. Get away from it all. A train to somewhere.'

'I've told you, I'm very tired. I'm not going anywhere.'

'When I think how different it could all have been. With my contacts and way with the ladies and your flair for cutting. Bron Heilpurn, you've thrown it all away.'

'Lilah, you've been telling me for the past thirty years how I ruined your life, so go to London, go to the wedding, go on the honeymoon for all I care but stop nagging me. I've had enough.'

'You've had enough? What do you think I've had? I've had it up to here, that's what I've had. I'm going and don't try to follow me!'

Bron picked up his jacket and made one of his slow-motion exits, mumbling something about fish. A few minutes later the front door closed. It was a quarter to twelve.

Lilah stood in the bedroom looking at the unmade bed. She went and sat at the dressing-table. She parted her lips to have a good look at the new tooth. It was definitely greyer. It was almost as grey as her hair. Well, thank God it tones in with something, she thought. She opened her bag and counted the notes in the brown envelope Mrs Leroi had put in her hand earlier that morning. Sixty pounds in tenners. Then she took out her musquash coat, chose a nice pair of matching brown court shoes and some gloves, and picked up her bag. She paused for a moment before the mirror and for some reason decided to take the two framed photographs. She stuffed them into a plastic carrier and left the room.

She was walking. She was excited. She wasn't sure where she was walking to. A passing car splashed her thirty deniers. She was walking to the station. Sixty pounds in cash. Usually she put the money in a post office account, saving it for a rainy day, she explained to Bron, but today she thought, it's raining, it's raining. She felt exhilarated. She caught the twelve twenty-five to London.

She sat in the train and thought about Polly. It would be nice to have a quiet talk to her before meeting Doug and all going out to dinner. It had been such a long time since she'd seen her. She remembered the photos in the carrier and took them out. Lilah kissed her grand-daughter's face, leaving a smudge of lipstick on the glass. She must remember to remove her lipstick before kissing Polly. Then she looked at the wedding photo. Bron was smiling. His eyes were bright and stared arrogantly into the camera. His bride stood beside him, her face framed in a white veil. She was smiling too, but with less certainty and her hand rested lightly on her husband's arm. Lilah looked at herself. The eyes in the photograph had an expression that made her look closer. What was it, that look? Was it a dream of artificially-lit rooms, and the smell of rich women's perfume, of smoked-salmon sandwiches and of Bron pulling at a roll of cloth and holding it draped over his arm, a dress, before his scissors had made the first incision? That man could make sackcloth look like silk, Lewis used to say. She smiled and put the photographs away. She looked up, still smiling and saw her face reflected in the train window. A full mouth of teeth. They looked really nice. Of course, if Bron had been there, he'd have made some joke about missing the gap. The funny thing was that she felt as though he was there, but tucked up safe in the plastic carrier. She folded her hands in her lap and imagined the time to come.

She and Polly would make all the arrangements. All right, it wouldn't be the same as when she was a girl, but she was prepared to compromise. She could even make the wedding dress in denim if that was what was wanted, but a wedding was a wedding and the most important day in a woman's life. It must be done properly, with good food and music and lots of pictures to look at afterwards. Bron would have to buy a new shirt and he'd wear his dark suit. He would lead off the dance with the bride and she would follow with Doug. Later, Bron would make a speech and he and Lilah would exchange looks and smiles and grimace at the jokes like all couples do who've weathered the storm and lived to tell the tale. As long as everyone could be together it would all have been worth it. The fact that everyone was together proved it had all been worth it. Yes, everything would be all right. She sat absorbed in her thoughts, with her neat grey hair, her face lined and slightly sagging at the jaw, but with eyes bright with the same expectancy as the young bride in the photograph. She didn't notice the row upon row of suburban houses and later the factories and finally the tower blocks of Stepney and Bethnal Green.

The guard's voice came over the tannoy system, 'Ladies and gentlemen. We are approaching London, Liverpool Street. We shall be arriving at our scheduled arrival time of one thirty-five. We hope you have had a pleasant journey. Thank you. This is the age of the train . . .'

Oh yes, thought Lilah, a train . . .

CHRIS BARLAS

Proceedings

Everything should be so sharp about the past. Crystal clear, indisputable. No one should be able to argue if presented with the facts of history, public or private. Things happen or they don't happen. It should be no problem.

The way I remember it, the sun shone continually for three years. We lived on a new housing-association estate, built on the edge of town so there was nothing between us and nature except a few piles of rubble. We'd go for walks across the fields from the flat, past the cows which didn't give us a second thought as we trespassed. Long days of blue skies and larks singing in the fresh air. I don't remember any of the other tenants going for walks. Probably they never stayed that long. They seemed to move in and out so fast the windows looked like a great kaleidoscope, with constantly changing cheap curtains. Afterwards we'd come back and make love in the late afternoon sunshine, on top of the duvet, before watching television in the evening.

Hazel remembers nothing of this. She says it rained the three years we lived there. Didn't I remember the time the tiles had to be relaid in the hall because water coming under the front door lifted them? And traipsing through the mud when I insisted on going to the pub and when we got there the landlord was rude, the bitter cloudy and I complained? She assures me we weren't happy.

'Let me get the divorce, I'd like to.'

For Hazel most incidents could be made the subjects of a small, intimate play. We'd lived apart for the statutory two years and she thought it would be sensible if we got divorced at last.

'We might as well,' she said, with her switch-on smile. 'There's no point in staying like this.'

I said I thought it might stop her getting married again, which was true. She said it was most unlikely that she would ever get married again and mentioned that she'd been very savagely bitten, which I thought unfair. Besides, it was no business of mine any more what she did with her life.

So we agreed. And thrift being mutually necessary, we opted for a do-it-yourself arrangement. Which suited me fine since I disliked solicitors and their dusty offices. And their close-set eyes.

'I'll pop into the legal stationers and pick up the forms,' she said. 'No problem.'

'When'll we sit down and do it all?'

'Let's have a drink in about a fortnight. I'll ring you.'

She didn't. I waited for the call, throughout November and December. It was now the new year and no point in waiting any longer. I went out myself, found a legal stationers and bought the forms. I only hesitated when the assistant asked, 'For the husband or the wife, sir?'

She'd said she wanted to file for the divorce but I decided she'd forfeited that right when she didn't call me. I got the husband's, three sets and a sheet of instructions to school you in the ways of legal jargon.

Filling them in was a nostalgic, occasionally painful process over a bottle of whisky late one night. I could hardly remember the date of the marriage. The form seemed to me irrelevant with its demands for specifics. The way I remembered it, the process was gradual, only half perceived, meeting, meeting again, sex somewhere in between, nights out at the pictures, moving in together. And nowhere a date you could accuse or point the finger at. Parting the same. My love didn't cease on a given day, it wore out rather, over months. The actual day of leaving home was far too painful to remember. The only way I'd have of telling would be the receipt for the transit van I'd hired to move my things. Probably lost now, anyway.

The following day I phoned Hazel.

'Nick, the last two months have been hectic, absolutely rushed off my feet.'

Which explained why she hadn't done anything about the divorce. She still had the power to hurt me, when she made it clear I wasn't the shining light in her universe any longer, nor even a dim rock at the edge. When we parted we'd swapped the conventional comforts of still being friends, respecting each other, remembering birthdays. I told her I felt ignored and she said, quite reasonably, that that was my problem. It smarted.

We met in a Greek restaurant in Charlotte Street, in late February. Over the taramasalata, I told her about the forms I'd filled in. She scowled.

'But I wanted to do it.'

'I waited and waited but nothing happened. I had to set the ball rolling.'

Between courses, she looked at one of the completed forms while I made fidgety noises about getting fingermarks on it. As a matter of fact, her fingers had always been somewhat distasteful to me. They were long and bony, not artistic, the fingers of a shrew. And she always wore rings, a pair of large diamonds that glittered in the light, making her harder and colder than she really was.

She shook her head.

'It was June,' she said.

'What was?'

'You've written under 'date since when the petitioner and the respondent have lived apart' that it was May. It was June.'

I was certain on this. I remembered.

'It was May because I watched the snow out of the window of my bedsitter when it snowed on the first of June that year. I'm sure of that. I'd moved in by then, so we parted in May.'

She tucked her lips together and sucked air in.

'Perhaps you went to have a look at it, then. But you were still at the house on the fifth, I remember, it was my dad's birthday and they came to see me.'

'Maybe they came a week early.'

'They wouldn't.'

We argued for a bit but she insisted she was right. In the end, May/June was written under the date of separation, since neither of us would budge. Hazel made it clear that she expected me to pay for the meal which I did, reluctantly. Perhaps she was put out because I'd pre-empted her on the divorce.

In a fortnight the forms were returned by the court, with a letter of the delete-what-is-not-applicable variety with 'incorrectly completed' underlined. They wanted a specific date of separation. It could hardly have been because they cared, either for the truth or for us, but doubtless the bureaucratic soul craved things tidy. Birth, marriage and death all have their dates, so why not separation? Explaining that a total failure to agree on anything had been one of the symptoms of a bum marriage wouldn't excuse us. They asked for definite dates, they expected definite dates.

It was spring, so we met in a pub by the river. We sat outside, shivering in the chill breezes that blew across the water as, one by one, the other drinkers decamped inside, to the warmth of the gas fire and low ceiling.

Hazel said, 'Are you cold?'

'No, I'm fine.'

'But you're shivering.'

'So are you.'

'It's too smokey in there.'

'Quite,' I said.

It had always been so during our marriage, deferring to each other and ending up doing what neither wanted. It was as if the only things we could agree on were those which inconvenienced one or the other. I showed her the letter, which she read and threw on the table.

'Oh, it's so silly, what does it matter.'

'Obviously it matters to them whether it was May or June. Why don't we just say it was May. It gives us an extra month to make certain.'

'Because it wasn't, that's why. It was June. Besides, you only need two years separation, it doesn't matter about the extra month.'

'If only you'd got the forms like we agreed in the first place, instead of forgetting all about them.'

'I was busy, I told you.'

'It's you who wants the divorce.'

'Don't shout.'

I was shouting but felt irked that she'd told me, especially in that pompous, point-winning way. I counted to ten. The thought occurred to me while counting, that if we hadn't been sure about divorcing at the start, we were now, or at least I was. Somehow, the law ensured that the process of divorce made you loathe the other person.

'All right, let's say it was June,' I said. 'It still gives us two good years of separation.'

'As a matter of fact,' Hazel was producing a set of forms from her handbag, 'I've got hold of the wife's forms and filled them in. Look.'

They were much neater than mine, less full of crossings out and smudges. They had a professional appearance.

'Let me do it after all,' she said.

I couldn't say no, so we went inside and had another drink to seal the bargain. She told me about her new job, interviewing in an employment agency. Her enthusiasm bubbled like boiling mud as I stared around absently at the knots of drinkers. I suppose all of us like to talk about ourselves, only Hazel has perfected the technique. She doesn't need anyone to talk to, merely a co-operative physical presence. That evening made me realise why I only remembered the good times with her. I'd learned to shut off during the rest, the conversations that were monologues, the stubborn rows, the long silences. I'd been a sleepwalker through our marriage, into and out of it. No wonder she accused me one summer's day of eroding her confidence. I must have been like a brick wall.

A month later I received notice from the court that her petition had been accepted. There was a simple printed form, with a sheet for me to complete and return, agreeing to the proceedings. It seemed that this time we'd got everything right. A further two weeks brought another form, signed by Hazel in her spidery writing, announcing the day for the hearing. It said on the bottom that it was not necessary for either of us to appear.

I phoned her.

'Let's go, shall we?' she enthused. 'Have a drink after. We ought to.'

Another dramatic moment to be enacted in Hazel's life, but I wanted to go too. I was there at the beginning so I might as well be there at the end. The bureaucratic tidiness had finally affected me.

It was June, disputed June. We sat in the gallery of the court, pretending we were spectators. Our names were read out by the clerk. Objections were solicited and in default of wild-eyed relatives leaping up to rail at our broken pledges, the judge, tired and listless, like an animal in the zoo, pronounced the said Hazel and the said

Nick un-man and un-wife.

'Celebrating?' the landlord of the pub round the corner asked as he uncorked the champagne.

Hazel said, 'Yeah, we've just got divorced.'

'Very nice.'

We must have looked odd sitting there in the gloomy lounge bar at half past eleven in the morning, drinking champagne. Hazel poked around in her handbag and slipped me a scrap of paper.

'You said we'd go halves. All right?'

Item, court fees, £25; item, set of forms, 30 pence; item, champagne, £8.50. Total, £33.80. My half, £16.90. I reached for my cheque book and forked out. She tucked the cheque into her purse. I'd half a mind to ask for a receipt.

'That's that, then,' she said.

I felt as though I was one of her interviewees at the employment agency who'd just been told he didn't meet their standards.

'What'll you do now?' might have been the next question.

We finished the champagne. Half jokingly I said it had ruined the rest of the day for me. Alcohol before the evening always sends me to sleep. She said I was boring, you didn't get a divorce every day. I had to agree.

We kissed outside on the pavement and walked off in different directions, waving. I had been going her way, in fact, but I could scarcely walk with her. And as I hurried through the side streets back to where I wanted to be, I wondered if I could put my contribution down against tax.

JEAN BINNIE

A Patched Jacket

I drove back there, yesterday. I'd nearly passed the signpost, 'Mellinger'. I braked and turned the Jaguar's wheel, I slid into the turning and I found myself going back, backwards in time. Back past Major Blake's manor house, back down the lane where we used to toboggan, back to where we'd spent a year, when I was twelve.

'A whole year!' my mother had said, wringing her hands.

We'd gone and sat on the gate, swinging our legs. A whole year! It had been autumn and the two cottages had gardens stretching away, thick with vegetables and fruit. To us, it looked like England in a picture book. Coming back from India, there'd been nowhere to live. Furniture in store. Two separate schools for my sister and myself. Now we were to go to boarding school and come here for a year's worth of holidays. A whole year!

My sister and I learned not to talk much about school, even to each other. We came home for the Christmas holidays. It was the winter of '47 and once it had started snowing, like a child crying, it couldn't stop. We thought that was how home, England, always was and would be. The water pump in the old cottage froze, we chipped ice off jugs and buckets. It was so cold going to the outside lavatory, we used to put it off for a whole day at a time. We had bedside tables made out of orange boxes. No plates matched. When the coal wasn't delivered, we had to find things to burn.

'What shall we do?' my mother asked my father.

'What'll we do?' my sister said, half scared, half excited. I would never have imagined in the desperate heat of Calcutta that we would really need things to burn, to keep warm, in England.

'Ask the lady next door,' I suggested, 'ask Miss Barnes?'

'Mrs,' my father said quickly, 'Mrs Barnes.' There was an embarrassed silence, I had said something wrong.

'Darling,' my mother said, 'we can't just freeze?'

Looking onto the lane, the Barnes house was to our right. My father came back from there, snow still on his hair, with a sackful of logs. Just like you would, we thought, in England. The whiteness dazzled us, we were delirious with it swirling everywhere. We had enough to do, enough to see and find and explore those holidays, without wondering why we weren't supposed to go next door, why we could sometimes hear Mr Barnes, but only later, at night, when we were in bed with fires crackling. His deep voice would be raised, it would leak out of the windows and carry clearly across the snow; her voice was quiet.

One of our favourite places, for tobogganning, was the blocked lane. And for walks we had the Lovers' Lane where drifts were piled high as pillow-cases. The man Mr Barnes, from next door, helped my sister once, to climb out of the snow there, where she'd got stuck. She was half-giggling, half-crying. She always did things by halves.

He handed her back to me and looked at me, his blue eyes laughing too, his face brown against the dazzle, 'You off 'ome now?'

I nodded.

'Ere,' he said, undoing things, searching in folds of coat and jacket. He held out an envelope open along the top. He licked it, but I'd seen there was money inside. 'Jus' be droppin' this in nex' door, would you? Save me gettin' there — when I've this lot on,' he nodded towards the next field where a sheep bleated. I nodded. Then he turned and scrambled on all fours up to the hedge, scraped through the thorny twigs and out the other side. We heard the sheep, then his voice.

I knew not to mention the letter to my mother. After all, it wasn't a proper letter, I thought. Sometimes, we owed money to the Post Office shop, or the milkman, and I delivered it. I thought of it like that.

By the Easter holidays, we knew we were in paradise. My mother had started understanding the pump and the garden was awash with primroses and blowing daffodils. The fruit trees in the garden were thick with blossom and this holiday we were allowed to go round to the Barnes's house.

'Just run round to Mary, I mean Mrs Barnes,' Mother would say, 'I've run out of sugar.' Or it would be, 'The fire's not drawing, pop into the Barnes's, won't you, ask her what we ought to be doing?'

And my sister and I would fight over which of us would go. Father had got the wrong idea about Mrs Barnes. There was nothing shocking about her. She always knew what to do. She knew about pruning trees and cooking rabbits and the cat's kittens and barbed-wire cuts. She knew what it was like for my mother, with Father away, because she was left on her own a lot, too. 'Where's Mr Barnes go?' we asked Mother. She would purse her mouth and we knew not to ask again.

Sitting in the car opposite the cottages, I realised I could only remember bits of Mrs Barnes — her heavy, thickly shining, lustrous brown hair, her huge brown eyes and small hands. I remember more, across the years, of how it felt to be near her. She gave out calm and stillness like some places do. Though feminine, it is more an asexual quality. It's having an inner, sure place, that nothing can shake. It is also personal and caring. Warm and rich.

My sister and I took to dropping in on her, taking round women's fashion magazines which she loved and pored over. Not many other people went to see her and she didn't go out much, I don't know why.

We'd tap on the back door and knew we had to wait for her to say it was all right to go in, or we were to go away until later.

'Hello,' she used to say, going on with whatever she was doing, not stopping. She would lift a pile of magazines from a chair when it was clear that we'd gone round to talk and I or my sister would sit, chatting, while she peeled potatoes or plucked a pheasant or knitted or mended.

Once, when both my sister and I went round, she was mending a tear in a man's jacket which I could smell from across the dark kitchen. It smelled very strongly of man, and sweat and dirt.

'Is that your husband's coat?' asked my sister.

Mrs Barnes nodded. I could see danger ahead, but I couldn't see how to stop my sister without it being embarrassing.

'Why doesn't Mr Barnes live here?' she asked.

''E lives 'ere,' Mrs Barnes said, not looking up.

'Then why isn't he ever at home?' asked my sister.

'We'd better be going,' I said, not moving.

She looked straight into my eyes, not my sister's, and her brown eyes were large, ' 'E comes,' she said, 'whenever 'e can.'

'Oh,' I said. The way her eyes gleamed, you could see she loved him, and when he was away, it was like when my father was away, my mother was empty.

She did not need to explain, I understood, but she went on, 'It's bad when 'e's not 'ere.' My parents I took for granted, but the way she said it, I could see how loving like that could put you on the end of a string of elastic. You could stretch and stretch and pull and be pulled and still you'd go on giving, getting thinner, being pulled taut — anything, rather than letting go. Her eyes glistened, but her needle moved at exactly the same pace.

My sister said, 'Oh,' unsatisfied. She was jiggling her legs and she drew in a breath to go straight on before I could stop her. 'Why don't you have any children, then?' she said.

I knew that some people couldn't have children and that some people couldn't stop having children and I knew it was not the question to ask. I said, 'You don't ask that!'

Mrs Barnes over-sewed the thread and bit it with her teeth. She had her hair tied back, one curl escaped at the side. She looked small in the upholstered chair and her shoulders sagged. 'Some,' she said slowly, as if her mouth were dry or her tongue hurt, 'some people 'ave the person they're lovin' for life, and some 'ave 'em part-time.'

'Oh!' said my sister. 'Why?'

'In the snow,' said Mrs Barnes, 'if you'd been in that drift, and you wanted a suit to keep warm and somebody offered you a pair of trousers, would you say, no, not unless I can 'ave the jacket as well?'

'No,' said my sister, her legs still.

'Well, that's about it,' said Mrs Barnes and now she stood up. 'Time you went,' she said.

I thought I could understand about the children, but I didn't understand why loving somebody as she did could make you ache as she did. It made her eyes water and her shoulders bend. I noticed she held the jacket up to her cheek.

'I'm sorry,' I said unhappily. She shook her head. We were always the ones who said too much.

When we came back in the summer there was an abundance in our Eden, we knew England and paradise were the same thing. We walked further afield now, my sister getting tired before I did.

At church my father had found he knew Major Blake, and so we could wander over his estate too. Major Blake had a sort of keeper, he said, and he wanted us to meet the keeper and his wife so they would know us, and he went and got the man out of his house at the gates. It was our man, our Mr Barnes with the voice from next door, the man of the snow drifts, but he seemed not to know us. So my sister and I pretended not to know him either. Out of politeness.

We hid and played complicated games that summer and learned things and quarrelled. We watched birds whose names we never knew and found nests. We stalked rabbits and pheasants and played at jungles. Sometimes we went separate ways, my sister and I.

Walking alone, I came one day into the part of Major Blake's woods where they were planting young fir trees. New pines stomped away in lines to the right. To my left a wood fence held in wheat rustling like paper. Here the bracken had been burnt away. I marched on, singing, and nearly put my foot down on a snake. It was beautiful. I brought my foot back and stood and stared. It had zig-zag markings down from its head. It had been asleep in the sun, but now its head moved. The cobras in wicker baskets in India had never harmed me.

A voice behind me said, 'Don't move, still now, still.' I nearly jumped. The snake's head was rising, rising and weaving, its prettily forked tongue darted in and out, tasting the breeze. 'Still now.'

The snake seemed sluggish, its head sinking. I wanted his voice to go on, even when the snake had eased itself over a piece of bracken and slithered away.

'You're all right now,' said the man and turned me towards him. Major Blake's keeper-man was wearing Mr Barnes's jacket. It was the same jacket because it smelled the same and I could see the mended tear. His hand went on, resting on my shoulder. I liked it. It was warm, burning into me. I wanted it.

We stood so long, you might have thought we had to stand still for another snake. He stepped backwards, 'Ah well,' he said, giving my arm a pat. 'The adders 'ave 'ad their 'ome disturbed, see?' I nodded. He turned on the path and walked away. I watched him. He didn't look back once, though I wanted him to. I wished I had been so frightened he had been forced to stay. If I'd been younger he would have carried me. I wished I had been older and . . . and I could have made him stay.

Now, remembering, I looked at the cottages. That one, ours. There was the Barnes's house. So small. So long ago.

I started the car up and turned into a gateway and, wishing I hadn't come, went back to the main road. I had everything, didn't I? I had a second husband, I controlled my father's business entirely. I had power over other people twice my age and success in every company I took over. What I did not have was any inner calm. And I had nobody whose torn, smelling jacket I would mend and then hold, unconscious of what I did, against my cheek.